· HONEY MOUNTAIN SERIES ·

EVER Mine

USA TODAY BESTSELLING AUTHOR
LAURA PAVLOV

Entangled Publishing, LLC
644 Shrewsbury Commons Ave., STE 181
Shrewsbury, PA 17361
rights@entangledpublishing.com

Amara is an imprint of Entangled Publishing, LLC.

Visit our website at www.entangledpublishing.com.

Edited by Sue Grimshaw
Cover design by LJ Anderson, Mayhem Cover Creations
Edge design by LJ Anderson, Mayhem Cover Creations
Stock art by Olga Grigorevykh/Gettyimages, jcarroll-images/Gettyimages,
and kamchatka/DepositPhotos
Interior design by Britt Marczak

ISBN 978-1-64937-866-8

Manufactured in China
First Edition February 2025
10 9 8 7 6 5 4 3 2 1

· HONEY MOUNTAIN SERIES ·

EVER
mine

ALSO BY LAURA PAVLOV

Honey Mountain

Always Mine
Ever Mine
Make You Mine
Simply Mine
Only Mine

Magnolia Falls

Loving Romeo
Wild River
Forbidden King
Beating Heart
Finding Hayes

Cottonwood Cove

Into the Tide
Under the Stars
On the Shore
Before the Sunset
After the Storm

Jennifer DeJong,

I cannot begin to thank you for all of your support from beta reading, to making me the most beautiful book bibles and talking through the timeline with me. Most importantly, thank you for being an amazing friend. I am so thankful for you! Of course, Hawk is all yours (no worries, we haven't forgotten about you, Gray!), so I thought this would be a perfect book to tell you how much I love and appreciate you! xoxo

Ever Mine is a sweet and sexy small-town romance with all the feels. However, the story includes elements that might not be suitable for all readers, including the loss of a parent in the novel's backstory. Readers who may be sensitive to this, please take note.

Chapter 1
Everly

I took one last look around the house, folded the throw blanket on the couch for the third time, and blew out the candle on the counter because I didn't want it to look like I was trying too hard. Then I relit the candle because it should smell good in here. *I'm a professional, after all.*

The gorgeous house that the San Francisco Lions had rented for me while I'd be working with their star player, Hawk Madden, was completely magnificent. A gorgeous three-bedroom ranch house in the town I'd grown up in, Honey Mountain. It's actually the town both Hawk and I grew up in.

Fell in love in.

Lost our virginity in.

Broke up in.

I digress.

The house had a separate guesthouse on the property

where my sister Dylan was temporarily living. My baby sister Ashlan was in and out this summer as she had an internship back at school, but when she was home, she stayed with me or at our dad's house which was not far from here. The Lions appeared to be willing to spend big money on me, as they'd offered me a temporary job for the next few months during the off-season and paid six months' rent on this house in advance. *Cha-ching.*

They'd made me an offer I couldn't refuse. Though I really wanted to refuse it, because seeing Hawk after all these years—I wasn't ready for it.

I recently finished my fellowship as a sports psychologist with a professional basketball team back East, and it's time to find a job. With no other offers on the table, a boatload of cash and a free house were impossible to turn down. Even if it was temporary.

Even if it meant working with Hawk Madden.

Coach Hayes, the head coach for the Lions, had teased the idea that they might bring me on full-time, but it would depend on how things went with Hawk. Sports psychology was my passion, as I'd always been an avid sports fan, and the mental game for athletes had always intrigued me. But not every sport was on board just yet with how important the mental game was for athletes. Hawk had been drafted into the NHL after we graduated high school. He'd been picked up by the Lions almost nine years ago, and they'd won two Stanley Cups since. But due to a few injuries and what Coach Hayes called a temporary case of burnout, they wanted me to get his head back in the game. But getting my head on straight would be just as important to making this work. Behaving like a professional around Hawk would be a challenge—one I was certain I could handle.

The doorbell rang, and I smoothed my hair into place and took one last glance in the mirror in the front room as I made my way to the door. Did I mention that the furnishings in this place were something straight out of an HGTV renovation show?

Deep breath.

It had been several years since I'd last seen him in person. But of course, the man was splayed across every sports magazine, and I'd seen him on TV in numerous interviews over the years. We followed one another on social media, though we never commented on each other's posts. He was a big name in the sports world, and he'd been linked to several famous models and actresses over the years. I had muted his social media, as seeing him with other women still stung. He was coming here with his trainer, Wes, so that I could meet him as well, and we'd come up with a schedule that worked for everyone. I didn't know how much would be required, as Coach Hayes hadn't shared much of his plan with me.

The doors were glass, which allowed the natural light to flood the open space, but more importantly, it allowed me to get a glimpse of Hawk before opening the door.

My breath caught in my throat at the sight of him. His green eyes locked with mine through the glass, and I tried to calm my breathing. I pulled the door open.

"Ever," he purred. The man had more charm in his little finger than any one man should be allowed. Even as a boy... he'd always had a way of charming the pants off of whoever was near.

It was just usually me.

He'd always called me Ever, and for years he'd followed it with the word *mine*.

Ever mine.

"Hey. It's good to see you." I cleared my throat as my voice sounded gravelly and hoarse, and I took in the older man who stood behind him smiling.

"I guess they've hired you to fix me, huh? You think you're up for the task?" Hawk said as his lips grazed my cheek, and I squeezed my thighs together at the contact.

What the freaking hell was that about?

Men did not affect me like that. Not since I was a teenager, and with this man in particular. Well, he was more of a boy then, and now he was most definitely a man.

All man.

A confident, sexy, muscly man who smelled like mint and bergamot and birch.

I had a keen sense of smell, always had. And my bat senses were going off because oh my, did he smell good.

Like sex and confidence and success.

Umm… hello… you're supposed to be a professional here.

Jeez. I'd spent the past few years working around professional athletes, and I'd always been able to stay in control. What the hell was it about this man that made me lose all sense of reality?

The man standing behind Hawk cleared his throat before stepping beside him. "Hello, Everly. I guess we'll be working together. I'm his trainer, Wes Scout," he said, extending his hand.

I shook his hand as his eyes moved around the house.

"Nice to meet you," I said.

"Damn. She's got a much nicer place than I do, and don't even get me started on the McMansion they rented for your ass," Wes said, and Hawk laughed.

"I guess they think my head needs more work than my body." Hawk's gaze never left mine. "Okay, so I wanted you two to meet, talk about the schedule, and then Wes is going to head out for the day. We already did our workout this morning, and he's off the clock."

"Oh, okay. Well, I'm sort of at your beck and call, so I'll work around your schedule." I shrugged.

I mean, they were paying me an obscene amount of money over the next two months, so this was my focus. Whatever he needed, I'd make myself available.

Well, not whatever he needed. Unless, of course, we both needed it.

Oh my gawwwwd. Get your head out of the gutter.

I led Hawk and Wes into the kitchen and offered them each a glass of water as they moved to sit at the table. We worked out a schedule that allowed Wes to train Hawk twice a day, and basically, I'd attend most of those workouts to observe, and I'd work one-on-one with Hawk each day as well. They trained seven days a week, because apparently, when you've signed a forty-million-dollar contract over five years—you work out every day.

Hell, I'd work out daily for a hundred grand... just saying.

Hawk hadn't told me about his contract, but Coach Hayes had. They were looking to get him to agree to play one more year by offering him an astounding ten million dollars for one season. It was definitely his coach's way of letting me know how much they had riding on their star player. And apparently, it was also public knowledge, however, I just didn't follow the pay of NHL players. I was guessing I would know what everyone was making in the sports world moving forward, because the bigger the paycheck, the more likely they were to bring me on.

Wes moved to his feet. He appeared to be in his early forties, very fit, much smaller in stature than Hawk, and wound a bit tight. "All right. I'm going to go hit the grocery store, and I'll call you this evening to see how things went."

Hawk nodded. "Thanks, man. I'll see you tomorrow."

I pushed to my feet as I followed him to the door, while Hawk remained at the table, sipping his water. "Nice to meet you. Thanks for coming by."

"We've got a lot of work to do, Everly, and most of that falls on your shoulders." He kept his tone low as he looked past me to make sure Hawk hadn't followed us. "The guy is a bulldog, but he's lost a bit of his fire and I think a lot of that has to do with politics of the sport more than his head. But everyone is hoping you can help bring that fire back."

I nodded. I was here to make sure Hawk kept his focus on the game and kept his confidence intact. Play to his best ability. If he'd lost his fire for the sport—his love for the game, or had a problem with the people he was working with, that would be a different story. "I'll speak to him today, and we'll get the ball rolling."

He tipped his chin up. "I'll see you at practice tomorrow."

I closed the door behind him and made my way back into the kitchen. Hawk was staring down at his phone typing something.

Probably his girlfriend.

I cleared my throat to let him know I was back.

"Hey," he said, and the corners of his mouth turned up, making my heart pound.

I took the seat across from him. "Hey."

"It's good to see you, Ever. I've missed those eyes that always saw through my bullshit and that smart mouth of yours that liked to call me out on it too." His dark hair was a wild, disheveled mess, green eyes flanked by dark lashes that I'd always envied, and a chiseled jaw covered in just enough scruff to make him look sexy as hell. He was tall and lean with just the right amount of muscle, and I struggled to catch my breath in his presence.

Always had.

"I'm guessing you don't get called out much these days, huh?"

"Not particularly, no." He smirked, and I imagined that look had girls dropping their panties at his feet.

I reached for my iPad and pencil that I'd had on the table. His hand covered mine. "No, Ever. I didn't agree to work with you so that you could psychoanalyze me. Let's not take notes just yet. It's been years since we've seen one another, and I'd like to have a normal fucking conversation without being under the microscope. That's why I was willing to come to Honey Mountain. To work with you."

I nodded, taken aback a little by the edge in his voice. Hawk had always been confident and relaxed, but he had more of an edge now hidden beneath that carefree attitude he liked to portray.

"All right. So, tell me why you agreed to work with me." I

pushed my iPad out of the way.

"Because I trust you. Even if you ripped my heart out back in the day." He chuckled. But there was something beneath the laugh. Anger. Hurt. Maybe even disappointment. "I know who you are."

I sucked in a breath and shook my head. "I hardly ripped your heart out. And if I did, you sure seemed to bounce back quickly."

Well, that was unprofessional. But if I wanted to get through to this man, we'd need to find level footing. We had a history. We couldn't pretend that we didn't. So, this needed to happen.

He scrubbed a hand down his face before his green gaze locked with mine. "Hardly. But I survived. It's what I do. But like I said, I know who you are. I figured if anyone could fix me, it would be you."

"Why's that?" I asked as I pushed the tears that threatened to fall away. I didn't expect to feel so much just by seeing the man. But sitting here across the table from him—it brought all those feelings back.

Hawk Madden had been my first love, and unfortunately, he'd been my last love. But that was okay with me. Love was overrated.

I had a great life. A fabulous career that I'd worked hard for. A family that I loved, including my father and my four younger sisters.

I dated my fair share of handsome men, and I never let anything get too serious. It worked for me.

"Because you remember me before all of this. Before I became a man with a shit-ton of responsibility. I figured you broke me once, the least you could do is put me back together." He leaned back in his chair and crossed his arms over his chest, and the first tear broke free, rolling down my cheek.

I'd avoided him all these years because I'd never wanted to hear those words.

Because the truth was—I'd broken both of us.

And we'd both survived.

Now I just needed to survive being around him again.

"That's not fair," I said, swiping at my cheek before tucking my long hair behind my shoulder and pulling myself together.

"Who said life was fair, Ever?"

"I'd say you're doing all right, Hawk. You were offered a one-year, ten-million-dollar contract—that's after coming off of the largest five-year salary in the NHL—and you've been linked to several beautiful, famous women over the years. I think you put yourself together just fine."

He raised a brow and leaned forward. "You been keeping your eye on me?"

"I mean, don't flatter yourself. You're sort of hard to hide from. Your face is everywhere, and your private life is public knowledge."

"I'm a hockey player, not Brad Pitt. You'd have to search if you wanted to know what was happening in my private life." His lips twitched, and I looked away. "You've avoided me all these years, so I figured you didn't care to know what I was up to."

I looked back up at him, because as much as this conversation pained me, it also comforted me. I'd spent years thinking about this man, and here we were.

"I wasn't avoiding you," I lied.

"Come on. Are we going to do this? Do you really want to help me?" he asked, knocking his knuckles against the table.

"Of course."

"Then start with the truth. You left me and then avoided me for years. If you want me to talk to you, you have to at least admit that fucking much."

I nodded. "Fine. I avoided you. But you'll have to talk to me about what's going on before I give you any more than that. Deal?"

"Deal." He extended his hand, and I shook it before he pushed to his feet. "Was that so painful?"

"Umm, kind of. Yes."

He barked out a laugh. "That's enough for today. I'll see you tomorrow. Your number still the same?"

I nodded. "Yep."

My cell hadn't changed, but he hadn't reached out in years.

"I'll text you to let you know what time I'll pick you up tomorrow." And he walked right out the door.

I never expected this to be easy.

But I thought I'd at least be able to keep my heart in one piece.

And at the moment, I highly doubted that was going to happen.

Because Hawk Madden still held too many pieces.

Chapter 2
Hawk

Ever and I were heading to practice with Wes this morning. I'd picked her up on my way as she lived less than a block away from my rental. It felt fucking good to be back in Honey Mountain. Breathing in that crisp mountain air. The sun shining above and the lake glistening right outside every window in my temporary home. My parents were back in town too, as they spent most of their time in San Francisco attending all of my home games.

When Coach Hayes had brought up the idea of me working with someone in the off-season, I knew there was only one person I was willing to work with. The one person who knew me better than anyone.

How fucked up was that? We hadn't spoken in years, yet Everly and I knew one another in a way I'd never experienced with anyone else. When she'd kicked my ass to the curb, it felt like I was going to die at first. But being drafted into the NHL as a teenager had forced me to focus on the game. Not on the fact that the girl had jumped ship on me. I'd signed a hefty contract my first year and spent some time numbing myself on booze and ladies, which I wasn't proud of. But it got me through. Eventually, I'd pulled my head out of my ass and gone on to win Rookie of the Year my first season playing professional hockey.

I'd dated my fair share over the years. I was more of a relationship guy than a player. I'd had a few serious girlfriends over that time, but nothing ever made it past a year or so. My schedule and travel were tough on any relationship, but if I was completely honest, most had all ended because I compared everyone to Everly Thomas. And no one had lived up to the hype. Hell, maybe I'd built her up in my head all this time, exaggerating how good we'd been together.

I figured when it was right, someone would knock me on my ass, and I'd know it. But right now, I needed to figure out why the fuck getting on the ice was more work than fun these days. Why I was ready for it to be over most days and couldn't stand the sight of my piece of shit coach.

These past few months had been hell.

The endless expectations.

It had caught up with me.

So, when I heard Ever was looking for a job, I talked to Coach Hayes. I think the guy would do just about anything to get my head back in the game, especially after I'd mentioned retirement on more than one occasion. So, I'd tapped out of my daily life and hauled my ass back to where it all started.

Honey fucking Mountain.

My hometown.

Everly Thomas's hometown.

Wes greeted Ever and me as we walked up the driveway before he had me start running drills. Coach had found Wes a place with a massive yard so that he could set up a full gym in the back. I never minded cardio, as I was a center and I'd always been willing to do the work to stay at the top of my game. Hell, that wasn't the problem. I was still doing the work. It was second nature to me.

It was the rest of the bullshit that I had a problem with. Ever watched as Wes ran me through the routine. Her long dark hair was pulled up in a ponytail and she wore jean shorts, a white T-shirt, and flip-flops (*damn straight, I noticed*) as I'd warned her she'd be sitting outside for hours. She looked sexy as hell, and I forced myself not to stare. Sweat dripped from my head as the sun beat down on me. I glanced up to see her watching me intently. As if she were surprised by my work ethic. She'd probably thought I was tired of it, and that's why we were here. I guess we still had a lot of shit to unpack. Her sapphire blue eyes locked with mine, and the familiarity of being back with her again nearly knocked me on my ass.

She jotted something down on her iPad, and I didn't mind because this side of my life wasn't private. Hell, I never minded sharing the work with anyone who wanted to know exactly what it took to be at the top of your game.

"Great job, Hawk. I swear, if the guys on the team were willing to put in half the work you put in, we'd be heading to the Stanley Cup this season with no question," Wes said.

And there it was. It was always about getting there. The ultimate goal.

I'd been there. Done that. Still wasn't enough.

It was never enough.

I guzzled from the water bottle he handed me and dumped some over my head.

"Feels good to be back here where it all started," I said, winking at Ever.

"Yeah, this is a far cry from our air-conditioned facility, huh?" Wes griped before smiling at both me and Everly. The dude was loyal as hell. He'd been on this ride with me from the beginning, and I was grateful Coach Hayes allowed him to come with me for the next few weeks. Wes hated Hayes and everything he stood for. Hell, we had that in common. But he'd promised to work for the Lions as long as I was there.

"I could check with the high school and see if we could use the gym in the morning? School will be out soon, so I'm sure they'd be thrilled to have Hawk working out there," she said.

As Wes started to agree with her, I barked at both of them. "No. I don't want to be a spectacle. That's why I'm here. If the press got wind that I was training at the local high school, there would be a crew here in no time turning it into a big fucking story. This is about getting back to my roots. If that means sweating our balls off in the hot sun, so fucking be it."

Wes nodded, and I saw the apology there. He knew I'd wanted to get away from all of that, and that's why we were here. But Ever, she just studied me like she was trying to peel back every layer.

Good fucking luck with that.

There were a shit-ton of layers now. She'd missed the past nine years of them.

"You're right. And you're the one running your ass off out here. We're good. Let's stick with the plan." Wes clapped me on the shoulder, and I reached for my keys.

"You ready?" I asked her, and she nodded before following me to my truck. We drove in silence, and I pulled into my driveway.

"Are we working here today?"

"I need a shower. I figured you'd rather I do that here than at your place." I quirked a brow at her, and her eyes doubled in size. "Relax. It'll take me five minutes and then we can get to work."

I jumped out of the truck and led her up the walkway. I unlocked the door and motioned for her to enter first, and my gaze moved down to take in her tight ass and tanned legs as I followed behind her. I cursed myself internally for checking her out. I wasn't ever going down that path again, and we needed to keep this shit aboveboard. Getting over Everly Thomas proved more difficult than playing professional hockey. I'd learned my lesson. I wasn't looking for round two of heartache.

"Wow, this place is gorgeous. I knew the Sullivans had renovated it, but I haven't been in here in years."

"Yeah. It's a great house. I rented it for the next few weeks."

Her gaze narrowed. "A few weeks? The Lions rented my place for six months."

I nodded. I'd asked Coach Hayes to do that for her so she'd have a place if this gig didn't work out, which it most likely wouldn't. The Lions weren't looking for a full-time sports psychologist. I knew it, but they'd obviously not made that clear to her. They wanted someone to fix me, and that would be it.

One and done.

Coach Hayes was quick to dispose of things when they weren't of use to him anymore. My goal was to be off the team before I allowed him the pleasure of cutting me.

"Yeah. They probably wanted to sweeten the deal to get you to take the gig. But I'll be heading back to training at the beginning of September. So, I'm just here for the next eight weeks."

She nodded. Like she'd done the math already but maybe hoped they'd extend the contract. But even if they did, she wouldn't be staying in Honey Mountain.

"Yeah, I was surprised they'd pay the lease for that long. Dylan's thrilled. She's living in the guesthouse. She hates living with Dad. Ashlan comes and goes from school, so you'll get to see her too."

I laughed. The Thomas girls were some of my favorite people on the planet. Their big sister being at the top of that list back in the day. But that ship had sailed a long time ago. Didn't mean I didn't still care about Ever and her family.

"I can't imagine Dilly does real good with your dad's rules these days, now that she's lived off on her own at school. And Ashlan is a senior in college this year, right? She'll be graduating?"

"Who's keeping tabs on who?" She smirked as she sat down on the L-shaped couch in the oversized great room, clutching her iPad like it was the Holy Grail.

"Never said I wasn't. I'm not the one avoiding you when I come to town. I'm not the one who cut all ties. That's all you,

Ever." I arched a brow before walking toward my bedroom to catch a shower.

The look on her face had my chest squeezing. I know why she pushed me away. I knew it then, and I know it now. But that didn't mean I wasn't going to take a few shots at her. She'd not only been my girlfriend for years, but my best friend.

Losing Everly Thomas was the equivalent of losing a limb. She'd cut me deep, and seeing her all these years later brought that all back to me.

I rinsed my body, and I wasn't proud to say that I gripped my dick and closed my eyes as I thought of what it would feel like to claim that sweet mouth of hers again. To explore her body. Thoughts of the little moans she used to make when we couldn't keep our hands off one another back in the day only fueled me more.

I found my release quickly and gave myself a pass for being weak. Hell, this was a lot. My career was in unchartered territory. My future was up in the air. And my past was slapping me in the face like an evil bitch. One I hadn't thought would affect me this much. Hell, I'd put this shit behind me a long time ago.

Everly Thomas had been through some tough stuff. Losing her mom our junior year of high school. She'd started shutting me out shortly after. I was getting recruited by several NHL teams our senior year, and she was touring colleges. She'd grown more and more distant in the year that followed her mother's passing. She claimed that the distance would be too much for us to survive, but the kind of love Everly and I shared, hell, there was no distance that could have come between us. But grief? That was a different story. I'd tried hard for months to get through to her, but she'd put me in her rearview mirror and moved on with her life, and I'd eventually gotten the message.

I slipped on a pair of jeans and a tee and towel-dried my hair. I didn't do much because I'd be working out again in a few hours. My PM practice was usually solo. I'd go for a run on my own, and I'd probably swim in the lake a few days a week too. It used to be something I did daily growing up here, and it felt good to be back. I made my way out to the family room, and the smell of bacon flooded my senses. Everly was standing at the stove and it brought back memories. She and her sister Vivian were always in the kitchen cooking with their mom, and they were damn good cooks if memory served.

"What are you making?" I asked.

She looked up and smiled. "I made some scrambled eggs and bacon. I figured you'd be starving after that workout. I can't believe you do it twice a day."

I sat on the barstool beside the kitchen island. The space was massive. Far too big for one person, but Coach had set it up and I wouldn't complain. Ever placed a plate in front of me, and my stomach rumbled as I took it in.

She had a small serving for herself with a third of what was on mine.

"The afternoon workout is just a run. I'll get in a couple miles. Hey, do you still run? Why don't you come with me? You might be able to psychoanalyze me a little more when I'm huffing and puffing." I laughed before biting off half a piece of bacon and groaning at how fucking good it was.

She smirked like the wiseass she was. "No one is psychoanalyzing you, Hawk. But yes, I'd be happy to accompany you on the run today, if you think you can keep up with me."

I nodded. We'd always been competitive with one another, and I loved that even though she was small in stature, she was a fucking badass. Always had been. "Sounds good. So, tell me what your plan is to fix me then? I imagine you're good at your job, because you've always been good at everything you set your mind to."

"I guess it takes one to know one." She shrugged and reached for her water and took a sip. "Listen, no one thinks you need to be fixed. That's not what I'm here for. I'm here to help you reach your full potential. Potential that you've reached numerous times before. Coach Hayes thinks you're in a slump, and we're just going to help you find your way back."

"A slump? Is that what we're calling it?"

"That's what he calls it. I'm not sure I agree." She reached for the slice of bacon on her plate and took a bite.

"What do you think it is?" I asked before forking a mouthful of the best fucking eggs I'd ever had and reaching for my napkin to wipe my mouth.

"Well, Hawk... let's review. You scored forty-eight goals last season, you're the captain of your team, one you've led to three Stanley Cups, two of which you came out victorious. You have the highest-selling jersey in the NHL, and your stats have improved every year since your first year playing. According to your coach, your last few games have been a little off and he just wants to get ahead of it. But it doesn't sound like a slump to me."

I laughed. Of course, Everly Thomas did her homework. "So, what's your diagnosis?"

"That depends on what he means by your last few games being a little off?"

"I've sucked major ass the last few games." I shrugged. "Got my ass served to me out on the ice, and Coach Hayes just isn't used to that going down. But I can't say I minded seeing him flip out over the losses. The guy is an asshole, and there are days I'd rather not play if it means playing for him."

"Did you intentionally play poorly to punish him?"

"No. I wouldn't do that. I just meant that I didn't mind seeing him lose his shit."

"Were you injured?" she asked as she set her fork down.

"Hell, I'm always injured. I've got a rod in my leg. I've had numerous surgeries after separating my shoulder. Same story, different day. But physically, none of that holds me back. So, what do you make of it, Dr. Thomas?" I teased.

"Sounds like a head problem to me."

I rolled my eyes, but I knew she was right. I just wasn't sure I was fixable.

Chapter 3
Everly

Hawk was acting like his last few games hadn't been a big deal. They hadn't made the playoffs after they'd been expected to be one of the two contenders at the Stanley Cup. The loss had landed completely on his shoulders, and I was here to figure out why. I'd watched the tapes numerous times, and he hadn't had his usual fight in those games. I could see it in his eyes. In the way he maneuvered around the ice.

"Tell me what you were feeling in those games?"

He finished chewing and leaned back on the barstool, studying me like he was trying to decide how much to share.

"We play a lot of games, Ever. You can't always be on."

I nodded. "I call bullshit. You've played a lot of games for nine years, yet you've always managed to be on."

"Have I? Or have the expectations changed?"

"Meaning?" I asked as I took another sip of water.

"Meaning, I've had off games before. But there was more forgiveness back then, even over the years. But the further I get in my career, the higher the expectation. And trust me, I fucking get it. I get paid a ridiculous amount of money to do something that I'm supposed to love."

"You don't love it anymore?" I asked.

I'd spent years out on the ice watching Hawk play hockey when we were together. We'd started dating at the start of our freshman year of high school and broke up three days before I left for NYU, and he went off to start his career. I used to envy the way he shined on the ice. It was impossible to miss how much he loved it.

"I don't know, Ever." He ran a hand down his face and let out a long breath. "I know that when I first started and I won Rookie of the Year, I scored forty goals that year. Everyone lost their fucking mind. This year I scored forty-eight goals, and everyone's disappointed. I've got a metal rod in my leg, more aches and pains than any twenty-seven-year-old man should have, but it still isn't enough. We have a ton of rookies on our team because Coach cuts every dude that has an off-season, even though they've played their asses off for him for years. And I'm on the ice during our games more than any other player in the NHL. But sometimes that shit just doesn't work. You pass the puck, and the other guy doesn't make the shot. Or they pass it to me and the goalie fucking blocks it. It happened when I first started, and it happens now. But now there's no grace, so that means I'm in a slump."

My heart ached at his words. At the pressure he dealt with on a daily basis. Yes, it came with being a professional athlete. It came with being one of the highest-paid players on the ice.

But that didn't mean it didn't get to you.

"You don't think you're in a slump?" I moved my hand closer to his and my pinkie finger grazed his.

"I don't know. I'm fucking tired, Ever. Coach expected me to pull off a miracle to get us to the playoffs, but the truth is, we weren't equipped. Our team is young. We lost a ton of valuable guys this season, and I can only do what I can do, right? And yeah, maybe I'm getting older. Maybe I'm not what I used to be. I don't fucking know." He scrubbed a hand along the back of his neck when a knock on the door startled us both.

He moved to his feet and made his way to the door. I heard a familiar squeal, and I rolled my eyes.

I leaned back to see the front door as my baby sister flung herself into Hawk's arms. I knew she wouldn't stay away. It's not her style. Dylan was the feisty twin compared to Charlotte, who was most definitely the softer, less abrasive twin.

"I thought I told you that I'd bring him by to see you later in the week," I hissed as I moved to my feet and crossed my arms over my chest as they pulled apart from their embrace. Hawk had always been close to my sisters and my parents. He was my biggest support during the months my mom fought cancer and deteriorated right before our eyes. It had been hell, and after she passed, a part of me died with her, I think. I never was quite the same, and there was nothing Hawk could do about it.

"And I told you that I didn't want to wait. It's about time you two got past your drama and made amends. We've missed you, Hawky player."

His head fell back in laughter. He'd always loved my

sister's cute nickname for him.

"Hey, Dill pickle. Apparently, I'm a hawky player with a head problem these days. Hence the need for the big sports psych they've called in," Hawk said as he winked at me.

Dylan moved to my seat and picked up the piece of bacon on my plate and took a bite. "This is so delicious. Now that I live with you and I'm out of Dad's house, there's never any food in the fridge in the guesthouse."

"You have your own kitchen. That means you need to stock it. Don't you have class today?" I rolled my eyes as I sat back down on the barstool beside my sister and Hawk pulled out the one beside me.

"Nope. We're remote today. I was running an errand and saw the familiar truck in the driveway and beelined over here. I can't believe you get paid the big bucks, and you still drive the same truck as you drove in high school." Dylan laughed as she motioned for me to pass her the saltshaker, she added a few shakes to my eggs, and dove in.

Unbelievable.

"I love that truck. Plus, I have some good memories in there." He winked at me, and I felt my cheeks heat. I couldn't begin to count the number of times we sat in that truck for hours making out, among other things, parked over by the lake in the dark. "I've always been superstitious. That truck has been good to me. I drove to the meeting where I signed my first contract with the NHL in that truck. Now mind you, I may have a sports car or two parked at my place in San Francisco, but this truck will always be my day one."

I was surprised by how unscathed Hawk still was to me. He hadn't been tainted by the money or the fame, and if you told me he was flipping burgers at the diner instead of being paid millions of dollars to play hockey, I'd believe it. He seemed exactly the same. The fact that the man had been nicknamed the GOAT of the NHL last year, yet he remained his down-to-earth self, spoke volumes about him.

"I like that about you. But I wouldn't mind taking a spin in one of your sports cars." Dylan waggled her brows. "The girls are going to be so mad that I got to see you first."

"Yeah?" he asked. "How are they? I know Vivi and Niko got married. I was disappointed I couldn't be there. I was busy *shitting the bed* on the ice." He smirked. It was his way of saying he hadn't played well during the playoffs.

"Yep. And he already knocked her up." Dylan laughed.

"Yeah. Vivi's three months pregnant," I said, taking a sip of my water.

"I believe you owe me a hundred bucks," Hawk said, raising a brow as his gaze locked with mine. "I predicted that shit years ago. Niko's such a cool dude. I'm glad she dumped that douchedick, Jansen. I never liked the guy."

"You and me both." Dylan set her fork down and high-fived Hawk. "Charlie is teaching kindergarten. I don't know how she does it. The girl has the patience of a saint."

"She always did," he said. "I wasn't surprised to hear that at all. And you're in your second year of law school, and Ash graduates this year. The Thomas girls are kicking ass, just as I expected." He nodded as a wide grin spread across his face.

"Holla," Dylan sang out and pumped her hands in the air before moving to her feet. "All right, kids, I'm out of here. I've got to go run a few errands and then find an outfit to wear tonight. I have a date."

"With that guy in your class?" I asked.

"Damn straight. I finally agreed to meet him at Beer Mountain. You guys should drop by so I have an out if it's not going anywhere."

I couldn't help but laugh. My sister was quite the dating queen. She hadn't been in anything serious since she graduated college, and even then, she seemed one foot out the door.

"Yeah. I haven't been to Beer Mountain in years. And now I can actually get in without a fake ID." Hawk chuckled, moving to his feet and hugging Dylan goodbye. "See you later, Dill pickle."

She waggled her brows. "See you guys later."

"Are you going to Lulu's boutique to find an outfit?" I asked as we followed her to the door.

"Hells to the no. I'm an unemployed law student. I'm going to your closet, big spender. You've got the best wardrobe of all of us."

I let out a long sigh. "Text me and let me know what you're wearing."

She waved a hand over her head as she continued down the driveway, and Hawk and I returned to the kitchen.

"Damn. I forgot how much I missed your family."

My chest squeezed at his words. Hawk had always been a part of the family. He'd spent so much time at our house over the years. He'd been an only child, and he loved all the chaos at our house.

"Yeah. They're all excited to see you. How are your parents doing? I don't see them much. I know you bought them a place in the Bay Area, so they aren't here that often, huh?"

"They're back now. You know my mama, she can't be far from her boy," he said, and his voice was all tease even though it was true. The Maddens loved their son something fierce. They were a great family, and as much as he'd always loved hanging out at my house, I'd loved the calm of his house when we were growing up. Dinner at their house was easy conversation, whereas my house was always a three-ring circus. We'd spent time going back and forth between our two homes, and the thought of how long it had been since I'd seen Dune and Marilee Madden suddenly made me sad. I think I avoided them when I was home too, because for whatever reason, seeing any of the Maddens made my heart heavy. It made me long for something that I had no right to long for.

"I remember sitting at all the games with your mom and dad. I can only imagine how it is for them to see you play in the NHL now. You really did it, Hawk. You know? Such a small percentage make it in professional sports, and you're out there kicking butt."

He smirked. "Always wished you could have seen me play in a pro game. You'd been with me the whole way and then when things ended, that was it. I figured you saw me on TV once or twice."

"I've actually gone to a few games. I wanted to see you play in person," I admitted, but I couldn't look at him.

His hand found my chin, and his thumb and finger turned my face so I was looking at him. "You did?"

I nodded, the breath catching in my throat at his nearness.

"Yeah. Why is that so shocking? Of course, I wanted to see you play."

"Did you bring a boyfriend with you when you came to my

games?" he asked, and though he made sure there was humor in his voice, I didn't miss the way his shoulders tensed.

"Nope. I've seen you play three times, and I went alone to all three games." I shrugged. It was the truth. I sat in the nosebleed section, and I just watched the boy I'd grown up with shine on the biggest hockey stage in the world. I couldn't go with a friend or one of my sisters. I couldn't let anyone see the way it affected me. *The way he affected me.*

His hand fell from my face, and he smiled. "You should have told me you were there. I would have gotten you a good seat up with my parents."

"No. It wasn't about that. I just wanted to see you shine." My eyes watered and I looked away, a deep lump lodged in my throat, making it difficult to swallow.

"I used to love seeing you out in the stands when I'd play."

"Hey. I have an idea." I pushed to my feet, reaching for both of our plates and carrying them to the sink.

"What's that?"

"Let's go out to where it all started. The ice rink at Honey Mountain." I wriggled my brows. "Remember all the scouts that would come there to see the small-town phenom on the ice?"

There was an indoor rink and an outdoor rink, pending the season. Both were always freezing to me because even the indoor rink was kept at a ridiculously cold temperature, but I'd loved seeing him play so much that I'd never minded.

"You sure you want to take a trip down memory lane, Ever?" He came up behind me and whispered in my ear, and I shivered. He bumped me out of the way. "You cooked. I'll load these in the dishwasher, then we can head over to the ice.

I'm guessing this is part of your devious plan to get my head back in the game."

I chuckled.

But it wasn't about that.

It was just about reliving a special time with the boy I'd loved my entire life.

If it helped him rediscover his passion for the sport, that would be a win. But it certainly wasn't the motivation at the moment.

It looked like Hawk and I both needed to get our heads in the game.

Chapter 4

Hawk

Everly and I took the truck over to the ice rink. The place where it all started. Literally and figuratively.

My love for hockey started here, but it was also the first time I admitted I had a crush on the girl beside me. We'd gone to school together our entire lives and we'd been friends for sure, but I remember when we were in middle school coming out here for the first time and seeing her on the ice rink.

"Did you know that you're the real reason I even started playing hockey?"

"Shut up. That is not true," she said as we walked over to the outdoor area that was not currently frozen, but the rink was framed in wood and the bleachers were empty. Everly moved to sit on the metal bench, and I stood in front of her, running my hand along the smooth wood guardrail. The tall peaks surrounded us, and I breathed in the mountain air.

Damn, I forgot how beautiful it was here. Both the mountains and the girl sitting in front of me with sapphire blues that were so nostalgic it sent a sharp pain to my chest.

"It is. My dad brought me here in sixth grade to check out the hockey program." I laughed and shook my head. I remembered him telling me about his time on the ice. He never played professionally, but he'd been a very impressive player through high school. "And there you were. Sailing across the ice in that white leotard with the cute little skirt. Man, I remember that was the first time I realized my body was reacting to the presence of a beautiful girl." I wiggled my brows, and her head fell back in laughter.

"Oh my gosh, stop. I do remember that particular outfit though. My mom made it for me for an ice-skating competition. It had the white sheer skirt and the tiny rhinestones all along the neckline."

"Your long dark hair was tied up in a bun on top of your head, and I remember telling my dad you looked like a real princess." I stared back out at the rink.

"I can only imagine what Dune said to that." She smiled and shook her head.

I raised a shoulder. "You know him well. He told me to pull my head out of my ass." I laughed. "But boy, did he end up a sucker for Everly Thomas. You could do no wrong in that man's eyes."

I turned back to look at her and saw her gaze wet with emotion again. Man, every time we talked, it brought shit up. Shit I thought I'd put behind me a long time ago. I'd barely been home for twenty-four hours and here we were, digging deep into the past.

"I doubt he thought that after we broke up," she said, her voice just above a whisper.

I moved to sit beside her and wrapped an arm around her. "No one blamed you for that. Not even I could. I mean, I'll never understand why you cut me off the way you did. But I know you, Ever. I know that losing your mom was devastating. I know that grieving sucks major ass. Hell, I grieved the loss of your mama too, so I knew how bad it had to be for you. And I know that you handled it the best you could. I just wish you would have let me help you through it. But look at you now." I squeezed her shoulder, and she pushed to her feet abruptly. Putting space between us just like she had all those years ago.

"What are we talking about? This isn't about me? How did we get off track?"

She was still grieving, that much was clear. Just the mention of what happened had her on edge.

"We were talking about my first time here, which happened to involve you."

She paced in front of me before coming to a stop. "Right. Okay. And what happened after you saw me skating?"

"I told my dad to sign me up. And then I think I possibly stalked you all through middle school before you agreed to date me freshman year of high school."

A wide grin spread across her face. "That's not how I remember it."

"Tell me how you remember it, *Ever mine*?"

Her breath hitched as the words left my mouth. I didn't know why I was digging this shit up, but every time we tried to talk about my early love for the sport, it involved Everly Thomas.

She sat back down beside me and turned to face me. "I remember becoming great friends in middle school. I also think I got far more involved in ice skating once you started playing hockey." She shook her head and laughed. "And then on the first day of our freshman year, you taped a note to my locker and asked me to be your girlfriend."

I nodded. "Damn. I had mad game back then."

Laughter filled the space around us. "As opposed to now. Aren't you dating Darrian Sacatto?"

"There you go again, showing me your hand." I raised a brow. "You can ask me anything, Ever. I have no secrets. I dated Darrian for a bit, but it wasn't all that deep, you know? The press ate it up, and she liked that more than I did. We both traveled a ton, and it just wasn't something either of us was willing to fight for, but I do consider her a friend. Is this part of your inquiry about the reason my last few games sucked?"

Her cheeks pinked. "Yes, actually. I need to know everything going on with you if I want to figure you out."

"Well, if anyone can do it, I'm guessing it's you." I pushed to my feet. "My breakup with Darrian was not all that memorable. We're still friends, so that was definitely not a factor in how I play on the ice."

"Good to know," she said, and the corners of her mouth turned up. I tried not to react. I couldn't go back there with Everly, but I wouldn't mind having her back in my life to some extent.

Life was always better with Everly Thomas in it.

"How about you? You dating anyone serious?"

"Not at the moment." She pushed to her feet. "Come on.

Let's go inside and skate."

I rolled my eyes. "Seriously? You want to skate with me?"

"I do. I don't know. Being here, it makes me miss it."

Everly had been a competitive skater until the time her mom got sick, and then she abruptly quit the sport that she'd loved so much. She said she didn't want to take time away from her mother, and then she never went back.

"I'm not sure you can keep up with me anymore," I said.

"I'll be the judge of that, ole cocky one."

My hand grazed hers as it swung beside me, and I glanced down to see her cheeks flush pink. I pulled open the door and I'll be damned if Mr. Chanti wasn't still working behind the desk. The man was old back in the day and now he was just ancient.

"He's got to be over a hundred by now?" I whispered in her ear, and I didn't miss the goose bumps that spread across her forearm.

She backhanded me in the chest and laughed. "He's a spry ninety-eight. Vivi just made his birthday cake."

"Cake sounds really good. How about I smoke your ass on the ice, and we head over to the bakery to see Vivi?"

"Sounds like a plan," she said.

"Well, I'll be damned if it isn't the hockey star himself. Hawk Madden, what in the world are you doing here?" Mr. Chanti said. He was hunched over and couldn't be more than 5'4", barely standing as tall as Everly and almost a foot shorter than me.

"Mr. Chanti. Nice to see you. I figured you were retired by now," I said, shaking the man's hand.

"Nah. My son Stu is too fragile to run this place. These

teenagers run circles around him."

I couldn't imagine anyone being more fragile than the man standing in front of me. If I were to sneeze right now, I was fairly certain I'd blow him over.

"I see. Well, good for you."

"Hello, to the lovely Everly Thomas. Man, I remember watching you skate on this ice when you were young." He looked off as if he were imagining it now. "Like a beautiful fairy princess. You were a natural."

Everly laughed. "I mean, thank you? But this guy is a professional hockey player. I was a kid skater. I think those outfits my mama designed just made me look a little more magical out there."

"Well, Hawk wasn't as pretty to look at. In fact, I'm not surprised that he got drafted into the NHL because he was a bit of a brute out there. Sloppy and rough. I never knew who he'd take out. But you, Everly, you were like watching an angel the way you sailed around the ice. A real vision."

I chuckled as I looked around, seeing the walls were filled with photos of me at my games throughout the years. Honey Mountain is where it all started, and maybe this was the place I could get it all back, even if the old dude was crushing hard on my sports psychologist.

"She sure was. I could watch this girl skate all day." I winked.

"Okay, Casanova," she said before turning to Mr. Chanti. "Can we each get a pair of skates?"

"You'd think a fancy professional hockey player would have his own," the old man taunted me as we both told him our skate size.

"I've got my own at home. I didn't know the brilliant doctor here was going to take me skating."

"This is sort of spur-of-the-moment. It looks pretty empty in there."

"Yeah, until school gets out, it stays pretty quiet. You'll have the ice to yourself." He handed us each a pair. "You think I could get your autograph, Hawk? You may not be as pretty on the ice as Everly, but the people in this town are your biggest fans. I'd love to hang it on the wall."

"Absolutely." I signed the piece of paper that he handed me, and Everly and I made our way into the ice rink.

"Dang. I forgot how cold it gets in here."

"Well, I guess you need to get your ass moving on that ice if you want to warm up."

"Don't you worry about me moving on that ice, Hawk Madden. It's like riding a bike," she said as she sat on the bench, and we laced up our skates.

We both made our way onto the ice, and I skated backward as I waited for her to get her footing. Of course, it took no time. This was Everly Thomas we were talking about. The girl was good at everything she did.

She started skating faster, and I continued moving backward and laughing as she tried to keep up. Before I realized what she was doing, she moved to the center of the ice and reached behind for her leg and started twirling in circles as she pulled her heel up to the back of her head like it was no big deal. I glanced over to see Mr. Chanti watching her through the window from the front desk like he was watching a Broadway show. She laughed when she came to a stop, bits of ice spraying all around her and landing on her tan, toned legs.

"Damn. That was pretty fun. Now show me your stuff, Hawky player." She skated toward the wall and crossed her arms.

I started skating faster and faster around the ice, moving forward and backward, and cutting in different directions, making her laugh. I came to an abrupt stop in front of her, causing ice chips to gather around her calves.

"Impressive." She smirked.

"Come on, let's race," I said. And I'll be damned if it wasn't the most fun I'd had on the ice in a long time.

We were both laughing, and she begged me to do her favorite *Dirty Dancing* move and I rolled my eyes but happily played along.

"Nobody puts Baby in the corner," she shouted, as she moved to the far end of the ice before skating toward me as fast as she could. Her body flailed through the air, just like she did when we were kids.

I caught her with ease and held her high above my head as I skated backward down the rink.

She was gasping for air when I finally set her down.

"I forgot how fun this was."

"So did I," I said, my voice all tease. But there was truth behind my words. Because I had forgotten how fun it was.

"Time for cake?" she asked.

"Absolutely."

We returned our skates and made our way to Honey Bee's, Vivian's bakery.

"My, oh my, say it isn't so. Hawk Madden, you're even more handsome than I remembered," Mrs. Winthrop, who owned Sweet Blooms down the street from the bakery, said as she stepped out onto the sidewalk. She wrapped her arms around me. "Good to see you, sweetheart."

I patted her on the back and smiled. "Good to see you too."

It was. I didn't realize how much I'd missed this place until I came back. Hell, my life never slowed down. I didn't skate at local rinks or go get cake in the middle of the day in my world.

It was all business, all the time.

Practice and games and press conferences and interviews.

Everyone wanted a piece of me.

But here in Honey Mountain, I was just the local kid who grew up here. Hell, even Mr. Chanti knew Everly was a bigger deal than me.

And I reveled in it.

In the innocence.

In the grace of being able to go places without someone wanting something. Without being pulled in eighteen directions. The simplicity that was home.

I guess I needed it more than I realized.

Needed to make amends with the girl beside me more than I realized.

Chapter 5
Everly

We waved our goodbye to Mrs. Winthrop and I pulled open the door to Honey Bee's. My sister had done an amazing job with this bakery. Vivian was the heart of our family. The girl had given up a lot to stay close and help my dad with our younger sisters after our mom had passed away. My dad was the captain of the fire department here in Honey Mountain, and Vivian had passed up her college scholarship to stay home and help out. She'd encouraged me to chase my dreams, and I'd gone clear across the country to attend school in New York. Staying home wasn't even an option for me back then. Hell, even coming home was challenging for me most of the time.

I studied psychology in college and received my Ph.D. in sports psychology as well. You didn't have to be a rocket scientist to know that we all dealt with grief differently.

Fight or flight.

It was the basic survival skill in life. My sister was a fighter, and she didn't even know it.

I was all about running.

Fleeing.

I'd run from home. I'd run from Hawk. I'd run from everything and everyone that I loved.

It wasn't an admirable trait, and I wasn't proud of it. But we were all wired differently, and this was the way that I'd dealt with my grief. Hell, I was still dealing with it. I'd buried myself in school for years.

And nothing was lost on me with this job. Working with athletes trying to find their way definitely gave me more insight than I ever wanted into my own.

"Hawk," Vivian shouted as she ran around the counter and jumped into my ex-boyfriend's arms. They all loved him. We'd dated for four years, but we'd been friends since preschool. And my sisters all had my back when I'd ended things and refused to talk about it. They'd never pushed. Almost like they'd understood it was too painful for me.

Because it was.

"Hey there, little mama," he said as he hugged her and spun her around. "I hear you've got a bun in the oven."

Jilly, Charlotte's best friend, and Jada, Niko's younger sister, worked at Honey Bee's, and they both gawked at the man because his presence was larger than life. He set Vivi down and moved toward the two women, giving them each a hug.

Like I said, the man oozed charm.

"We're going to need to take a selfie together so I can hang up proof that the GOAT of the NHL was here," my sister said as she beamed up at him.

"How about you hang these in the bakery?" Hawk said, holding up his phone and scrolling through his photos as he showed them to her. I leaned in and my cheeks heated. He had taken several photos of me twirling on the ice.

"You skated?" Vivi's eyes welled with emotion.

"It's not a big deal." I shrugged.

Sure, I hadn't been on the ice since my mom got sick. It was something we'd always done together. My mother had been a competitive skater when she was in high school, and she'd coached me for years.

Vivian pulled me into a hug, and when I pulled back, I placed my hand on her little belly. "Maybe I can teach this little bambino a thing or two about skating?"

"Do you know if it's a boy or a girl yet? Maybe he'll be a little hockey player," Hawk asked as he glanced through the glass at the pastries.

Jada and Jilly were acting like schoolgirls with a crush the way they kept giggling and batting their lashes. They both had serious boyfriends, but I understood how the man could make you melt into a pile of mush. It's how I'd been around him most of my life.

"Not yet. We'll find out at the next appointment. Niko's excited to see you. We thought maybe you guys could come over for a barbecue?" Vivian said, shooting me a look. She knew I was trying to be cautious about how much time Hawk and I spent together, but seeing as we only had a few weeks, I thought the more time I spent with him, the more likely I'd uncover what he was struggling with.

"That sounds great. I was going to see if your sister wanted to stop by the firehouse after I eat one of everything you've got here, so we can see your dad and Niko. I heard Jace is a fireman now too, so I'd love to see him as well."

I nodded. "Sure. We can do that. And a barbecue sounds like fun."

"She'll need the food. We're going for a run later today, and I may be racing her in the lake as well."

I rolled my eyes. "Twirling around the ice, running, swimming... this job has never been so challenging."

"You bowing out, Ever?" he whispered close to my ear, and I shivered.

Vivian was busy filling a box with treats, and I studied his green eyes when he pulled back. His tongue swiped out to wet his lips, and I forced myself to look away.

"Never. Game on, Madden."

He whistled. "She talks such a big game. We'll see about that."

Everyone laughed, and my sister's gaze locked with mine.

Don't overthink it.

Sisters were the best. All five of us could communicate without speaking. Always had. I nodded.

Hawk hugged everyone goodbye, and I waved as we walked out the door and down toward the firehouse as he passed me a brownie.

"Damn, your sister can bake. This is unbelievable." He spoke over a mouthful of cake.

I chuckled. "You're just making the Honey Mountain rounds, aren't you?"

"Yep. And it feels damn good. I forgot how much I loved it

here. With my parents in the Bay Area most of the time, I don't feel the need to come here as much. But this is exactly what I needed." He reached in the box and pulled out a cookie, and I shook my head in disbelief at how much the man could eat.

"Yeah, I don't come home all that often either." I don't know why I said it, but I did, and I wish I could take it back.

Hawk came to a stop and studied me. "Everyone you love is here. Why wouldn't you come home?"

I shrugged. "I don't know."

"Looks like we're both in a slump," he said as he started walking again. I knew my dad would be thrilled to see him, as would Niko and Jace and all the guys who probably had man crushes on the hockey star. "We'll need to go by and see my parents soon too."

I sucked in a long breath. I'd been so close to them for so long, and when I left, I left all those relationships behind. I avoided them because I feared they hated me, and I couldn't stand the thought of that.

"Don't be a baby. They miss you. No one is angry at you. That shit is in the past. We were kids. Kids break up. They get their hearts broken. They recover. Don't make it bigger than it is."

Ouch.

I knew he didn't mean to offend me, but wow. "I know you're over it, Hawk. I hear you loud and clear."

He nodded as we approached the firehouse. I led him up the stairs, and he held his box of treats as well as the box that Vivi gave him for the firehouse.

"Hey," I said as Niko came around the corner.

"Hey, Ev," he said before his eyes moved to Hawk. "Hey,

dude. How are you?"

Hawk pulled Niko in for a hug. "Hey, yourself. I hear you're going to be a daddy. You know, I bet Ever years ago that you two were going to end up together."

"Yeah? Was I the only one who didn't see it coming?"

"Definitely," I said with a laugh.

"So, is Dr. Thomas figuring your shit out?"

"I guess so. She took me to the ice rink, and we saw Mr. Chanti, which is a walking miracle that he's not only still alive but still able to give me shit."

Niko laughed just as Jace came around the corner and pulled Hawk in for one of those bro hugs.

"The GOAT comes back to Honey Mountain. Good to see you, man. I don't think Niko and I have missed a game in nine years," Jace said, and Niko winced at me as if that was supposed to be a secret.

"What? Does she have you afraid to say that you're watching my games?" Hawk laughed and then shot me an offended look.

"No. I do not," I insisted.

"Well, Honey Bee says we aren't supposed to say your name around Ev, so I just don't talk about it."

"There's an awful lot to unpack there, am I right, Doc?" Hawk smirked at me.

I gasped, and my cheeks had to be flaming red.

Niko and Jace were both laughing just as my dad walked up, and I wanted to crawl under a table.

"Hawk. I heard you were coming home. It's good to see you, son. What a career you've had. And I'm the only one who isn't afraid to piss off my daughter. Your games are always on here at the firehouse and the Thomas house when you're playing." Dad hugged him tight, and I huffed beside them once again.

"I never told anyone not to watch your games."

"Just not to say his name, right?" Dad joked, and I raised my brows at him as if that was supposed to go to the grave.

"You're such a traitor. The superstar comes home, and you completely betray your firstborn?" I said, holding my arms out to the side.

"Damn straight, girl. People have already named him the greatest hockey player of all time." Dad shrugged, looking at Hawk. "So, is my girl going to fix whatever shit you've got going on?"

"I think if anyone can do it, it's Ever." Hawk winked at me. I think he actually felt bad that everyone was giving me a hard time. That's what had made it so hard when I'd called things off. Hawk Madden was the best person I'd ever known. A part of me hoped he'd come back and be arrogant and cocky. But he hadn't changed a bit. Obviously, he didn't have feelings for me anymore, but I thought he'd like to be friends, and I was thankful for that.

But being in his presence had stirred up a whole lot of feelings in me that I hadn't expected.

Desire.

Want.

Longing.

Things I made a point not to feel. And I was sure every woman within a mile radius of the man felt those things when they were in his presence. He was the whole package. Beautiful, strong, charming, humble, and kind. Throw in the fact that he was also a rock star on the ice, and it was almost too much.

And we'd only spent one day together so far. I knew I was in trouble, and the urge to run was strong. But I had a job to do, and I needed to stay focused on that.

We spent the next hour sitting around the table at the firehouse as all the guys drilled Hawk with questions. Rusty and Tallboy and Rook were there, practically drooling over him. Big Al, my dad's best friend, was a huge fan and actually asked me to take a picture of them together. Gramps, the oldest guy at the firehouse, just listened and laughed as the guys all acted like fools in his presence. And Hawk took it all in stride.

I caught my father watching me at one point, and I forced a smile. He winked, but I saw something behind his eyes that I couldn't read. Dad always worried about us girls, so he probably worried that I'd get hurt. But I'd learned how to protect myself a long time ago. That would not be happening.

Not that Hawk wanted anything to happen.

He didn't.

I didn't.

Did I?

The alarm sounded, and the guys were off and running. Hawk and I were sitting at the table, and I looked up to find him studying me.

"What's up? Are you exhausted from being fawned all over?" I chuckled.

"Nah. That was awesome. I'm just trying to figure out why no one was allowed to say my name all these years?"

I shook my head and pushed to my feet. "Well, we're not

psychoanalyzing me, we're psychoanalyzing you, remember?"

He nodded, but his gaze never left mine as he moved to his feet, and we made our way down the stairs.

"We'll see about that. This is give-and-take, Ever. You want to know things about me, you better be ready to share things about yourself."

I rolled my eyes as we made our way back to his truck, and I climbed into the passenger seat and buckled up.

"That's not how this works," I said, glancing over at him.

"We'll see about that. Ready for our run?"

"I was born ready, Hawk Madden."

He laughed and shook his head. "Remember, I'm a professional athlete now. I will not be going easy on you."

"You want to bet on it?"

"Sure. I'm not afraid to wager on my skills," he purred.

Damn, he was so ridiculously sexy without trying and my lady bits were all up in arms about it.

"How far do you want to run?"

"How about that five-mile course we used to do?" He turned down my street.

"Perfect. I run that course all the time, hotshot. First one to finish gets to ask anything they want."

"Deal. I have complete confidence in my abilities." He winked as he threw the car in park.

No doubt about it.

The man was gifted in all the things.

"Get ready to sing like a canary, Madden."

"You'll be the one singing, Ever. If memory serves, you used to hum after I'd make you cry out my name, so it should come easy for you."

My mouth dropped open after I got out of the truck, and my eyes doubled in size. *Did he seriously just reference us having sex back in the day?*

"You at a loss for words?" he said as he leaned close and his lips grazed my ear. "When you lose, you'll have no choice but to spill the beans."

I didn't say a word. I tried to calm my breathing and pushed the door open.

I was losing control of this whole situation.

I needed to reel it in.

First things first… beat his ass at the race.

And then make him start talking.

Chapter 6
Hawk

I came around the final turn and damn if I wasn't almost completely out of breath. But she continued to challenge me, and I was not about to back down. Hell, I'd expected to drop her after the first mile, but the girl proved she had incredible stamina.

I looked ahead at the tree right in front of the lake and pumped my arms like I was in a motherfucking *Rocky* movie. Still, I couldn't lose her.

She was gasping.

I was gasping.

And we both slapped the bark of the tree at the same goddamn time.

Was I losing my edge? I glanced down at my watch, and it was the fastest five miles I'd clocked in years. Maybe ever.

I wasn't losing my edge, I was racing a freaking running machine.

I leaned forward to catch my breath and she did the same thing.

"What the fuck, Ever? What was that?"

She was laughing as she dropped down on her ass and attempted to slow her breathing. "What? I've been training for a half marathon. Did I not mention that?"

I sat on the ground beside her and used both hands to push the damp hair out of my face.

"You could probably get hired by the team as a trainer." I chuckled.

"So, what happens now? I'd say that was a tie, hotshot."

"A tie means we both won, and we both lost. So, you get to ask me something, but I also get to ask you something."

She huffed and fell on her back, shielding her eyes from the sun shining down on us. The water lapped against the shore. Honey Mountain Lake was my favorite place in the world. The water was the darkest blue, and I'd always told Ever that her eyes were Honey Mountain blues.

The deepest and the darkest I'd ever seen.

"I get to go first. If you're actually honest with me, I'll answer one of your questions," she said, sitting forward and shaking out her long, dark ponytail to free it of any leaves.

"I'm always honest, Ever. I'm not the one who's got anything to hide."

She rolled her eyes. "Fine. Here we go."

"Bring it on." I leaned back on my elbows and stared out at the water.

"Are you happy, Hawk? I mean, does hockey make you happy? Does the life you're living make you happy?"

I laughed. "That's so you—get a turn asking *one* question

and ask three."

"It's one question, it just needed clarification." She smirked.

I reached for a twig resting beside my hand and peeled back the bark as I thought over her question. "I'm happy to an extent."

"That is not going to cut it, Madden."

I turned to look at her. "Do I love living my life under a microscope? My worth being judged by how many goals I score? The whole city being angry at me every time we lose a game? Not particularly. But did I love lacing up those skates today and gliding across the ice? Hell yeah, I did. And most of the time, I'm happy with what I do for a living. My teammates are like family to me. We work hard and we play hard. My coach is an asshole, and I don't trust him as far as I can throw him, but I've been dealing with his shit for the past nine years, so it's not a deal-breaker. But I don't know. I feel like there must be more to life than this, you know? More than just scoring goals and making money."

I turned to look at her and her gaze searched mine. "Like something's missing? What do you think it is?"

"That's the million-dollar question, Ever. Either something's missing, or this just isn't enough anymore."

"That's fair. And it's honest. I appreciate it."

I nodded. "All right, so it's my turn. Tell me why no one was allowed to say my name for the past nine years. Hell, Ever. I talk about you with my parents every time they come back home. I ask if they saw you or your family. What's the deal with you not wanting to talk about me to anyone?"

Her lips pursed, and she looked away. It was something

she used to do when things were on her mind.

She cleared her throat. "Why are we talking about me when I was hired to figure out what's going on with you?"

"Says the queen of deflection. Answer the goddamn question, Ever. You've never been one to renege on a bet."

She let out a long breath. "Talking about you hurt too much, Hawk. There. Are you happy?"

She pushed to her feet and stormed down toward the water, and I followed. This wasn't done.

She skipped a rock across the lake before bending down and grabbing another. She wound her arm back and chucked it along the surface, and it moved along the water with perfection. Bouncing every few feet as it disappeared in the distance.

I placed a hand on her shoulder and squeezed. "Don't run every time the conversation gets uncomfortable, or we'll never get anywhere."

"I'm not running. I just don't know why we're talking about the past. We're here to fix you, remember?" She shrugged, her gaze staying directed at the water, but her cheek leaned in toward my hand, craving the warmth I was offering.

I pulled my hand away. What the fuck was I doing? She was right. We didn't need to dig up the past. I didn't come here to figure out why Everly Thomas had run from my life. I'd moved on. We both had.

"Well, we can either talk more or go dive into the water." I bumped her with my shoulder, and she swiped at her cheeks and chuckled.

"You really want to swim after that run? I swear I heard you gag a few times toward the end there." She turned to look at me with a brow raised in challenge.

"Whatever. I'm out on the ice for hours during games. That was nothing," I lied. I'd pushed it harder than I had in a long time on that run. "Sounds like you're the one bowing out."

"Never. I just don't have a suit here."

"Your house is about a quarter of a mile in that direction," I said, pointing at the dock in front of her rental. "We can strip down and hide our shoes and clothes under this tree and race to your house. Then I'll swim back and grab our things and get the truck because I'm assuming you'll need to lie down on the grass and recover."

"You're so full of yourself, aren't you?" She tugged her black tank over her head, exposing her fitted black sports bra, before she reached for her shorts and pushed them down her thighs. She wore black panties that matched her bra.

Holy fucking hell.

I'd dated my fair share of gorgeous women. None had ever come close to Ever. And seeing her strip down all these years later... she was absolute perfection.

Toned and tanned and gorgeous.

She snapped her finger in front of my face.

"It's not like you haven't seen this before. And seeing as you date supermodels now, I don't think there's any need to gawk, Hawk." Her head fell back in laughter because the last two words rhymed.

Gawk and hawk.

Yeah, that shit never got old. I rolled my eyes. "I'm not gawking. Don't flatter yourself."

I yanked my tee over my head, and her eyes doubled in

size as she scanned my body. I pushed my running shorts down and glanced down to see my dick sticking straight out of my fitted navy boxer briefs.

Damn. It was hard to pretend I wasn't reacting to her when the big guy showed up out of nowhere.

She put a hand over her mouth, and her shoulders quaked as she tried to control her laughter.

"It's been a while, that's all." I stormed toward the water because the last thing I needed was to walk behind her and find out if her panties were a thong. The thought of her tight ass had me hurrying down to the lake.

"Don't be a bad sport just because you can't handle seeing a girl in a sports bra. It happens to everyone, I'm sure of it," she said over her laughter as she caught up behind me.

My feet hit the water, and I knew the cool temperature would work in my favor with my current situation. She squealed when she stepped in, and I turned around to face her.

"Well, who's talking a big game? Looks like your body isn't numb to a hot man because someone's got her headlights on, and you're practically blinding me." I laughed and motioned to her chest. Ever's tits were works of art. I'd always been a big fan. Those tits gave me my first erection out in public, and I swear I'd spent four years memorizing everything about them.

She looked down and then folded her arms over her chest. "The water's cold."

"Sure, it is." I smirked. "So, if I win, we get dressed and then go pick up dinner and take it to my parents' house. Time to rip off that bandage."

She glanced out at the water, dark hair falling from her

ponytail around her face. "What if I win?" she whispered.

"We pick up dinner and take it to my parents' house. Come on, Ever. They want to see you."

She nodded, before surprising me and running out deeper and diving in. I was still standing there with my jaw on the ground, because yes, Everly Thomas was wearing a thong, and her ass was just as toned and tight as the rest of her. I hurried after her, stretching my arms over my head to pull me through the water as fast as possible. I'd always been a stronger swimmer than her, and I caught up quickly. I settled beside her, and we moved stroke for stroke down to the dock.

The sun was shining above, and it was the first time in several years that I felt completely at peace. There were no cameras. No coaches. No fans.

No expectations.

Just me and the girl who knew me better than anyone ever had, swimming in Honey Mountain Lake.

I looked up and reached my arm above to grab the base of the dock in front of her house. Ever stumbled a bit as she tried to grab the post, and I reached for the top of her arm and helped steady her. She shoved the hair out of her face.

"Tie?"

I laughed, because it wasn't even close, and she knew I could have smoked her. "Sure." I smirked.

A Jet Ski blew past us, but the lake was fairly calm today. The weekends were always crazier this time of year.

"So, I'll need to shower and get ready before we go to your parents," she said, and her gaze moved from mine back to the water quickly.

She was fucking nervous. I knew her well enough to know

that. But her eyes swept across my chest, and I didn't miss the way her sapphire blues darkened as they took me in.

"Yep. I'll swim back and grab our things. I'll pick you up in an hour. Hopefully, you'll be recuperated by then. And take a cold shower to calm your ladies down, all right?"

She slapped her hand down hard on the water and laughed as a gush of water hit me in the face. I walked backward before turning around and pushing the hair out of my face.

When I glanced over my shoulder, I winked.

I knew she was watching me.

Hell, we never could keep our eyes off one another.

Some things never changed.

Chapter 7
Everly

I took a quick shower and decided to let my long hair air-dry after I brushed through it. Between skating for the first time in years today, the run, and the swim, my legs were complete jelly. I'd need to talk to Hawk about this. I wasn't his trainer. I was a sports psychologist. That did not require working out with the athlete.

I closed my eyes for a minute when I thought about the way he looked in the water. His green eyes had locked with mine, and little flecks of amber and gold sparkled in the sun shining down on us. Hawk had always been the best-looking boy I'd ever laid eyes on, but to say he'd grown into an even more attractive man would be an understatement. And he made it look effortless. His dark hair falling all around his face as water droplets moved over his broad shoulders. I'd fought the urge to move closer to him. The urge to lick the water droplets from his shoulders.

I covered my face with both hands and let out a long breath.

Pull yourself together, for god's sake.

My phone vibrated and I glanced down to see Brad Weber's name flash across my screen. We'd dated on and off the last few months that I lived in New York. It never got all that deep and with me moving back home to look for a job, we'd called it quits. But he'd reached out a few times since I'd moved, which had surprised me. Our friendship wasn't even all that strong. We'd just enjoyed going to movies and dinners a few times a month, and we had a couple mutual friends.

"Hey, Brad," I said, putting him on speakerphone as I rubbed lotion all over my face. I was naturally tan, but my cheeks and nose were a little pink from all the sun today. Never in a million years did I think I'd be swimming in the lake in my panties and bra with Hawk, but that's how it always was with him. You never knew what to expect.

"Hi, Everly. I wanted to let you know I'd be coming that way for a bachelor party with a college buddy of mine."

"Really? Honey Mountain is not the most popular bachelor party destination," I said over my laughter.

"Yeah, that's what I thought. Apparently, Doug spent his summers there when he was growing up, and he loves the lake and the mountains, so there ya go."

I applied a little lip gloss and flipped my head over, running my hands through my now damp waves before flipping it back over.

"That sounds great. What are your guys' plans?"

"We rented a big house on the lake, and it's got a boat and

Jet Skis, so we'll be kicking it on the water. I thought maybe we could meet up for a drink?"

"Of course. That would be great. When are you coming to town?"

"In two weeks. I'll text you all the details and you let me know when I can see you. I miss you, Everly."

Um... what? That came out of left field.

I chuckled. "Really?"

He laughed. "Don't sound so surprised. You're easy to miss. You probably don't know that because you're always one foot out the door, so you don't let people get close enough to miss you."

That struck a nerve. He nailed my MO though, and maybe that's what bothered me most.

"I knew I was leaving New York after my fellowship, so no point letting anything get all that deep. But I'm sure you're doing just fine, Romeo." I shook my head as I looked myself over once more. There was no doubt that Brad was a total player, and I recognized it from the start. It didn't bother me because I wasn't looking for anything serious. "Text me the details, and I'll meet you somewhere for a drink."

"Looking forward to it. Talk soon."

There was a knock on the door, and I ended the call before slipping on my sandals and hurrying out to open the modern glass-pane door for Hawk.

"You look pretty," he said, clearing his throat. "I thought we'd grab some pizzas and head over. I didn't tell my parents you were coming. I thought it would be more fun to surprise them."

My stomach churned because I loved the Maddens so

much, and the thought of them being upset with me made me physically ill. I'm sure they didn't understand why I'd ended things so abruptly, and at such a big point in Hawk's life, because even my own family hadn't understood it.

But I knew I'd done the right thing.

For Hawk and for me.

"Sounds good," I said, grabbing my purse as I followed him out the door.

We picked up pizzas from our favorite local spot and made our way to Hawk's parents' home. It was right down the street from my dad's house, and I was suddenly overcome with nostalgia as we pulled into the long driveway.

Of all the times I'd run over to this house growing up. Of the long talks with his mom, Marilee, at the kitchen table. Of his dad talking to me for hours about ice skating and hockey. The man was a sports fanatic, and we'd always had that in common.

"Ever." Hawk turned off his truck and looked at me. "There's nothing to be nervous about."

I nodded. "I know. I just really miss them, I guess."

"Why is that so hard for you to say?"

"I don't know?" I shook my head and blinked a few times to stop the tears that threatened to fall. I wasn't a crier. I'd learned a long time ago to control my emotions, but somehow being home, being around Hawk—it made it all a lot more challenging.

"How do you eat an elephant?" he asked, and I laughed.

I used to always say that to him when he'd complain about our calculus homework. And our English homework. Come to think of it, he'd say it about all of our schoolwork. When

Hawk was young, he always wanted to be outside swimming or skiing or skating. He'd get very impatient when we had a stack of homework to complete and I'd always reference said elephant.

"One bite at a time, Mr. Madden." I unbuckled my seat belt, and we both got out of the truck.

He placed a hand on my lower back and led me up the walkway before pushing the door open and guiding me inside.

The smell of pineapple and coconut flooded my senses, and it reminded me of home. Of my childhood.

Of laughter and fun and sunshine.

Marilee loved her candles and she obviously had remained loyal to that one scent.

"Hello? I'm home," Hawk shouted.

"Do I smell pizza?" Dune asked, and his wife chuckled as they both stepped into the kitchen and saw me standing there.

Marilee's jaw dropped open and something crossed her face that I couldn't read. It was a brief look of panic before she shook it off and hurried toward me.

"There she is. Oh, how I've missed you, Everly girl."

She wrapped her arms around me and before I could stop it, the tears started to fall. I hugged her back and sniffed a few times to try to stop the sob from escaping.

"Oh, for god's sake, Marilee. Let the girl breathe. Bring it in, Everly girl." Dune stood there with his arms open. The man was large in stature like his son, though he'd been bald since as far back as I could remember. Hawk definitely got his thick dark hair from his mother.

I hurried over to Hawk's dad and heard Marilee mumbling to her son about something being a little awkward. The panic in her voice had my haunches up, but I couldn't imagine she would hug me the way she just did and feel uncomfortable about my presence.

"Hey there, handsome," a sultry voice said, and I pulled back from Dune's embrace to see none other than the famous actress, Darrian Sacatto, standing in the middle of the Maddens' kitchen.

Hawk set the pizzas on the table and looked between his parents, to me, and back to the gorgeous woman standing in front of us.

She was much taller than me and had to be pushing six feet tall. Long blonde waves fell down her shoulders, and her bright red lips were impossible not to stare at.

"Darrian," Hawk said as he cleared his throat, and she stepped into his arms. I couldn't look away. They looked like a Hollywood power couple when they stood beside one another. I don't know why it happened, because I thought my heart stopped working a long time ago, but I swear on all things holy, it shattered right there in the kitchen I'd spent hours upon hours in when I was growing up.

I was thankful that Dune must have picked up on it because his arm came around my shoulder protectively, and Marilee glanced over at me with the most empathetic gaze I'd seen since my mother's funeral. I now understood why she'd acted so nervous when I walked in.

"What are you doing here?" Hawk asked. Was he putting on a show for me? Were they really together and he just didn't want to tell me?

But why? We were nothing. And that was my doing. My fault.

But why'd it hurt so damn much to see him with someone? I'd seen him with her in the media before, but seeing it in person. The way she looked up at him like he was hers. I hadn't felt a pain like that in a very long time, and this was the type of feeling that I avoided. Working with him was a huge mistake.

This was too much for me.

My need to run was strong.

Stronger than it had been in years.

And it made no sense.

"Well, I knew you came back home to get your head back in the game," she purred, and her hand ran up his chest possessively, long red nails that matched her lip color. She was staking her claim. And he was all hers. "I hadn't heard back from you, and I don't know, Hawk. I missed you. I have a red-carpet event coming up in a few weeks, and I was hoping I could talk you into going with me."

So, he hadn't lied. They weren't technically together. But it wasn't because she didn't want to be. He kissed the top of her head in adoration, and my hands fisted at my sides, and Dune glanced down at me with a brow raised as he chuckled.

"Darrian surprised us, showing up at the door just a few minutes ago," Marilee said, glancing over at me to make sure I knew this wasn't planned. But she hadn't known I was coming over and it shouldn't matter either way. They had dated and obviously she wasn't done just yet.

"Dar, this is Everly Thomas. She's working with me on my head game."

"Hi, Everly. I'm Darrian. It's nice to meet you." She extended her arm to me, and I shook her hand.

"Nice to meet you, too," I lied. It wasn't. I was an asshole. A complete hypocrite. I hated this woman, and I didn't even know her. I hated her for reasons that were completely unfair.

"Have you figured out what's going on with my man?" Darrian said as her tongue swiped out to wet her lips then looked back up at Hawk, and it was like a missile had just blasted through my chest.

My man.

She wanted him. This woman could have anyone she wanted. They'd probably end up getting married and have beautiful children, and they'd grace the covers of every magazine. They were the Hollywood *It* couple.

"We're working on it," I said as I cleared my throat. Was it closing? Was anyone else struggling to breathe?

"Who wants pizza?" Hawk said, ignoring Darrian's comment and reaching for some paper plates in the cupboard.

"Um, excuse me. I just need to run to the restroom," I said, moving away from Dune as Hawk's gaze studied me.

I wanted to run out the back door.

Run home, pack my bags, and get the hell out of Honey Mountain. Everything hurt here.

That's why I left.

Being home was bringing it all back. And it was awful.

Chapter 8
Hawk

My mother glanced over at me as Darrian stepped out onto the back porch to take a phone call. I handed my mom the plates and left to find Everly.

She had that wild look in her eyes.

The one that told me she was ready to flee.

The panic. The fear. It was all there. Hell, had it ever left?

That's the way she'd been nine years ago when she'd ended things. Like a scared animal not willing to hear anything because her need to run was so strong.

I knocked on the bathroom door lightly. "Ever."

"Oh, hey. I'll just be a minute."

"Open the damn door," I said, keeping my voice calm and making sure no one heard me.

She cracked the door open, and I pushed inside and closed it behind me.

"What are you doing?" she gasped before leaning up against the wall and huffing.

The girl used anger to cover her fear, and I understood it. But it wasn't necessary with me. I knew her. She knew me.

"You don't need to run. Nothing is going on here." I moved closer.

"I'm not running. Why do you think you know me so well?" she hissed, taking a step in my direction, her chest hitting mine as she tipped her head all the way back to look up at me.

Had there ever been a more beautiful woman? I don't think so. Her skin was flawless, lips naturally plump, and eyes soul-searching.

"Because I do. Stop being a stubborn ass. Darrian's a friend."

"Why would I care what Darrian is to you?" She moved until her back hit the wall, but I went with her, our chests still touching.

"I don't know, Ever. Why don't you tell me?"

Without any warning, she pushed up on her tiptoes and her mouth crashed into mine. She kissed me with the hunger I felt. Her lips were soft and lush. My tongue dipped in before I could stop myself. Tasting and claiming her in every way, as I pressed her against the wall.

But I couldn't go there. Not like this. Not when she wouldn't open up to me. Not when she'd already run from me once with no warning. She must have felt it because she pulled back, and her hands landed on my chest.

"That was a mistake." She shoved me back, and I rolled my eyes.

"Do you ever get tired of your own shit?" I said, moving to the sink and turning on the water to wash my hands because I needed to do something to distract myself in this small space. My dick was raging. I hadn't wanted anyone like this in... nine years, if I were being honest.

"And what shit is that?" She rubbed her temples and shook her head.

"You ran to the bathroom, probably trying to plot your escape. Then you kissed me before calling it a mistake. What the fuck, Ever."

She reared back. "You kissed me, you arrogant jackass."

"I don't think so." I smirked, turning off the water and drying off my hands on the towel hanging beside the sink. "Now get your ass out there and eat some pizza and talk to the movie star and visit with my parents. They love you."

"This is a lot, Hawk. And it's really only our first day working together. It's just bringing up a lot of things." She shrugged.

At least she was being honest.

"Just calm your ass down. You don't need to overthink everything. You felt the urge to kiss me, and you took your shot. Kudos, girl." I laughed and reached for the bathroom door.

"I did not kiss you. When did you get so arrogant?" She pinched my arm, and I yelped before peeking out the door to make sure no one was listening.

I turned around and leaned down and her eyes widened, but I moved my lips close to her, grazing her skin as I spoke. "Not arrogant, just honest, Ever." I nipped at her ear, and she let out a loud squeak.

"Everything all right?" my mother called out, and I heard Darrian step back into the kitchen and apologize for taking the call.

"Go," I said, pointing for her to start walking down the hall.

"Why do I have to go first?" she whisper-hissed and shoved at my shoulder for me to go.

"Because you left first. Do you want it to look like you have a bad case of the shits?" I raised a brow, and it took everything I had not to laugh at the panic in her eyes.

"Fine." She whipped around, her long hair slapping me in the face before she stalked away.

I stepped back into the bathroom and splashed some water on my face. Everly wasn't the only one struggling with our reunion.

The connection was still there, all these years later. Hell, a part of me had hoped I'd see her and realize I'd built her up in my head. But she was still the same girl I loved all those years ago. And I wasn't a dude who stopped loving someone just because we weren't together.

But I wasn't the same guy I was when we were young. I didn't have blind faith that the universe would just deliver everything I wanted simply because I wanted it. I knew what it felt like to have your heart split in two. And the beautiful girl I'd just kissed in the bathroom was the one who did that. I'd be wise to remember it.

I made my way back out to the kitchen and everyone was sitting at the table with pizza on their plates. Darrian was talking a mile a minute to my mom about the current movie she'd just finished working on. Everly looked up and her gaze locked with mine before she quickly turned her attention back to my father.

"You haven't played since we last saw you? You were the reigning champ!" my dad shouted.

"Oh, for god's sake, Dune. We're all right here. You don't need to shout." Mom handed me a plate and shook her head at my father.

"What were you the reigning champ of?" Darrian asked as she peeled the cheese off her pizza and set the crust on my plate. I didn't miss the way Everly tracked the movement. It wasn't all that deep. Darrian didn't eat carbs and I was the carb king, so when we'd dated, I'd been all too happy to oblige. Her showing up here was completely unexpected, but we were friends and I'd never turn away a friend in need. It just wasn't who I was.

"Um, well, I guess I'm the reigning queen of *bullshit*. It's a dice game," Everly said, and she chuckled because apparently saying the word bullshit to a complete stranger embarrassed her.

"Oh. I've never played." Darrian took a bite of her cheese.

"What is the world coming to? This one hasn't played in almost a decade and this one has never played?" my father said over a mouthful of pizza.

"Don't worry about it. There's plenty of bullshit in your life," my mother said, and she leaned into Everly, and they both laughed hysterically.

Darrian watched them and turned back to me. She studied me for a long moment before returning to her odd meal of cheese and pepperoni.

My father insisted on playing a few rounds, and Darrian

said she'd just be an observer as she had to take a few calls that came in over the next hour.

My dad and Everly were dangerous together. Always had been. He liked to make his own beer and she was the only person on the planet who liked it. He poured us each a glass, but Darrian had declined because apparently beer has a lot of carbs.

Laughter flooded the space as Everly held on to her title as she pushed to her feet and shouted, "Bullshit!"

"Damn, girl. You've always been able to read me." Dad crossed his arms over his chest after lifting his cup and showing his hand.

"What can I say? Once a champ, always a champ." Everly shrugged as she took a sip of beer.

"Can we head back to your place? I'm getting tired," Darrian said.

Everly spewed beer all over the table. Her eyes widen with disbelief as everyone jumped back. My dad's head fell back in a fit of laughter, and my mom jumped to her feet to get a towel. Apparently, Everly didn't like the idea of Darrian staying with me.

"Oh my gosh. I'm so sorry. It just went down the wrong pipe, I think." Everly grabbed the towel from my mom and started cleaning up.

"Shoot. I think a little got on my blouse." Darrian moved to the sink, and she didn't hide her irritation.

"You're in trouble now, Everly girl," my father sang out as he elbowed her in the side.

"Darrian, I'm really sorry. Do you want to borrow a T-shirt, and I'll take your blouse home and try to get that stain out?"

"That's all right. It's one hundred percent silk. It needs to go to the dry cleaners." She forced a small smile at Everly before looking at me.

She wanted to leave.

"All right. We're going to get going. We'll drop you off on the way home, Ever."

When I used the nickname, Darrian's head snapped up to look at me again. What the hell was her deal? We'd broken up weeks ago. We'd hardly talked. She occasionally texted, but they were short and sweet.

We'd had an amicable breakup.

We were friends.

I was good with that.

"Oh, you don't need to do that. I can walk." Everly's words slurred, and she moved to her feet.

I reached for my keys. "You're not walking alone at night, especially being three sheets to the wind. Get in the truck."

"Was he always this bossy?" she directed her question at my mother.

"I believe he was. You just always held your own with him." Mom wrapped her arms around Everly and hugged her tight.

I turned to see Darrian watching intently before she stepped up and gave my parents each a brisk hug. Darrian Sacatto wasn't overly warm. She was friendly enough, beautiful, smart, and independent. But hugs and small talk weren't really her thing. She was more of a red-carpet girl, and she handled her growing celebrity very well.

When we got to the truck, Everly climbed in the front

seat on instinct and then hiccupped unusually loud before breaking out in a fit of laughter. She'd had three beers with my dad and his beer was not low on the alcohol count. This was why I'd only had a few sips.

"Oh, you probably wanted to sit up here by *your man*," she sang out ridiculously loud. "I can just scooch over."

Awkward did not begin to describe the situation. Darrian climbed in the truck, which I knew she wasn't a fan of. When we went out, she always preferred the sports cars. The three of us were packed in the front seat like sardines, Everly in the middle, as I pulled down the long driveway.

Everly let out a loud sigh. "That was really nice. I can't believe how much I missed your parents."

"I told you they'd be happy to see you," I said as she leaned her head against my shoulder and burped before laughing hysterically once again.

I pulled in front of her rental house and glanced over to see Darrian looking highly annoyed.

"Sorry about that!" Everly shouted. "I swear that beer is pure alcohol."

"Yeah. It gets stronger every time I see him." I went to get out of the truck, but before I could, Everly Thomas shocked the shit out of me.

"No. I've caused enough trouble already tonight with spewing beer on you, Darrian. And the burp..." She stopped me from climbing out and shifted her body onto my lap, her ass hitting the steering wheel and causing the horn to beep, startling Darrian. "Anyhoo, I can just climb right out of here without causing you two any more trouble."

She reached for the door handle and her tits hit me

smack-dab in the face. Her ass was in the air, and she tried to maneuver around me. The door sprung open, and she slid down the side and one hand landed on my knee, while the other hand literally gripped my dick.

I yelped and grabbed her wrist to stop things from going from bad to worse, and she looked up at me just before her feet hit the ground. "Oops. Sorry about that, big fella. I'm sure we can both attest to that, am I right?" She winked at Darrian, and more ridiculous laughter bellowed from her body.

Had she lost her fucking mind? She was acting insane.

"It's fine." I tried hard not to laugh. "There was no need for all that. I'm still walking you to the door." I glanced over at Darrian who was no longer irritated. She seemed rather entertained by the whole spectacle. "I'll be right back."

Everly started up the walk before I was out of the car, and my eyes doubled in size when I realized her sundress must have gotten caught on something when she exited the truck like a fucking Sumo mud wrestler, and her entire ass was exposed.

I jogged up and took my time admiring it one more time today before grabbing the hem of her dress and yanking it down.

"What are you doing?" she hissed and smacked at my hand.

"One full moon is enough for tonight, *am I right*?" I mimicked her crazy words and raised a brow.

She fumbled with her keys and looked up at me. "What? Too much?"

"Get some sleep, Ever. I'll see you tomorrow."

Her face grew serious at my words, and she glanced back

at the truck. "Yeah. Sure. Thanks for the ride."

I waited until she was inside and made my way back to the truck. As soon as I pulled away from the curb, Darrian started in. I knew it was coming.

"So that's her, huh?"

We'd talked about our pasts. People we'd dated. None had been more memorable than my first love, who also happened to be my last love. I'd never told another woman that I loved them. I'd been in plenty of relationships over the past nine years, but I'd never gotten to that point. I wasn't a bullshitter. I'd never say it if I didn't feel it.

"Yeah. That's her."

I parked the car in the driveway and turned to look at her as I waited for her to respond.

"She's kind of freaking adorable. And I hate that she looks like that and chugs beer and eats carbs, yet has that rockin' bod. Life is not always fair, is it, Hawk?"

"Hey. What's this about? I thought we were good?"

"We are. I don't know. I had this spontaneous moment and decided to come here and find out if you missed me as much as I missed you."

I reached for her hand. "I'm always happy to see you, and you're always welcome."

"Ouch. Why aren't you pining for me?" she said with a laugh. "Never mind. I already know the reason. I just saw it with my own eyes."

"I promise you there is nothing going on there, Darrian. Just a lot of history." I shrugged, because it was the truth. But that didn't change anything between me and Darrian. She was romanticizing what we had.

"Hawk Madden, are you really that clueless? There is a lot more than history going on there," she said, unbuckling her seat belt and climbing out of the truck.

Maybe she was right.

The connection was impossible to miss.

But it didn't mean either of us should act on it.

Chapter 9
Everly

I woke up with a massive headache and dragged myself to the bathroom just as Dilly flew through the door.

"Morning, sunshine. I'm borrowing a bagel," she called out from the kitchen.

"Borrowing implies that you are going to be returning said bagel. Just say you're stealing it. Don't you have your own house?" I walked out to the kitchen.

"To-may-to, to-mah-to." She dropped it in the toaster before turning to look at me. "Oh my... you look like hell."

"You steal my food and insult me all at the same time?" I sat down on the barstool, rubbing my temples as the door flew open.

Charlotte and Hawk walked through the door, and I quickly adjusted my little pajama shorts and camisole and moved to my feet.

"Relax, girl. I'm fairly certain I saw more of you yesterday between our lake swim and your striptease exit from my truck last night," Hawk said, moving to the kitchen and pouring two cups of coffee. He handed me one and then took a sip of his.

"Hey, Sissy," Charlotte said, planting a kiss on my cheek. She was the more subdued, gentle twin in comparison to Dylan, and seeing as I had an incredible hangover this morning, I was more in the mood for gentle. "I was driving by and saw Hawky player getting out of his truck in the driveway."

"Ohhh, give us the deets. What kind of striptease are we talking about?" Dylan asked, spreading a layer of cream cheese all over her bagel and hopping up on the counter.

"It was nothing. Hawk's girlfriend surprised him with a visit, and I was just trying to get out of his truck without causing them any trouble." I shrugged.

He barked out a laugh and Charlotte rested her head on my shoulder to comfort me. She was good at reading people, and she knew I wasn't in the best place right now.

"You still dating Darrian Sacatto? She's hot, but the lip injections are a little much, if I'm being honest," Dylan said over a mouthful of bagel.

Hawk laughed at the comment. "I'm not. We're friends."

"She called him her man, so I'm fairly certain the movie star would disagree," I hissed. It came out harsher than I meant it to. Darrian was nice enough. I just had an overpowering urge to scratch her eyes out.

That's normal, right?

Charlotte studied me and smiled before turning to Dylan. "I thought you were meeting me at Pilates, Dilly?" I could always count on Charlotte to save me and change the subject when I needed her to.

"I am. I just needed some fuel." Dylan shrugged before biting into her bagel once again, jumping off the counter. "See ya, Hawky player. Get some rest, Ev."

"Let's go." Charlotte paused to hug Hawk again, and Dylan did the same. They both gave me a squeeze before they headed out the door.

Hawk moved around my kitchen like he owned the place, dropping two bagels in the toaster and turning to look at me.

How did he look so damn good?

"Was I the only one who had too much to drink last night?"

"Nope. I'm fairly certain my dad had several more than you, and my mom was right there with you." He chuckled, completely unfazed.

I sipped my coffee and thought about the night.

The kiss.

Darrian claiming her man.

The spew of beer on the movie star's pretty blouse. The burp. And I had a hunch my exit from the truck wasn't as graceful as I'd thought it was.

I groaned. "I think I may have embarrassed myself."

"You're fine, Ever."

"I thought you two were broken up?" I asked, bracing myself for the answer. Why did I care? Hawk Madden was not mine. He hadn't been for many years. Why was this such a big deal to me?

"We are." He reached for two plates when the bagels popped up in the toaster and topped them both with cream cheese before handing me one. "Eat."

"Thank you." I took a bite and we sat in silence. "Why

was she here then?"

I sounded desperate, but I just wanted to know.

I'd survived nine years of my ex being a famous hockey player. Seeing him in the press with women. It had always hurt, but not the way seeing him in person with someone did.

Like a knife to the heart.

The pain was indescribable.

Why the hell did I have to meet my soulmate at fifteen years old? That wasn't fair, right? That allowed me far too much time to mess things up.

I knew I'd never find anyone like Hawk, and I hadn't. But I'd been okay with that because I didn't want to love that hard.

Love that deeply.

The man was a reminder of everything I needed to avoid.

"She missed me. We're still friends."

I took another bite and nodded. "Are you going with her to the red-carpet event?"

"I told her I'd be there if she wanted me there."

He was being very straightforward, but he wasn't giving me much. Breadcrumbs at best. Almost like he was forcing me to pry even more.

"How long is she staying?"

He rolled his eyes. "She left this morning. Is there anything else you need to know?"

I shook my head and sighed. But if I were being honest, I had a ton more questions. I really wanted to know where she slept. If they were still having sex. But it seemed like I'd already pushed my luck asking what I had. Why was this so freaking hard? I could do a lot of things. I'd run two marathons over the years. Climbed some of the highest peaks in the US during college when I joined the rock-climbing team.

But spending time with Hawk Madden... was torture.

In the best and worst way.

"Come on, burpin' Barbie. Go get dressed. Wes will be waiting for us."

I jumped off the stool and jogged down the hall before shouting back at him. "It was one burp."

I piled my hair in a messy bun on top of my head and slipped on some running shorts and a tank top. It would be warm this morning, and I had no idea what Mr. Hotshot would expect from me today.

I slipped on my tennis shoes and joined him in the kitchen. Grabbing my mug, I went to put it in the sink, but we each moved in the same direction and my chest slammed into his.

"Sorry about that," I squeaked.

"That's all right. I thought you were going for another kiss." His laughter echoed off the kitchen walls, and I crossed my arms over my chest.

"I did not kiss you. You kissed me."

"Whatever you need to tell yourself, baby." He waggled his brows and led me out to the truck.

It was going to be a very long day.

• • •

The rest of the week went by in a blur. Hawk and I had found our rhythm. We spent long days together, with me attending his practices, us going on runs and swims in the lake, and eating most of our meals together. He hadn't brought up the kiss again, and I was thankful. I was writing that off to a moment of weakness after not seeing one another for all those years.

Did I want to do it again? Of course. I'm human and the man was sexy as sin.

But I'd learned years ago that loving Hawk was too much for me.

Too intense.

Too strong.

Too much to lose.

Like willingly walking toward the flames.

We'd had hour-long sessions twice a day and I felt like we were making progress. He was opening up. Coach Hayes was touching base with me once a day for updates. I didn't care for the man. I hadn't liked him nine years ago when he came to Honey Mountain to recruit Hawk, and I didn't care for him now. He wasn't concerned with what was going on with Hawk, he just wanted to know that he was going to extend his contract for one more season.

"Did you fix our boy?"

"Well, that's not really how this works," I said. *"But I think we're getting to the root of things. He's got a lot of pressure—"*

He cut me off before I could finish my sentence. "He makes the big bucks and that's what comes with it. You've got to toughen him up on that or give him some outlet, that's what I hired you for. My interest is if you can get him back on the ice or not."

"I'll keep you posted," I'd said before ending the call. *He wasn't interested in what was going on with his player. He was interested in having a winning season, and he needed Hawk to do that.*

My personal assessment? Hawk was fine. He was definitely

tired, maybe even a little burned out. Physically, the man was in the best shape of his life. And oddly, he was just as strong mentally. The question wasn't whether or not he could show up mentally and physically this upcoming season—the real question was, did he want to? We were still working on that. I'd logged hours of our conversations to track the reason for his loss of interest in hockey. I'd documented his workouts and noted his focus each and every time. We'd been back to the ice-skating rink several times as well. We'd come today to skate during the free skate time, as we had every day this week. Word had traveled around town, of course, so now it was packed with kids on the ice. Mr. Chanti thanked us profusely for increasing business, but he still took his shots at Hawk. Hawk didn't mind it because there was no press here, and skating with the kids was a lot of fun for him.

"We'll see you tomorrow, Mr. Chanti." I waved.

"You sure look pretty out there, Everly. Your sidekick is a different story," the older man said, and Hawk laughed.

"Couldn't agree with you more, buddy," Hawk said.

We headed to the bakery for lunch because Niko and Jace had texted Hawk and asked him to meet them there, and I always loved to stop by and see my sisters. Vivian was pretty much always at Honey Bee's, and Dylan worked there part-time. Charlotte was also helping out when Vivian needed an extra set of hands while she was on summer break from teaching. Ashlan was home for a few days as her internship had given her a week off before they'd need her to come back. She'd been staying all over the place. She spent a night with me, a night with Vivian, a night with Charlotte, a night with Dad, and last night she'd slept in the guesthouse with

Dilly. That was the beauty of having a big family. It was never boring. I didn't know if she'd be here today, but she usually stopped by.

We pulled the door open and Niko, Jace, and Tallboy were sitting at the table in the corner by the window, and Ashlan was sitting there giggling like a schoolgirl.

What was up with that?

Maybe she had a thing for Tallboy. He was a sweet firefighter who worked with my dad and the guys over at the firehouse. Hawk went over to greet them, and I made my way toward my sisters behind the counter.

"You just missed the rush. It finally slowed down," Vivian said.

"Hey, Everly." Jada paused to give me a hug.

"Hi, how's little Mabel doing?" We all loved Jada's little girl, as Niko and Vivian brought his niece over to the house for Sunday dinner often.

"That girl is a ball of energy. Me and Rook are taking her to the lake to swim today. I'll see you tomorrow, guys," she called out as she made her way to the table and hugged her brother goodbye.

"She and Rook are still going strong, huh?" I asked. Rook worked at the firehouse with my dad, and he was still a newbie—or as the guys called it, a probie, but with the new recruits coming up, they may need to think about giving him another nickname.

"They are," Dylan said, coming around the corner. "I watched Mabel so they could have a date night last night, and they are pretty damn cute together."

"Seems like you and Hawk are spending a lot of time

together," Vivian said, waggling her brows.

"Yeah, apparently, our big sissy did some sort of striptease, sexy time for him a few days ago," Dylan said.

I glanced over my shoulder to see Hawk deep in conversation. "That did not happen. Zip it, Dilly!"

"Come on, let's get you all fed." Vivian led us back to the group and we ordered our sandwiches, and I joined the guys as they pushed two tables together to make room for everyone.

"How are the girls?" Hawk asked Jace, who had two young daughters, Paisley and Hadley. His wife, or soon-to-be ex-wife, had apparently left town with some random guy a few months ago, and Jace was raising his girls on his own.

"They're a handful, man. I took them to skate yesterday, but I guess I'd just missed you guys." Jace took a sip of his iced tea before setting the cup down on the table. "All the kids were talking about the big hockey player coming out there, but Mr. Chanti only had eyes for Everly."

Everyone laughed as the older man was known for being harsh to the guys and sweet to the girls.

"Yeah, she's a sight to see on the ice. Always was." Hawk winked at me. "You and Karla are done, I heard? I'm sorry to hear that."

Jace's shoulders tensed at the mention of his ex-wife. I'd known they'd been rocky for a long time. Forever really. Karla had gotten pregnant after she and Jace had a one-night stand. He'd dropped everything and married her, and they'd had their second daughter, but apparently, they'd always struggled. Karla was a known party girl, and I couldn't imagine her staying home and raising kids. But I felt bad that Jace was doing it on his own.

"It's for the better, dude. The main problem is finding a reliable nanny to watch the kids when I'm at the firehouse. Right now, my mom is picking up the slack, and of course, the Thomas girls all help out when I'm in a pinch," Jace said with a tight smile. I'd known him for a long time, and asking for help wasn't something he was real comfortable with. "But I need to find someone consistent."

"For sure. That's got to be rough. But you'll find someone. It just might take some time," Hawk said.

"I can come today and take the girls to the park," Ashlan said. Our baby sister was one of the most empathetic people I'd ever known. A true caregiver down to her core. It didn't surprise me that she had offered, but the blush climbing up her cheeks had me wondering what was going on.

"I can go with you, I'm off today," Tallboy said, and Ashlan looked a mix between nervous and annoyed. I couldn't quite read her.

"They'd love that. Thank you." Jace nodded at my sister.

"So, are the Lions going to hire Ev, or are they just stringing her along?" Niko asked, and he squeezed Vivi's hand when she set down his sandwich. She leaned down and kissed him and I couldn't look away. The way those two loved one another was a sight for sure. I looked up and found Hawk watching me as I watched them. He narrowed his gaze to study me before turning back to Niko.

"I don't know. They weren't big on hiring a sports psychologist, but I pushed hard to work with her," Hawk said, and my mouth gaped open.

"I didn't know that."

"I told you I wanted to work with you. I knew you'd be the

best," he said with a half-shrug. He thanked Dylan as she set the last of the sandwiches down and then joined us.

"But I assumed they were interviewing a few, and you just pushed them to hire me?" I reached for my turkey on rye bread and took a bite.

Have I mentioned how incredible Vivian's food is?

There was nothing better.

"You know what happens when you assume, Ever," Hawk purred, and the guys all laughed.

"Hey, how about a barbecue at our house this weekend?" Niko asked, pulling Vivian onto his lap.

"That sounds great," Hawk said, and everyone agreed.

And just like that, this man was inserting himself back into my life in every way.

And I only wanted more.

Chapter 10

Hawk

"You're getting faster," I said as we sat beside the lake staring out at the water, both trying to catch our breath after our swim. We'd just raced over a half mile, and Wes had kicked my ass this morning, so I was feeling it.

"Well, if you keep bringing me out here and making me race you, it's bound to happen." She tipped her head back, letting the sun beat down on her face. I took a minute while her eyes were closed to check her out. Couldn't help myself. She was wearing a white bikini as she'd refused to swim in her panties again, so she usually came prepared.

We'd been spending a lot of time together, and I liked it. I looked forward to waking up and seeing her. It was a dangerous combination.

"Niko texted me about the barbecue tonight."

"Yeah. You want to walk over together?"

"Sure. All the girls going? Did Ash go back to school?" I asked.

"Yep. She's interning for this big marketing company, but she said she definitely doesn't think that's what she wants to pursue. She's unsure, but I think she'll find her way."

"Not everyone finds it as easily as you did," I said as I used my hands to shake off some of the water in my hair.

"Takes one to know one." She laughed.

"Yeah. I think we're lucky. We knew what we wanted to be when we grew up, there was never any doubt. But sometimes you've got to try a few things before you get that lucky." There was more meaning behind my words, and I didn't even realize it until they left my mouth.

Everly and I had met at such a young age, and she'd been it for me. I think I'd been it for her at one point too. But life threw us a curveball, and we went our separate ways. I had a feeling we'd both been searching ever since.

"Ash said you guys chatted at the bakery about it. What did she say?"

"She just asked if I always knew that I wanted to play hockey. I think she's nervous being a senior in college and not really sure about what happens next."

"What did you tell her?" she asked as she pulled her tank top over her head and twisted her ponytail to wring out the water.

"I told her she doesn't have to know what happens next. She doesn't have to have it all figured out. She'll know when it's right."

"You've always trusted your gut, haven't you?" she asked.

"It hasn't failed me." I shrugged. "So, how about you? You

love your profession, that's obvious. Is there anything missing in your life?" I wondered if everyone felt this need to have it all. The job. The great love. Success. Happiness.

I sure as fuck did. I wanted it all.

"I love my job and I'm focused on that. But I agree with you, it's okay to find your way as you go. I haven't always had it all figured out."

"No? That surprises me."

She gazed out at the water and thought about it before turning back to look at me. "I always had a plan, you know? And then my mom got sick and everything happened so fast, and she was gone. So everything I thought I knew kind of changed."

"You still went to the school you always wanted to go to, and you always said you were going to be a sports psychologist, so I think you stayed the course," I said.

"Well, I guess I mean more personally. I hadn't thought you and I were going to go our separate ways, and I never expected to avoid coming home all those years the way I did. I'd always beg the girls to come visit me. Anything to avoid being here."

I looked up to see so much sadness in her eyes, and my hand rested right beside hers on the towels sitting between us and the grass. My finger reached out and intertwined with hers.

"You were grieving."

"My sisters were grieving too, and look at them. They didn't feel the need to run away."

"You may have been away at school, but I know you. You called them incessantly to check on them. You were still there,

Ever. You just needed time to process."

"I thought I was helping by leaving. You. Them. But you especially."

"How so?" I asked, my tone easy, as I didn't want her to shut down.

"Well, when you're drowning, the last thing you want to do is bring the people around you down with you, right? So I reached for a life raft and came up for air, I guess."

"I get that, Ever. I really do. You did what you needed to at that time."

"Hey, aren't I supposed to be the psychologist here?" She laughed as she swiped at the single tear running down her cheek.

"Hey, hockey players can go deep." I bumped her with my shoulder and pulled my hand away.

I liked that she was opening up to me. Unpacking all the hurt. It was closure for me in a way, because it helped me understand why she did what she did all those years ago. She wasn't running away from me. In her mind, she'd been protecting me. I didn't agree with it, but I understood it.

"Okay, that's enough for today. Coach Hayes isn't paying me the big bucks to talk about myself." She pushed to her feet. "And we've got a barbecue to go to. All this swimming has worked up my appetite."

I jumped to my feet and reached for my towel before snapping it lightly in her direction. She howled before her head fell back in laughter. It was one of my favorite sounds in the world.

Always had been.

We'd spent a lot of time out here on the water growing

up, and being here with her...it was bringing it all back to me.

"Why am I blindfolded?" Everly asked as she gripped my hand hard.

"You are such a control freak. You can't stand that I'm in control right now, can you?" I teased as I led her down to the water behind my house.

"Well, the ground is bumpy, and it's freezing out here. I can hear the water, so I just don't know what you're up to. I swear if you throw me in that icy lake as a joke, I will not forgive you, Hawk Madden," she said over her laughter as she continued to ramble. "It's Sunday, so that means all the guys are coming to dinner, and my mom will not be thrilled if I come home soaking wet. And then I'll get pneumonia, which will mean I'll miss my ice-skating competition next weekend. And you know my mom hasn't been feeling good, so I don't want to stress her out. Hawk! Tell me what this is," she shouted as she grew more and more frustrated that I wasn't telling her what we were doing.

We'd been dating for just over two years, and it was Christmas in a few days. But I couldn't wait any longer. I'd been picking up hours at the hockey rink when I wasn't at school and practice to save up for this.

Her heavy ski jacket was bulky, and her hat was pulled down over her ears. I'd put a blindfold over her eyes, and all I could see were her perfect pink lips and the bottom of her rosy cheeks.

"Will you relax? You're going to ruin the surprise," I said, my voice calm even though I was so excited to give her this gift.

We came to a stop just before the dock, and I let go of her hand.

"What are you doing? I can't see anything." She panicked. The girl was always so in control.

"Relax," I said over my laughter. I untied the bandana that was around her eyes and shoved it in my coat pocket. She blinked a few times as she stared out at the dock.

"What is this? I mean, I know it's the dock to your house. But what is that?"

I reached for her hand and led her down the dock to the little firepit I'd set up. There were two sleeping bags for us to bundle up in as we sat around the fire. Graham crackers, chocolate, and marshmallows filled the little pail that sat by the fire. Thankfully, my mom was all about coming up with romantic ideas and she'd helped me pull this off. I helped her sit down in the sleeping bag and then pulled the rest up around her shoulders before I moved to sit beside her.

"I wanted to give you your Christmas gift now."

"Really? But I have yours at home. I should have brought it."

"I just couldn't wait anymore." I shrugged and pulled the box out of my pocket. "It's not fancy or anything, but it's just something I wanted to give you."

Her eyes gaped open at the black velvet ring box. "What is it?"

"I think we're a little young to get married." I chuckled. "But this is a promise, Ever. I know we might go off to different places next year, and I know you worry about me getting drafted and you being in school, but I wanted you to know that you're it for me."

I pulled off my glove and opened the top of the box to show her the little white gold band I'd gotten her.

"Oh my gosh, Hawk. I can't believe you did that. It's a promise ring?"

"It is. And I had it engraved just for you," I said, pulling it out and handing it to her.

She tilted the ring up to read the inscription. "Ever mine."

It's what I'd been calling her for the longest time and I wanted her to have that with her even when we weren't together.

"Someday I'll get you a big ring, but for now, it's a promise. And you know I never break my promises."

Tears were streaming down her face, and she slipped the ring on her finger.

"I promise to love you forever, Hawk Madden."

"Forever will never be long enough with you, Ever mine."

She pushed up on her knees and wrapped her arms around my neck and kissed me hard.

"It'll never be long enough for me either."

And then we roasted marshmallows on these little sticks and made s'mores, and I ate more than my share and kept sneaking bites of hers.

Laughter filled the air around us, because when we weren't talking or kissing, we were laughing.

Me and Ever mine.

"I can't believe you did that." She tried to grab the towel from me, and I wrapped it around my hand so she couldn't pull it away, and she rolled her eyes.

"Come on. I'm starving too. And I suddenly have a taste for s'mores."

Her eyes blinked a few times when she looked at me.

She remembered too.

These memories may have faded, but they were most definitely not forgotten.

Chapter 11
Everly

Dylan and Charlotte strode through the front door just as I came walking out of the bedroom. We laughed because we were all similarly dressed. That happened a lot with sisters.

We were all wearing jean cutoff shorts, and I had on a silky white tank, Charlotte wore a ruffled floral blouse, and Dylan wore a Rolling Stones ripped black T-shirt. We all had our own looks.

"We were just talking to Ash. She's really hating that internship. I think she's ready for school to start. I can't believe she's graduating this year." Dylan set her purse on the counter and glanced at the platter with Caprese salad that I'd made.

"Oh, was I supposed to bring something?" she asked with a laugh.

Charlotte held up the bag of tortilla chips and salsa. "You're lucky we both thought of it, so you can just skate on by."

"Good, because I'm starving." She flipped her blonde hair over her shoulder.

"Anyway... I guess the good thing is that Ash knows what she doesn't want to do, right?" I asked as I slipped on my sandals. "Did you guys pick up on anything at the bakery the other day with her and Tallboy?"

"Tallboy has a girlfriend." Charlotte raised a brow. "Were they flirting?"

"No. Not at all. It could be nothing. I just noticed she got all giggly at the table, and her cheeks were flushed."

"Ummm," Dylan said dramatically with a devious smirk. "Tallboy was not the only guy at that table. I'm guessing every woman who comes within a few hundred feet of Jace King blushes... the man is seriously hot."

"Jace is like ten years older than her, and he has two kids. Not to mention that he's recently divorced and a family friend. No way." I grabbed the salad and started walking toward the door.

"*Yes* way, girl. A hot daddy is nothing to shrug off. And a sexy single dad. I can't even go there. The man fights fires for his profession and then raises those two little girls all on his own. It's hot AF if you ask me." Dylan tore open the bag of tortilla chips that Charlotte asked her to hold and ate one.

"Those are for the barbecue," Charlotte snapped.

"Listen, walking to their house is part of the gathering. Once I got dressed and blew out my hair, it was go time. So, we're eating these as an appetizer while we walk."

I laughed. "You know you're ridiculous, don't you?"

"I think I just do what everyone wishes they had the balls to do. Speaking of balls, where's Hawky player?" Dylan asked over a mouthful of corn chips.

"There are no balls in hockey? I don't get the reference."

"Doesn't he have balls of his own? I think he's probably got a set of two. Must everything be a hockey reference?"

Now Charlotte laughed too. "Damn, girl. You don't need to bring any snacks when you bring all the entertainment."

"Thank you. It's nice to be appreciated. So, where is he?"

"He had a call with Duke Wayburn, the owner of the Lions, and he said he'd meet me at Vivi and Niko's." I shrugged. But I noticed that I didn't like being away from him now that we were spending so much time together.

And that scared the crap out of me.

How could you miss someone after spending just a short time together after being apart for so many years?

Nothing made sense when it came to Hawk Madden.

"So, what's going on there?" Charlotte asked.

"Just working together. I mean, obviously we have a history. So it's been really nice to spend time with him after all these years."

"It's okay to say you missed him," Dylan said as we walked up the driveway. "You two ended so abruptly and I'm sure that was hard."

I blew out a breath. "Yeah. We've been talking about that. I'm glad to know he doesn't hate me."

"Of course he doesn't," Charlotte said, resting her head on my shoulder and patting my cheek.

"Girl. That boy most definitely does not hate you. The sparks flying between you two are crazy." Dylan waggled her brows before pushing open the door.

Jace and his girls were there, and Jada and Rook were

there with Mabel. Tallboy and Samson were standing outside with Niko, helping him at the grill.

We made our way into the farmhouse kitchen, and I set the salad on the counter as I hugged Vivian. She was wearing leggings and a tank top, and the tiniest little bump was starting to show.

"I can't believe you're not out there cooking," I said to my father as he stood at the kitchen island chewing on celery and carrots and sipping a beer.

"You know what, I'm passing the torch to Niko. I do it on Sundays, but the other days are open for whoever wants to jump in." He pulled me into a hug and kissed the top of my head. "So, how's it going with Hawk? You guys working well together?"

"Yes. Of course. It's going well. I think he's going to be just fine no matter what he decides to do at the end of summer."

The door swung open, and Hawk strode in carrying a case of beer and a bouquet of pink and white flowers.

Always so thoughtful.

He picked up Vivi and swung her around before hugging Dylan and Charlotte. The twins took him on a quick tour of the house, as Vivian and Niko had done a ton of renovations to the place.

I looked up to find my dad watching me.

"What?" I raised a brow in challenge.

"Nothing. You just seem lighter lately."

"Lighter? Is that a good thing?"

"You seem happy, sweetheart. That's always a good thing. I think home has been good for you. Among other things." He smirked.

I laughed just as Hawk and the girls walked back into the kitchen. I helped Vivian get everything set up on the island, but every time I looked up, I found myself searching for Hawk. Our gazes locked a few times, but he continued making small talk with everyone, and my dad had cornered him with endless hockey questions. He took it all in stride. He moseyed over to stand beside me and nudged me with his elbow.

"Hey," I said, feeling my cheeks heat. What the hell was wrong with me? I spent every day with him. Why was I suddenly nervous?

"What's up? Did you miss me?" he teased.

But I did. I wasn't about to admit it and make a fool of myself, but I definitely needed some boundaries when it came to this man.

"I survived. How did your meeting go?"

"Duke Wayburn is a cool dude. He cares about the team and about the players. He just gave me a little pitch about coming back." His tongue swiped out and moved along his bottom lip as he moved a little closer to me. "It's always nice to be wanted." He winked before pushing away from the counter and moving outside.

Did it just get hot in here?

Did that have more than one meaning?

I'm sure it is nice to be wanted.

"This is what I'm talking about, Sissy. That little exchange," Dylan whispered before glancing around to make sure no one was listening.

"What little exchange? I asked how his meeting went."

"Well, Hawky player just eye-fucked you right in Vivi's kitchen, while her unborn child is stirring around in her belly, and Dad is standing five feet away reciting hockey stats to try to impress the guy. That's not nothing where I come from."

I closed my eyes and shook my head. But I'd be lying if I didn't say I'd had to squeeze my thighs together when he'd been talking to me. There was a dull ache that resided there now, pretty much twenty-four seven, ever since the hockey star arrived in Honey Mountain.

I wasn't that girl.

I didn't get hot and bothered over a good-looking guy. I'd always been able to stay in control. But at the moment, I felt anything but.

"Time to eat. We're not as fancy as Jack's house, so you just kind of make a plate and sit wherever you want," Niko called out, placing an enormous platter of brats and burgers on the island.

I made a plate and went to sit in the family room on their enormous sectional. Dylan, Vivi, and Charlotte took the seats beside me, and Charlotte had Ashlan on FaceTime so she could be part of the dinner. Jace's older daughter Paisley took the phone and started gabbing with our baby sister, while Hadley sat on Jace's lap out back.

I glanced up and looked out the window, and Hawk's green eyes locked with mine. Then he winked at me, and I could barely pull my gaze away.

"You're actually panting, Sissy. You might want to pull yourself together, there are children here, not to mention our fath—" Dylan stopped speaking when our dad dropped in the chair across from us.

"You okay, Ev? You look like you might have a fever?" he asked before taking a bite of his burger.

Dylan put her clammy little hands on my cheeks and cracked up. "Yep. Someone is definitely burning up."

"I hate you," I whispered over my laughter.

"Maybe you should take something, sweetheart." Dad studied me with concern.

"Oh, she should take something, all right. She's got a bad case of *desire*." Dylan coughed to mask the last word before correcting herself. "Sorry. Dehydration."

"Oh yeah. All that running and swimming you've been doing with Hawk is probably more than you're used to. You need to double up on that water."

"That's definitely it." Dylan smirked, and I set my plate down before taking hers from her hand and placing it on the coffee table and diving on top of her.

She was laughing and I was laughing, and Vivi was smiling as she watched us.

"What are we doing?" Charlotte asked as she jumped on top of us.

"Just having some fun!" Dylan shouted.

"I want to play." Little Paisley clapped her hands together as we were behaving like we were four years old.

"What did I miss? Are we playing suffocation?" Hawk's voice startled me as he stepped inside, and I jumped off my sister and smoothed my hair into place.

"Nothing. Just Dilly being Dilly." I tried to pull myself together.

"Dilly being Dilly, my ass. Someone's got a fever!" She hysterically laughed and Paisley clapped her hands harder.

"Ass is a bad word."

Well, that will sober up a room quickly.

"Oh, no." Dylan shoved Charlotte off of her and sat up and smiled at the little angel. "I said *Dilly being Dilly, hard pass.*"

"What's a hard pass?"

"It's something I do to most of the boys who ask me out." She waggled her brows proudly at how quickly she could think on her feet.

But when I looked up, Hawk was watching me. He mouthed the words, *"Are you okay?"* And the care that I saw in his gaze nearly took my breath away.

I nodded.

But I was most definitely not okay.

Chapter 12
Hawk

Niko: Hey. You guys want to meet at Beer Mountain tonight? Everly's got some dude in town, and Vivi wants to go because Dylan and Charlotte are going to meet the other guys he's bringing. You guys in?

Jace: Let me see if my mom can watch the girls. If so, I'm down.

Me: Count me in.

I wouldn't fucking miss this for the world. Had she lied to me? Were they still together? I was sure as fuck going to find out.

"So, you love the game. That hasn't changed," Everly stated as she sat on her couch with her tanned legs crossed beneath her. Her dark hair was up in a messy knot on her head, and she was wearing these sexy-as-hell black glasses and typing on her iPad.

"Yep. But we've already been over this." I leaned forward and dropped my elbows to my knees. The girl tracked my workouts, asked me endless questions, and documented everything. What more was there to discuss?

"Don't be a stubborn ass, Hawk. I'm just trying to figure out what's going on. Coach Hayes wants something concrete." She shrugged, pushing to her feet and grabbing both of our water glasses and heading to the kitchen to refill them. I glanced over my shoulder to watch because I couldn't resist how fucking good she looked in her little running shorts. She returned with our water glasses and set mine in front of me before placing hers on the coffee table in front of her.

"Of course, he does. He can't just accept the fact that you can't be on"—I use two fingers on each hand to make air quotes when I say the word—"every game, all the fucking time. I'd say my track record is pretty decent, but listen, I'm human. And that's the truth. You can analyze the shit out of me. You're not going to find a single event that made me play differently. I told you… it's just a whole lot of everything."

"I get that. I do. It's a lot of pressure. And I think you handle it really well."

"Can't you fancy that shit up into some sort of medical terms and give him something that keeps him happy?" I chuckled.

She smiled and reached for her water. "I guess he just wants to know you're coming back, full steam ahead. Are you getting a lot of offers from other teams now?"

My gaze narrowed. "You working undercover, Ever? Did he tell you to ask me that?"

Her mouth gaped open. "I would never do that."

"But he asked, didn't he?"

"He asked if you've mentioned anything, and I said that you hadn't. But even if you told me, I would never share that. I'm working for you. He's just paying me."

I nodded. Everly Thomas would never go there, and I knew that. It wasn't her style.

"I have a few offers. But if I play, I plan on playing for the Lions. Those dudes are my brothers. My agent, Joey, handles any offers I get, but he knows where my heart is and the dude always has my back."

"Well, you're clearly physically and mentally strong enough to keep playing. The question is… do you want to?"

"I'm leaning toward it. How about you? Do you have offers on the table when you're done fixing me?" I asked. I wanted to know. Needed to know what her plans were for reasons I couldn't wrap my head around.

She shrugged. "No formal offers as of yet."

"It'll come. The sports world is more than aware of how important the mental game for athletes is."

"Yeah. The basketball team I had my fellowship with was amazing. But the guy I worked with is still there, and they don't need two of us. Plus, I think it's even tougher with me being a woman, you know?"

"You're the toughest woman I know, Ever. Just keep pushing. I'm sure Coach Hayes will consider hiring you if you send me back in one piece." I chuckled. The reality that I could get her the job if I agreed to go back was definitely weighing on me. She deserved the job. But Coach could be a selfish prick. I knew better than anyone how he worked. I watched players come and go over the years. I was his golden boy, so he'd never been anything but supportive of me, but having a few off games had given me a small taste of how cutthroat the man could be. I had zero respect for him. He cared about winning and nothing else. But it was a business. I wasn't naive about that. I was only as valuable as I performed.

"I want you to promise me something," she said, leaning forward and untucking her legs. Her sapphire blues locked with mine. "Don't agree to anything on my behalf, Hawk. I know how you are."

"How am I?" I smirked.

"Loyal and kind and genuine." She shrugged. "And I don't need the job. I mean, obviously I want it, but you know I believe that things always work out the way they're supposed to. I'll get hired somewhere. I'm too good not to, right?" She laughed.

"Damn straight, girl."

"Promise me you won't agree to anything just to help me out. That would be an epic fail on my part. I'm here to help you."

"I promise." I leaned forward and offered her my finger. The girl had always made me pinkie swear on everything when we were young.

Her finger wrapped around mine, and her warm breath tickled my cheek before she bit down on her juicy bottom lip.

"Is it tiring playing so many games? I mean, your season is really long," she said, pulling away quickly and leaning back.

"Hell yeah, it is. It's also amazing when you're in it. But the reality is, hockey players don't have long life spans. Me retiring at twenty-seven is pretty normal. It's hard to have a normal life when you're traveling that much."

"That's why it worked so well with you and Darrian, right? You both have to travel a ton for work."

"You sure are concerned about my relationship with her." I raised a brow, and a pink hue climbed her cheeks.

"Just curious. Aren't you supposed to be going to her event tonight? Are you leaving for the weekend?"

"We're friends. I'm not going. We talked about it, and it's better if I hang back on this one."

"Why?"

So fucking curious about my personal life.

"Because she wants more than I do, and I was straight with her. We'll always be friends, but it's better not to complicate things right now."

"How are you so unaffected by all of this?" She threw her hands in the air. "You were dating one of the biggest movie stars out there right now. You're on the cover of tons of magazines. How are you so... *you*?"

I laughed. "That might be the best compliment you can pay me. I see what money and ego do to people, and I made a conscious decision never to let any of this shit go to my head. It's temporary. I'm just here to do it and have a good time, and when I'm not, it's time to walk away. I know I'm close. I either play one more season or I walk now."

She smiled and reached for her water. "I've gotten to work with a lot of athletes over the past few years, and you're definitely in a league of your own."

"Hey, don't give me too much credit. I know I'm a badass on the ice. I just know that it doesn't define me."

"Good attitude."

"It's a realistic one." I leaned back in the chair and studied her. "So Niko and Jace texted me and said they were going to Beer Mountain tonight. Something about you meeting some dude who's bringing a lot of other guys with him?"

She groaned. "There are no secrets in Honey Mountain. Brad is my ex-boyfriend. We dated a few months. He's here for a bachelor party."

"Why'd you guys end things?" I couldn't stop myself from asking. I wanted to know.

Needed to know.

"It wasn't all that serious. It was nice having someone to attend events with, you know? I took my job seriously, so I wasn't about to get too invested in anyone when I knew I was most likely leaving."

The girl was still so cautious when it came to protecting her heart.

"Hey, I have a favor to ask you."

"Anything," she said, setting her glass back down on the table.

"I have this event I have to go to in two weeks back in San Francisco. The team will send a helicopter to take us there and we'd stay the night. You'd have your own hotel room obviously, or you're welcome to stay at my house. I'd rather not take a date and make it a big thing, and since we're spending so much time working together, I thought maybe you'd come with me."

Her eyes widened and she nodded. "Sure. I'll go with you, Hawk."

Why the fuck was I pushing this with her? We were already spending so much time together. We'd fallen into a routine. It was the most peaceful I'd felt in a long time. I wasn't sure if it was being home or if it was all Everly.

"Thanks. I'm going to go hit the showers. You want to just walk over to Beer Mountain together, or is Brad picking you up?" I asked, acting unfazed even though the thought of seeing her with him had my chest squeezing.

"No. I'm just meeting him there."

"All right. I'll see you in a few." I knocked on the coffee table with my knuckles before pushing to my feet. Being around Ever was stirring something in me that I hadn't felt for a long time. But I knew her better than I knew myself at times. And with my future up in the air and hers being the same, there was no sense acting on it. Hell, maybe it was just nostalgia. I didn't know, but something was building between us.

The only reason we ended was because we had moved far away from one another. This pull had always lived there between us, hadn't it? But I didn't know if she felt it. Or if she did, if she'd be willing to take another chance. She was still guarded. Cautious. I wasn't about to rock the boat where Everly was concerned. Because when she jumped ship again, I didn't know if I'd survive the second time around.

"Hawk," she called out as my hand wrapped around the door handle.

"Yeah?" I asked, turning around to face her.

"Thanks for inviting me to the event. I'm looking forward to it."

"You know you've always been my favorite, Ever. Distance didn't change that." I winked before heading back to my house to catch a shower.

Niko and Jace had both texted to let me know they were on their way. My hair was still wet, but I made my way back to Ever's. She opened the door and I whistled. She wore some sort of black tank top that exposed her tanned back and a pair of white skinny jeans. She looked sexy as hell as I followed her into the kitchen. Dylan and Charlie were standing there sipping a glass of wine and smiling at me.

"Looking good, Hawky player. I'm sure you noticed, Ev?" Dylan purred before falling back in a fit of giggles.

"Could you not be weird for one night?" Everly hissed.

We made our way out the door and walked the two blocks down to Beer Mountain, and the twins talked nonstop the entire way.

"So, are you ready to meet the tool—Brad?" Dylan asked, and Everly whipped around and glared at her sister.

"He is not a tool. You met him once. Don't be so judgy," Everly barked at her sister.

"Oh, I'm sorry. He just mentioned that he knew the owner of the football team in New York, that he grew up in a wealthy family in the Hamptons, and made sure I knew he drove a two hundred-thousand-dollar car. Sorry, Sissy, that's cheesy in my book."

Charlotte rolled her eyes. "He was fine. I think he was just nervous."

"He's a poser," Dylan grumped. "And you had nothing in common."

"We lived in the same city, and we both liked good food and our jobs. That was enough. Why don't you focus on you for a bit?" Everly raised a brow at her sister as she paused at the door before we entered.

"Well, hopefully he has hot friends. He was good-looking, I'll give him that."

I loved the Thomas girls and the way they bantered back and forth. I'd witnessed my fair share of arguments with them, but at the end of the day, they always had one another's backs. I was curious to see the kind of man Ever was dating these days.

Niko was standing at the bar beside Jace, and they had a round of beers ready for us when we walked in. Vivian hugged me before moving on to her sisters. We clinked glasses, everyone holding the mug filled with house brew aside from Niko and Vivian, who were drinking water. He didn't drink and she was pregnant.

"Cheers to having you back in town, brother." Jace held his glass up before chugging it.

"Cheers to hot boys, good beer, and the best friends." Dylan tipped her head back and took a long pull as everyone laughed.

A few people walked over and asked me to take a selfie with them, and I set my glass down and smiled. When I glanced up, I didn't miss the way Everly was watching me, her lips turned up in the corners.

"Does that ever get old?" she whispered when I stepped back beside her.

"Nah. It comes with the territory. I don't mind it."

A loud ruckus had us turning around as a group of men came through the door, laughing and cheering and looking sloppy as hell. They were wearing suits, which made them stand out like sore thumbs in Beer Mountain. Hell, Honey Mountain wasn't a formal place.

One of the guys, who was wearing a navy blue-fitted suit and a pair of aviator sunglasses, walked our way. It was dark outside and he was standing in a bar—he looked like a complete douchebag. His hair was black and slicked back, and he stood a few inches shorter than me as he sauntered right toward Everly.

"Why in the hell is he wearing sunglasses?" Dylan hissed under her breath, and Vivian and Charlotte both elbowed her in the side.

"Everly Thomas, it's been way too long," he said as he pulled her against his body. My hands fisted at my side as I watched. Niko clapped my shoulder and raised a brow when I turned to face him.

Calm the fuck down, man.

I had no claim to Everly. But I could still be protective. We were friends, right?

"Brad, I know you've met my sisters, but this is Hawk, Niko, and Jace."

She pulled out of his embrace, and I didn't miss the way she shifted away, putting a little space between them. His arm looped around her waist as he extended a hand to each of us.

"Oh, wait. You're the hockey dude, right?" Brad said.

"I'm the hockey dude. Yes." My tone did not hide my irritation.

"He's the GOAT of the ice." Niko smirked as he shook the asshole's hand.

He appeared to be the most sober one in the group as the other guys were shouting orders at Tanner, the bartender. Their words were slurring, and they looked like a bunch of douchedicks from where I was standing.

Dylan let out a dramatic groan. "This is so not what I was hoping for."

Everly covered her mouth to keep from laughing at her sister before turning to Brad. "Yeah. Hawk was voted MVP of the league this past season. He's the player I'm working with, remember?"

He nodded. "Yeah, yeah. A dude's got to be secure enough with himself to date a girl who works with a bunch of jocks, am I right?"

Everly closed her eyes for a minute before turning to him. "Hey, why don't we order some food so you guys can eat and sober up a little?"

He nodded. "Sounds good, baby."

Her shoulders stiffened at his words, but she took his hand and led him over to a table. She wanted to get him away from us. That much was obvious.

"Damn. The douchekabob's friends are all slimy too." Dylan dropped down on a barstool and pouted. I laughed, but I kept my eyes on where Everly was sitting with the dude currently trying like hell to touch her. If she gave me any sign that he was crossing a line, I wouldn't hesitate to knock his ass out.

"They do seem really douchey," Charlotte said with a laugh.

"That's because Hawk's the only decent guy she's ever dated," Dylan said as she held her glass up for a refill.

"Well, it's easy not to get attached to an asshole, right?" Vivian said, and her gaze locked with mine. "I think that's the goal."

And damn, if it didn't hurt like hell to see Everly Thomas

with another guy.

Maybe this was why she'd acted so insane the night she saw me with Darrian.

Maybe it was time I pulled her into the bathroom and went for round two.

Tanner brought us over another round, and I took a long pull from the mug. But my gaze locked with Ever's when I glanced her way.

Game on, girl.

Chapter 13
Everly

"You want me to stay at your place tonight?" Brad asked as he set his phone back down after texting someone. I glanced down and my mouth fell open when I saw a photo of a woman flashing her boobs at the screen. "Oh, ignore that. That was one of the girls, Brianna, who just danced for us back at the hotel. Skeeter had them brought in from San Francisco. She keeps texting me. I guess she likes what she sees." He flipped his phone over, and I tried not to laugh.

Dylan was right, even if I'd never admit it to her. Brad was a tool. When we'd go out alone, he was a decent enough guy, but in a group or with any amount of alcohol involved—his inner douche always came out. And was he seriously asking to spend the night with me while he was texting some random girl? I couldn't really blame him. She did have magnificent boobs.

"I think you'd have better luck with Brianna," I said, raising a brow at him.

"Listen, Everly. That shit doesn't matter to me. I don't care if you have big tits."

Oh my. This was worse than I thought. He'd clearly had a lot more to drink than I'd realized. Because even when Brad acted like a haughty asshole, he didn't behave like this.

"I'm so happy to hear that. I think you guys are definitely in the wrong place. Maybe you ought to head back to the hotel and catch up with those girls." I moved to my feet. There wasn't a deep friendship here or anything I was holding on to with Brad, so calling it a night seemed like the best thing to do at this point.

I could see the other guys in his group were irritating the locals who were here playing pool and having a good time. They'd already broken a few mugs and knocked over a barstool, and that wouldn't fly for very long here.

Tanner called out from the bar, "The bachelor party needs to head out. I've called two cabs and they are on their way."

"Fuck that," one of the guys said, and Niko, Jace, and Hawk pushed to their feet. When the guys took them in, they quickly realized that even though there were six of them, they wouldn't stand a chance against those three.

They held up their hands and started backing toward the door.

"We didn't like this lame-ass place anyway," one of them spewed.

"Wise choice," Dylan said, as she flashed him the bird.

"I thought you and I had a moment?" the guy said to Dylan.

"Yeah, you definitely thought wrong." She rolled her eyes.

"Baby, I want to go home with you," Brad said, reaching for my arm. He reeked of bourbon and cigars, and I pushed his hand away. In all our time together, he'd never called me *baby*, so I didn't know where the hell this was coming from.

And I definitely didn't like it.

"Brad. You need to go. That is not happening." My tone was direct. I didn't want to embarrass him, but I doubted he'd even remember this conversation tomorrow.

"You guys head out. I'm going home with my girl," Brad shouted at the group now heading for the door.

I looked up to see Hawk watching us intently, and Niko and Jace turned their attention our way as well.

"Listen to me. You are not coming home with me. You need to go get in that cab with your friends."

He wrapped a hand around the back of my head and yanked my mouth to his. I was so stunned by the move, it took a minute to process what was happening. My mouth stayed sealed shut as he tried to shove his tongue in, and my hands came up and shoved at his chest hard.

Before I knew what was happening, his body was yanked off of mine.

Hawk.

He threw Brad into the table like the man was a rag doll. "Get your fucking hands off of her!" Hawk shouted, eyes wild as he yanked Brad to his feet.

I grabbed his shoulder and gasped. "It's fine, Hawk. Brad, you need to go. Now."

"Easy there, hockey dude. This is an eight-hundred-dollar suit," Brad hissed, swiping down the front of his jacket as he shrugged Hawk off of him and glared at me. "I guess I'll be calling Brianna."

I backed away from him and shook my head with disbelief. "Take care, Brad."

He saluted me and then flipped off Hawk as he made his way to the door.

"Can I call a tool a tool or what?" Dylan said with a wicked grin on her face.

"Well, that was eventful." Vivian shook her head and tucked closer to Niko.

"I had it handled," I said as I looked over at Hawk.

"I don't think so, Ever. I gave him more room than I should have," he said, reaching for his beer casually, like he didn't just throw a man across a table.

"Are you not fazed by the fact that you just chucked a grown man across a bar?" I gaped, and everyone looked at me with ridiculous smiles on their faces.

"That's a bit dramatic, yeah? He was groping you and I stopped him. He's lucky I didn't put his head through a wall for the way he kept coming at you."

"I don't need your help, Hawk!" I shouted, startling everyone around us. "I was fine."

"Oh, yeah? Why don't you stop acting like you've got everything figured out, and just admit that sometimes you need fucking help." He ran a hand through his hair and studied me.

How dare he act like I'm some damsel in distress. I grabbed my purse and stormed out of there. I didn't need Hawk to defend me. I didn't need anyone.

And I liked it that way.

I huffed down the street when an arm wrapped around my bicep, and I whipped around. My chest slammed into Hawk's hard body, and I glared.

"How dare you!" I shouted.

"Stop being a stubborn ass, Ever."

I pushed the hair out of my face and yanked my arm free of him. "I'm not the stubborn ass. That title belongs to you."

He stepped forward, and I backed up. My back hit the brick building, and I looked up at him. His green gaze locked with mine, and the corners of his lips turned up.

"You think I'm a stubborn ass?" His voice was gravelly, and his hand cupped the side of my face.

"What was that back there? You think I can't take care of myself?"

"Shouldn't have to, Ever. He's an arrogant tool. Dilly was right. And I know you can take care of yourself. That's not why I pulled the prick off of you."

My hands found his hard chest and they tingled at the contact. Itching to move and trail down his muscular body. My breaths were coming fast, as his closeness did something to me. I closed my eyes and leaned into his hand on my cheek. "Why'd you do it then?"

"Because I didn't like seeing him paw all over you. Hell, I didn't like it even when he didn't have his hands on you. I don't like seeing you with another man."

My eyes flew open.

"Why?" I whispered, my tongue coming out to wet my lips.

"I don't know, Ever. Same reason you didn't like seeing me with Darrian."

He was right. I hated it. Hated her. Hated the way she touched him. Looked at him.

"Maybe it's just old feelings coming up," I said, my voice low and filled with need.

"Maybe it's new feelings coming up," he said, his mouth moving closer to mine.

"This can't go anywhere. You're my client." Fear gripped me, but the need to feel his mouth on mine was stronger.

"You worried I'm going to tell Coach Hayes that my dick has been having a meltdown since I laid eyes on my sports psychologist?" he said, his lips grazing mine, and I squeezed my thighs together.

"Hawk," I said, shaking my head. "We shouldn't do this."

"Definitely shouldn't. But you already kissed me once, Ever." My breaths were growing more rapid, and my thoughts were blurring. "You're going to need to tell me what you want."

"I just want to kiss you," I said, and the need in my voice made it unrecognizable.

"I want to kiss you too, baby."

Why did I love the sound of him calling me *baby* when hearing Brad say it had repulsed me?

"It can't go anywhere," I said again, making sure he knew this was a one-time thing. Well, seeing as we'd kissed the other day, it was a two-time thing.

"I got the message loud and clear," he said. His mouth covered mine, and my fingers tangled in his hair. I pushed him back, and he looked down at me with the sexiest smirk I'd ever seen. I tugged his hand and pulled him around the corner, where it was a little more private.

"Where were we?" I teased as I pulled his mouth back down to mine. His hands cupped my ass and lifted me off the ground, but our lips never lost contact. His tongue slipped in, and I groaned into his mouth.

My body started grinding, and I gasped at how hard he was beneath me. His hands found my hips, helping me move up and down, as his erection had me losing my mind. I loved the feel of his thick, dark hair against my fingers as our kiss grew deeper. Needier.

His tongue tangled with mine, and we made out in the back alley until my lips were sore and my need for him grew more desperate.

My core tightened, and my hips moved faster.

"Come for me, baby," he whispered against my lips as my body exploded in the most unbelievable way. Our mouths remained locked as he continued to kiss me as I rode out every last bit of pleasure, and my head fell back against the wall as I gasped for air.

"Oh my gosh," I said, my eyes opening to find him watching me. "That was… um, wow."

"I'll take *wow* from you any day of the week," he said, and the pad of his thumb traced my bottom lip.

"You make it easy," I admitted.

"I make what easy?"

"Being with you, it's just so…"

"Hot?" he teased, and I didn't miss the hunger that still danced in his gaze.

"Familiar." I smiled. "But it's hot too."

"Why do you have to make everything so hard?" he asked, pushing the hair away from my face.

"Speak for yourself," I said with a laugh as I ground along his erection slowly again.

He groaned and gripped my hips firmly to keep me still. "Careful there, Ever. I wouldn't mind making you come again, and I have a feeling I could do it fairly easily." Now he slid my body back down and up again before his lips found my neck, and my head fell back with a sigh.

"Oh, you think you have all the power?" I said, doing what I could to contain the fact that my hips were already moving again of their own volition. I fought the moan climbing my throat and threatening to give away the fact that this man had my body reacting in a way it hadn't in a long, long time.

"Well, I'm not the one who just cried out your name, am I?" He nipped at my bottom lip. "Damn, I want you something fierce, *Ever mine*."

At the sound of my nickname leaving his lips, I felt my eyes well with emotion.

"This is so unprofessional. How can I sleep with you tonight and then work with you tomorrow?" I asked, my mind racing. I wanted this. I wanted him. But he was the opposite of what I should want. I'd learned that the hard way, and it had taken me a long time to move forward.

"This wouldn't be the first time, Ever. Do you think I forgot how it feels to have you? A lifetime wouldn't be enough time to make me forget. And I've behaved professionally so far, haven't I?" he said, his voice all tease and sex.

I groaned. "Says the man who has me backed up against a wall in the side alley of Beer Mountain."

"This is us. You and me. You can keep fighting it if you want, and I'll just be here waiting until you admit what we both know." He continued kissing down my neck.

"And what's that?" I whispered over a moan.

"That when we're together, we want one another. You can move across the country and run from that shit, or you can just admit it."

I was panting now. "I do want you, Hawk. But it ends tomorrow. We can have one night. For old times' sake. Then we go back to normal."

His head raised. Eyes locked with mine. A wicked grin spread across his face. "You're mine until the sun comes up."

He smacked a chaste kiss to my mouth before sliding me down his body and steadying me as my feet hit the ground, and I already missed the feel of him beneath me.

"What are you doing?" I asked as he reached for my hand and led me back into the bar.

"We're saying goodbye, and we're leaving."

Hawk hurried me into the bar, and I smoothed my hair into place with my free hand. I hugged my sisters goodbye, and Dylan was three beers deep and still complaining about the pack of douchekabobs. Her word, not mine.

"All right. I've got to get up early for practice. We're out." Hawk gave Jace and Niko one of those bro hugs, and he kissed the top of each of my sisters' heads abruptly.

"Someone's in a hurry," Vivi said with a laugh.

"We've just got to be up early." I waved, trying to hide the blush I knew was giving me away.

They were all laughing as they shouted their goodbyes and the minute we were out the door, Hawk tossed me over his shoulder, fireman style, like I weighed nothing.

"What are you doing?" I shouted, and he started jogging.

"I've got till sunrise to have my way with you. I'm not wasting time waiting on your pokey ass." He laughed, and I couldn't hide the smile taking over my face.

I knew tomorrow I'd kick myself for doing this.

But tonight, I was going to enjoy every last moment.

Because I wanted this more than I'd wanted anything in a very long time.

Nine years, to be exact.

Chapter 14

Hawk

"You know I can walk, right?" She smacked my ass, and I howled.

"I'm aware. You had me puking up breakfast this morning on our run." I pushed through my front door and carried her to the kitchen, where I set her down on the large island and moved to stand between her legs.

Her face was flush, hair mussed and falling in sexy waves over her shoulders, eyes wild with want, and lips parted. "I can't believe you just ran with me for two blocks."

"I'd carry you miles if it meant I got another chance to be with you." It was the truth. I'd grown used to missing Everly and had found a way to move forward. But now that I was here, I didn't know how I'd lived so long without her. We were entering dangerous territory. This arrangement was temporary. I had no idea what the future held for me, or where

I'd go, and I knew she was hell-bent on spreading her wings and being independent. After seeing the last dude she'd dated, it was apparent that Ever was still running. But it would be worth the hurt to get a little taste of all that goodness.

I tucked her hair behind her ears as her gaze locked with mine, and then I held her face between my hands and took her in.

"What are we doing? This is so unprofessional. I don't even have an official job yet and I'm going to sleep with my first real client?"

"We have a history. At the very least, we're friends. Don't lump me in like I'm some fucking stranger," I said, and her hands were already in my hair.

"Did you sleep with Darrian last week?" she asked. Was she trying to find a reason to run right now?

"No. We haven't been together since we broke up a while back. You don't have to look for a way out, Ever. If you don't want this to happen, it's not happening."

My mouth was so close to hers that it took all the restraint I had in me not to cover her mouth with mine. But I wasn't about to push her into something she didn't want. Hell, I knew she wanted it. But for whatever reason, she didn't want to allow herself to go there.

"I want you so bad, but I don't want it to be weird tomorrow," she whispered.

"It won't be weird for me. But I'm not thinking about tomorrow or next week or what anyone else fucking thinks. I'm thinking about you and me. Right now. It's going to happen, Ever. You know it and I know it. Whether it happens tonight or next week or next year... this thing that lives between us cannot be ignored."

"One time? Get it out of our systems?" she said, her hands moving to my chest and making their way down to the hem of my T-shirt. I hissed out a sharp breath when her fingers moved beneath the fabric between us, heating my skin as she ran her hands slowly up my stomach and chest. I yanked the damn thing over my head with one arm, moving even closer.

"Whatever you want." My lips moved to her neck, and peaches and honey and sweetness flooded my senses.

She groaned as she tugged my head up, my mouth on hers. Our tongues tangling and exploring once again. My fingers moved down her stomach in search of the hem, and she laughed against my mouth.

"It's a bodysuit," she said when I found no end in sight.

"What the fuck is a bodysuit?" I pulled back and shook my head.

"It snaps at the bottom, like a bathing suit." A pink hue covered her cheeks, and I fucking loved it. Loved that after all we'd been through, she'd still be shy with me. She liked to act unaffected, but I knew she was as affected by me as I was by her.

"Lean back," I said, my voice gruff. She did as I said, lying back on the island as she propped up on her elbows watching me.

I pulled off her sandals one at a time before moving to the button on her jeans. I studied her, waiting for a sign that it was okay, and she bit down on her juicy bottom lip and nodded just enough to let me know she wanted me to keep going. Her chest was rising and falling rapidly, and my dick was ready to burst through the denim of my jeans, but I took my time.

Hell, I'd waited nine long years for this moment. Haunted by memories of the only girl I'd ever loved. I'd take a day, an hour, or a minute with her—that's how fucking strong the pull was that lived between us.

I unbuttoned her jeans, and she lifted up just enough for me to pull them past her tight little ass as I slipped them easily down her legs and dropped them to the floor.

"Ever, I could stare at you all night long. Right here. Just like this. Looking like every fantasy I've ever had." I ran my hands up her thighs gently and goose bumps spread across her skin. "Spread your pretty little thighs for me." My voice was strained with need, and I didn't give a shit. I had nothing to hide. I wanted her. Hell, I didn't have a memory where I didn't want this girl.

Not a single one.

Not the first time I kissed her or the last time I kissed her.

Not when she ended things and said goodbye.

And not when I walked through the door and saw her for the first time after all these years.

Her legs dropped open and I gently moved closer, grazing her thighs with the tips of my fingers before I found the snaps to her bodysuit. She sucked in a breath when I reached for the fabric, purposely taking my time to unsnap it one at a time. Each snap making a little pop that caused her legs to twitch just a little.

"Hawk," she said in frustration.

When the last snap was open, I tugged it up her stomach and reached to pull her up to sit. "Nine years, Ever. If you think I'm rushing this, then you don't know me very well."

Her hand landed on my cheek. "I know you."

I nodded and tugged the fabric over her head, her arms going up to make it easier. She wasn't wearing a bra which had me nearly coming undone right there, and I tossed the bodysuit on the floor beside her jeans and just took her in. The light from the moon was coming in through the oversized window in the kitchen and the family room, and my tongue swiped out to wet my lips because my mouth went dry at the sight of her.

"So fucking beautiful, Ever." I leaned her back down to lie on the island, and my fingers grazed over her perfect tits.

Her hands came over mine, urging me on, and she arched into my touch, and I swear I'd never seen anything sexier. My mouth came down over one hard peak and she yelped, as I took my time lavishing one and then the next. She writhed beneath me on the kitchen counter, and I found the hem of her white lace panties and slipped them down her legs.

"I've missed the taste of you for nine long years," I said before burying my head between her thighs.

"I've missed you too," she groaned. "So much, Hawk."

My tongue swiped along her most sensitive spot, and my hands continued massaging her breasts. It was the most erotic thing I'd ever experienced. The emotional connection, the physical attraction—everything was heightened. I slipped a finger in as my mouth worked where she needed me most. She was writhing and moaning and begging for her release. But I took my time. Savoring every last moment that I had with her. I could literally feel her body quaking against my mouth.

Her moans filled the space around us, and I didn't let up.

I wanted to enjoy this moment.

My dick was raging, but watching Everly Thomas come

undone was far better than succumbing to my own needs.

Her body was covered in a layer of sweat now, I continued to slowly work her into a frenzy.

"Hawk," she begged, and that was all it took. I chuckled before moving faster, knowing exactly what she needed. Her hips bucked, her fingers tugged at my hair, and she cried out my name as she went over the edge. I stayed right there, letting her ride out every last bit of pleasure before I pulled my hand away and pushed up to look at her.

Tears were streaming down her face, and I was startled at the sight.

"What's wrong?" I asked, pulling her to sit up and pushing that wild hair out of her face.

She shook her head, and her words broke on a sob. "I just missed you."

My heart shattered right there, because I understood it. I'd missed her in a way I couldn't explain. Like I'd spent the past decade searching for something I couldn't find. Because I'd already found it. And nothing ever compared after.

Like finding the missing piece to a puzzle you'd been working on for years.

"I get it, baby. Don't cry." I scooped her up, and her legs wrapped around my waist, her face buried in the crook of my neck. Tears falling against me as I held her close. And fuck, if I wasn't the most content I'd ever been in my life. I hadn't even gotten off, and it didn't matter. Pleasing this girl, being here with her—there was nothing fucking better.

I carried her down the hall to the bedroom and set her down on the bed, reaching for the throw blanket to cover her up, before climbing into bed beside her as we both rolled on our sides to face one another. I swiped away her tears with the pad of my thumbs and stroked her hair until her breathing calmed.

"I'm sorry. I can't believe I'm crying." She shook her head.

"When you bottle up all those feelings, I imagine it's a lot when you finally stop thinking and let things go."

"I, um, I just haven't felt that connection in a long time." She shook her head, and her voice cracked. "It's a little overwhelming."

I nodded. "It is."

"We can still have sex," she said, and her words broke on a sob combined with a laugh. "Oh my gosh, like you'd want to be with a blubbering mess…"

I laughed and pulled her closer, tucking her beneath my chin. "That shit doesn't matter to me. But we're not having sex tonight, baby. I think you need to just feel everything right now."

She sucked in a few breaths as I ran my fingers down her bare back.

"But this was a one-time thing," she reminded me. Because fear had gripped this girl fiercely, and the thought of feeling these things for more than today terrified her.

"Sure, it is," I said, as my eyes closed. Of course, my dick wasn't happy with this arrangement, but he'd have to settle his ass down and be patient. Because nothing about this was a one-time thing. It wasn't over nine years ago, and it wasn't over now. "If you're done tomorrow, then we'll go back to normal and pretend nothing ever happened. Sleep, Ever mine," I whispered.

Her breaths tickled my neck, but I could feel when her

body gave in to sleep. And I drifted off right with her.

I woke up to a raging erection, and I slipped out of bed and made my way to the shower, where I relieved myself with thoughts of Ever coming undone for me twice last night. I wrapped a towel around my waist and walked out into the bedroom to find her wearing one of my button-up shirts and sitting on the bed.

"Hey," she whispered. "I'm sorry if last night didn't go as planned."

I chuckled. "If you think that I could have come up with any version better than what happened last night, you're wrong."

She nodded, her hair a wild mess surrounding her. "Thank you for that. It was... one for the books." She laughed.

"I've never heard that before, but I'll take it."

"I'm happy you're back, Hawk," she whispered.

"I am too. We went too long without speaking, Ever, and that shit wasn't right. You're too big a part of my life to pretend we don't care about one another."

She nodded, and her eyes watered with emotion. "After my mom died, I don't know. I think a part of me died with her. I've never been the same."

"I don't think a part of you died," I said, pulling her onto my lap and wrapping my arms around her. "I think you were grieving, and I think you're still grieving. And when you finally admit that and let yourself feel all of those things—let yourself just be sad instead of always feeling the need to be strong, you'll start to heal."

She swiped at her face. "I cannot believe I'm crying again. You know I hate to cry."

"Let it go, Ever. It's okay to be sad. I was there that day when all your sisters broke down, and you just went around hugging each one of them, holding all of that grief in. Not allowing yourself to be taken care of."

She let out a sob and covered her face. "That was the worst day of my life. And I've always felt so bad that Vivi was the one who was there with her. She was alone with her, Hawk. She tried to bring her back. And I should have been there."

I wrapped my arms around her and held her against me, stroking her hair and comforting her any way I could. Hell, a decade ago I'd tried everything to get her to break down like this, on the night Beth Thomas had lost her battle to cancer. And I'd tried every day afterward for the next year, as I watched her shut down a little more each day. Vivian had been there the day their mother passed, and she'd tried to revive her until the ambulance got there.

"She wasn't alone, Ever. Niko was there. And Vivi wanted to be there. We all knew that time was coming, and she insisted on staying home with your mom. I don't think she'd change a thing."

"And I'd been at school going on with my normal life. Pretending that she wasn't sick. Avoiding all conversations about cancer and hospice and what was going to happen," she said, as she pushed back to look up at me. Her eyes were swollen, cheeks red, and eyes vulnerable.

"You were a fucking kid, Ever. We all deal with grief differently. But you shut down after your mom passed and bottled all that sadness up. And from what I can tell, you haven't let it out."

"Until now." She chuckled as she swiped at her falling

tears. "I knew you'd be the one to break me. I knew it then, and I know it now."

"Is that why you ran? Cut me out of your life?"

"It was a lot of things." Her fingers traced along my jaw as she spoke. "I don't know how to let it go, Hawk. I'm scared that the people I love will be taken from me. I wake up having nightmares about it sometimes. I used to have them about you that year after my mom passed away. I'd wake up in a cold sweat, certain that I was going to lose you."

"So you pushed me away," I said. I'd always known it, but hearing her say the words gave me some sort of closure that I'd always wanted. "Why then? Why right before we left?"

"The distance terrified me. I knew we were on different paths. And then Coach Hayes came to get you to sign with the Lions, remember? He took us and your parents out for dinner and swooned all over you," she said with a laugh as she moved off my lap and sat beside me. Like the closeness was too much for her.

"Yeah. I remember. It was the happiest day of my life, followed by one of the worst, next to the day your mom died. Because you broke up with me, and it came out of left fucking field."

"He and I waited outside while you ran to get the car, and your parents were using the restroom. He told me that we were young, and you were on a very exciting path, and he was right. Having a girlfriend would have held you back. He told me that real love meant letting people go fulfill their destiny. And I wanted that for you. I really did."

"What the fuck?" I yelled, shaking my head with disbelief. "Hayes told you that?"

"Hawk, you were signing a twenty-million-dollar contract back then, which I know seems like chump change now," she said with a chuckle, trying to make light of the situation. It wasn't working. "Listen to me. He was right. And I was an emotional wreck back then. Hell, I must still be because I've been crying for the past twenty-four hours. I needed to let you go, or I would have drowned us both. And I couldn't do it with us staying in contact. It was better for both of us."

Fury coursed through my veins, and I pushed to my feet. "Wrong, Ever. It wasn't better for either of us. He did it because he wanted me committed to the team. He didn't want me missing my girlfriend and flying across the country to see you every time we had a day off. And he's a fucking asshole for saying that to you when you were vulnerable as hell. The guy is a selfish prick. He has zero loyalty to anyone and takes what he can from people before disposing of them the minute they don't serve his needs. I can't fucking believe he said that to you."

"Come on, Hawk—don't blame him. It worked out for both of us. We're both fine. I chased my dreams and you chased yours."

"We could have been chasing them together."

"Your career took off. That wouldn't have happened if you were focused on your grieving girlfriend. You're the GOAT of the NHL. There couldn't have been a better outcome."

She was wrong. There absolutely could have been a better outcome.

One where we were together.

Chapter 15

Everly

I was exhausted from all the crying, all the digging up of old memories, all the thoughts of my mother. Thoughts of the day Coach Hayes and I spoke, and I made the decision to change my plan. It was the right one, even if Hawk didn't want to admit it. I was in a bad place, and I needed to pull myself together and not drag him down with me in the process. I'd already felt a ton of guilt over my sister Vivian being the only one there when Mom passed, and I sure as hell wasn't going to do anything to hurt Hawk.

No. It was better this way.

I'd studied psychology for the past nine years. I was more than aware that I had not recovered from my mother's death. That I pushed people away whenever they got close to me. That I was drawn to relationships that had no depth. That I distanced myself from the people I loved because it hurt too much to be close sometimes. That my fear of losing loved ones wasn't rational. I had all the knowledge and all the tools to help others, but helping myself wasn't something I'd been able to do. Because the truth was—I wasn't sure I wanted to fix myself. To allow myself to feel that kind of pain ever again. And loving people was a risk, and the fewer risks I took, the easier life was.

Pouring myself into work had been the perfect distraction. And as for relationships? Well, the more incompatible, the better, so I'd never have to worry about things becoming too permanent.

But now that I was home and spending time with Hawk, I was being pushed out of my comfort zone. And it scared the hell out of me.

"He's a selfish prick. He never should have said that to you. Damn, Ever, you should have talked to me. I mean, I deserved that much, don't ya think?" Hawk was angry, and I understood it, but I still wouldn't have changed a thing.

"So you could have done what? Gotten in a fight and not signed with the Lions? I was leaving for college. It wouldn't have worked. You were a professional athlete, traveling all over the US and—as Coach Hayes so kindly pointed out—you'd just signed a multimillion-dollar contract. You were not going to stay with your high school girlfriend. It was an exciting time for you. I was a college freshman drowning in grief. I did the right thing." I was on my feet, and I reached for his hand.

He shook his head. "That wasn't your decision to make."

"Well, I made it. And look at you now," I hissed. "This is all getting too complicated. We need to just go back to normal. It's too much."

He pulled away from me and walked to the closet, dropping his towel and pulling on some briefs before grabbing a pair of gym shorts. "Yeah. Look at me now. I'm back here with you, trying to figure out my fucking future. Deciding if I want to play another year for a man who would sell his soul to the devil for a Stanley Cup win. Getting psychoanalyzed by the only girl I've ever loved who spent the night in my bed and can't run out of here fast enough. Not sure that's the best place to be." He yanked a tee over his head. "But right now, I need to go to fucking practice because Wes is waiting for me, and as you've pointed out many times, I make the big bucks, and this is what matters in life."

"I can't believe you're mad at me. I did it for you!"

"Whatever gets you through the day, Ever. You're the only one who believes your shit. Do you know that? You didn't do this for me. You were looking for an out. Terrified I'd turn my back on you, so you made the decision for me. Which tells me that you don't know me as well as I thought you did." He stormed toward the door.

"Wait. I'm supposed to be at practice with you. We still need to work together whether you're mad or not. This is exactly what I was afraid of," I shouted, following him down the hallway.

He whipped around, his chest crashing into mine. "This is what you were afraid of? Hell, you're afraid of everything. You're so hell-bent on being strong, but you run from everything and everyone. And of course, after all that I just said to you, all you're worried about is your fucking job. Not the people you leave in your wake. Don't worry, Ever. Coach

Hayes isn't going to find out that you were writhing beneath me just hours ago while you slept naked in my bed. You were right, this ends now. You want to be professional, you got it. Meet me at practice after you wash the feel of my hands off your body."

And then he stormed out the door. I stood there with my jaw on the floor.

What the hell just happened?

I was honest with him. We'd agreed to go back to normal today. Of course it would hurt, but I thought I was doing the right thing.

I slipped on my jeans and my sandals and shoved my bodysuit in my purse as I made my way out the door. I walked down the street toward my house, fighting back the tears. A car pulled up behind me and I startled.

"Doing the walk of shame, Sissy?" Dylan called out with a laugh as she put the window down on her SUV. When I turned around to look at her, her face dropped. "Oh my gosh. Get in the car."

I climbed in and buckled my seat belt before the floodgates opened and I lost it. There was no more holding back. Sobs racked my body. I told her everything that had happened. Everything that we'd said to one another, and Dylan remained silent for the first time in her life. When we pulled into the driveway, I got out of the car and my sister was there with her arm around me, helping me inside. I dropped onto the couch, and she sat beside me, holding my hand. I looked up to see tears streaming down her pretty face. Her long blonde hair falling in a braid over her shoulder.

How many people could I possibly hurt today? Coming

home was a mistake. This was too much.

"I'm sorry, Dilly."

"I'm not crying because you did something to me. I'm crying because seeing you in pain makes me sad. Seeing you hurt—it hurts me. It hurts all of us, Ev. We've all grieved Mom. We've spent years talking about it. But you spent the year after her death taking care of everyone, and then you left for school and never talked about what happened again. You left us. You left Hawk. He's right... you are so determined to be strong, but that's not being strong." She swiped at her cheeks. "And you never told any of us that Coach Hayes said that to you, because I would have junk-punched that rat bastard. That had to hurt you so much, and at a time in your life when you'd recently lost your mother and you were about to go away from home for the first time. You kept it all bottled up. You're a freaking psych major, for god's sake. You know this isn't healthy."

I covered my face with my hands as the door flew open, and Vivian, Charlotte, and Ashlan came walking in.

"I'm home," Ashlan said, waving her hands in the air. "Surprise."

"We wanted to come find out what happened with you and Hawk last night..." Vivian stopped mid-sentence as she took us both in, and the smile on her face fell. "Oh my gosh. Is Dad okay?" Charlotte asked.

"Jeez, Dad is fine! Is this entire family so traumatized that no one can cry without everyone thinking someone died? Our sister is having a breakdown. Hawk called her out on her shit. Mind you, it was after some serious hot-and-heavy sexy time. Anyway, we're all fucked up. That's the bottom line. But she's the worst of all." Dylan waved her hands over her head before turning to our baby sister. "Welcome home, Ash. But no offense, it seems like you come home every other week, so I don't know why it's made into such a big thing." Dylan fell back against the couch as if she were completely exhausted, and I burst out in a fit of laughter and couldn't stop.

Vivian came to sit beside me with a look of concern, and Ashlan fell between us on the couch, half on my lap and half on Vivi's, and she hugged me tight before she laughed right along with me.

"I don't know what's going on. You lost me at hot-and-heavy sexy time," Charlotte said with a shrug.

Dylan and I took turns filling them in. Her version was much harsher than mine, painting me as a complete asshole, but probably more accurate. Reminding everyone how fearful I was. What a coward I'd been with Hawk. I told them how much guilt I'd carried over our mother's death, and we all cried some more.

"I was exactly where I wanted to be," Vivian said. "I hate that you carry guilt over that. I don't have any regrets. We all had different roles, Ev. And you were taking care of everyone. Going to the twins' games and making all the meals and doing laundry and managing the entire house."

"Because I was scared," I croaked. That was what it all came down to. I was scared to sit beside my mom because I didn't want to admit that she was dying. Hell, I had a hard time admitting it even after she was gone.

"That's okay. It was scary," Charlotte said, reaching for my hand. "I turned to my schoolwork and my friends and any form of escape I could during that time. We all cope the best that we can."

"I found my inner feminist during that time. Remember Charlie, I hosted that rally that girls should be allowed to play on the football team at Honey Mountain Middle School."

"Um, yes." Charlotte rolled her eyes. "You made me get everyone I knew to sign the damn petition, and you won. And then you announced that you had no plans on playing."

"It's not about playing football as much as it's about having the right to play. Why the hell would I want to be tackled by a bunch of sweaty boys? Well, I mean, now I might feel differently," Dylan said as she waggled her brows, and we all laughed once again.

"I don't remember much about it, if I'm being honest. I was in fifth grade, and I don't think I fully grasped what was happening at the time. I knew it was bad, sure. But I didn't understand the heaviness of it all. I just remember sitting bedside and reading Mama all the stories I'd write when I'd get home from school. I think that's when I found my love for writing."

"Maybe you should consider being a writer," I said. "You've always loved it."

"Yeah, but it's not practical. I need to get a job and make money when I graduate," Ashlan said.

"I don't know. The more I pour myself into my career, the more I wonder if I'm just using it to hide from what really matters." I wiped away the last of my tears. It was time to pull myself together.

"And what's that?" Vivian asked.

"Look at what you and Niko have. You're living the dream. You wake up every day excited to build your business up and go home to the man you love. Charlie, you have a passion for teaching. You love it. That matters. And Dilly, you're going to kick ass in a courtroom. You're chasing it." I pushed to my feet. "Ash, your passion is writing. Don't run from that. You'll make it work."

"How do you know?"

"Because you trust your heart. Mama always said that trusting your heart would lead you down the right path. I haven't trusted mine since the day she left us. I've been using my job as an escape. The problem is, I don't know how to change it."

"I think that's the first step. What if you did the unthinkable?" Dylan said, raising a brow in challenge as she looked at me. "What if you made an appointment to see a therapist? I know you think you know it all, and you probably do. But having someone else to talk to that isn't one of us… I think it would help. What about Lala?"

There'd been one person I'd allowed myself to get close to in college. My best friend, Lala. We'd been roommates at NYU and she knew me well. She'd always offered an ear because she knew I had a lot of walls up. She was a family therapist now and had a booming business.

It wasn't a horrible idea. I knew I was in need of help. I just hated that I couldn't fix it myself. But I'd been trying to do that for almost a decade, and it hadn't worked. Isn't that what I preached to my clients?

There was no shame in asking for help.

"I could do that. Lala has always encouraged me to join her client roster." I shrugged. "Thanks to modern technology, I can do it via Zoom."

"Please do this, Ev. You deserve to be happy. I love you so much," Vivian said, wrapping her arms around me. "And if anyone can pull things out of you, it's Lala."

"I promise I will. So, this was... a lot today, right?" I chuckled as I folded the blanket on the couch and pushed to my feet. "And now I need to get to practice and try to repair things with Hawk."

"What are you going to do?"

"I'm going to make an appointment with Lala and just see how he acts at practice. I have a hunch he's done with me, and he has every right to be." I moved to the kitchen and pulled out five bottles of water as they each came over and grabbed one.

"I don't know that he's ever truly been done with you," Vivian said.

"It sure doesn't sound like it after last night." Ashlan's cheeks flushed as she fanned her face.

"Yeah. And that's my kind of man," Dylan said. "He pleased his lady with no concern for himself. I mean, men just don't do that anymore. I will never look at his kitchen island again."

Everyone burst out in a fit of giggles and I tried desperately not to join in, but I couldn't help myself.

"Okay, can we please stop talking about that? This is why I don't tell you things." I crossed my arms over my chest.

"So, are you just going to show up at practice?" Charlotte asked.

"I think you should act natural and follow his lead." Ashlan unscrewed the lid from her water bottle. "Apologize when he seems open to it."

"Invite him to Sunday dinner. He used to love coming. That would be an olive branch. Let him know you're trying." Vivian reached for her keys and wrapped her arms around me. "Love you. I've got to get to work. Call me later."

My sisters each kissed me on the cheek, and I made my way to my bedroom and took off the button-up I was wearing of Hawk's. I held it to my nose and breathed it in.

Bergamot, birch, and mint.

Loyal and kind and genuine.

He was all of those. And he made me feel things last night that I hadn't felt in a long time.

He was turning my world upside down, and for the first time in a very long time—I wasn't sure it was a bad thing.

I picked up my cell and texted Lala, asking her to get me on her schedule. It was time to own my shit, as Hawk would say.

Lala: I've been waiting for this day to come. How about this afternoon? I have an hour free, and I think I should get you talking while you're willing. <winky face emoji>

I hesitated as I chewed on my fingernail. Was I ready for this? I walked to the dresser and pulled on a fresh T-shirt, making my way to the bathroom. I pulled my hair into a messy bun on top of my head, brushed my teeth, and reached for the phone.

Me: That will work.

Chapter 16

Hawk

"Good workout, Hawk. Coach Hayes has been all over my ass, asking how you're doing. The dude is relentless," Wes said as we walked to the table on his patio, and I chugged two waters. It was hot as hell out, and I'd pushed it hard today.

I was still pissed at Everly. After last night and all we'd shared, she still couldn't run for the door fast enough. And that shit didn't sit well with me. And the mention of Coach Hayes's name had my blood boiling.

"He's a selfish dick. Always has been. The only reason he's decent to me, or appears to be, is because I'm still valuable to him. But the minute I'm not, he'll be gone without a thought. Nine years I've played for the guy, and that's as deep as our relationship runs. And that's not inspiring, you know?"

Wes nodded. Hayes's reputation was known in the business. He was a cutthroat dude, with a lot of winning seasons. He'd do whatever it took to get there—that was no secret. But I had friends who'd been traded over the years, and they'd shared how they considered their new coaches to be like family. They may not win the Stanley Cup as often, but they'd formed a relationship that would last beyond the years of playing. But Hayes wasn't that guy. I had no respect for the man and the way he treated people. And after hearing what he did to Everly, the thought of playing for him again sounded less appealing than the day I'd come here.

"It's who he is. You know he's not going to hire Everly, right? I mean, you could probably negotiate that into your contract if you sign, and he'd pay. But he's just appeasing you by hiring her temporarily. And that pisses me off, because she's working her ass off. He doesn't give a shit. He just wants you to sign. Hell, the only reason I'm on payroll with the team is because you and I are close. When you're gone, I'm gone."

Wes and Coach weren't friendly. But Wes had been with me from the start, and cutting him wasn't an option if I was there.

"And you aren't pressing me to sign?" I asked, running a hand through my hair and reaching for the towel on the table to wipe my face.

"Nah. I know where you're at, Hawk. And if you stay, I'll be right there beside you. But when you jump ship, I'll be leaving the organization. Hayes thinks I'm lucky to be there because you've made that happen—but I wouldn't work for that asshole if you weren't there. I've had other offers, and I'll be just fine when you make the decision. You need to do you, Hawk."

"Thanks. I appreciate that more than I can say. Man, it's

hard to know who's got your back in this business, you know? And I get it. I get paid a lot of money to do what I do. But I'd still like to know that my coach has my back. He never has. Yes, he kisses my ass because he needs me. But I don't trust the guy as far as I can throw him."

"So why haven't you left before now?"

"I love my team, brother. The guys are my family. My parents live there, and the fans have been loyal as hell most of the time. It's hard to turn your back on that."

"I get it. And Everly will be okay, just like me. She's damn good at her job. I've seen a lot of change in you in the short time we've been here."

"Such as?" I asked as I took a long pull from my water bottle.

"You seem lighter. Happier. You two competing is funny as shit. The way she races you and holds her own. You're laughing half the time and it's good to see. She's good for you, Hawk."

You're preaching to the choir, brother.

"We just have a history. We grew up together, and there's a comfort there," I admitted. Even if she never would.

"Speak of the devil. He's a little exhausted right now, but I bet you can get him to race you later today," Wes said, and I turned to see Everly walking up to the table. She wore a pair of black leggings and a black tank top. Her hair was piled on her head, her face free of makeup and shimmering as the sun beat down on her.

"Bring it on, Madden."

Wes slapped the table and laughed. "I love seeing this tiny little thing challenge you. Hey, I'm starving. How about the three of us go grab lunch at Honey Mountain Café?"

I glanced at her to find her watching me as she spoke. "I'd like that."

"You two go ahead and go. I've got plans to meet my mom today. I'll catch you later." Wes and Everly had grown close, and I needed some space from her at the moment. I was done playing games, and when she was ready to own her feelings, we could talk.

"All right. Let me go grab my wallet," Wes said as he jogged into the house.

"Hey." Everly kicked at the dirt with her shoe.

"Hey."

"Are we still working out later today?" Her voice was low, and she bounced on her feet, letting me know she was nervous.

"Sure. You're here to fix me, right?" I pushed to my feet. "See you later."

"Hey, Hawk," she called after me.

"Yeah?" I hit the unlock button on my truck and heard it beep in the distance before turning around to meet her gaze.

"I, um, I wanted to see if you'd want to come to Sunday dinner. I know you used to love those. And Dad's making his famous burgers and dogs." She bit down on her bottom lip, and visions of her coming undone on my kitchen counter flashed through my mind.

"Sure. I'm not the one who's afraid to admit that I miss things from my past." I turned on my heels and left her standing there gaping at me.

I made my way to my mom's house and tried to shake off my bad mood. I walked in the door, and she had the table set for two. I'd called her this morning when I left Everly and told her I needed her. Hell, I wasn't ashamed to admit I was a complete mama's boy. I had no shame in my game. My mom was amazing. She'd always been my constant. She never missed a game, supported me through all the ups and downs, cursed out reporters when they wrote shit about me when we lost, and celebrated my every win.

"Where's Dad?" I asked when I paused to kiss the top of her head.

"He's golfing. I thought you and I could spend some time together today. You've been working so hard since you got here, and I figured a nice homemade lunch would do you good."

My mother was a fabulous cook and the fact that she'd pulled together barbecued chicken, mashed potatoes, and a big green salad for lunch—I was most definitely not complaining.

I paused at the sink to wash my hands before joining her at the table.

"Tell me what's troubling you. I heard it in your voice this morning on the phone."

I took a bite of chicken and chewed as I thought about how much to share. "Well, Coach Hayes is riding my ass. He wants an answer. And I think he's going to cut Everly if I don't go back and play for him."

She nodded as she reached for her water. "What does Everly say?"

I groaned because there was too much to unpack there. "She doesn't want me making any deals on her behalf. God forbid anyone help her out. She's a complicated woman, you know?"

She chuckled. "I don't find her to be that complicated."

My mother was true-blue when it came to the people she loved. And there was no doubt about the fact that she loved Everly Thomas. Always had, always would.

"She's just so guarded. Every time I think I'm breaking through, she reminds me that this is temporary. It's just a job." I shrugged. "What she hasn't even processed is the fact that if I go back and they offer her the job, we'll be working together."

"How has that been? Working with her every day? Every time I see the two of you together, you're laughing. Although when I drove by the lake two days ago, I saw you both sprinting down the street toward the water, and it sure didn't look friendly." She laughed. "I love that she challenges you and never backs down."

"Aside from having a real conversation or going deep with her. She fucking runs, Mom. Every goddamn time. Even all these years later."

My mother raised an eyebrow, probably at the fact that I'd just sworn in her kitchen. "Well, maybe try a different approach."

"Meaning?"

"If she runs every time you try to go deep with her, stop doing it. Give her time to come to you herself. She's been through a lot, Hawk. I can't imagine losing my mama at that age. Grieving isn't something that has an expiration date. And losing people you love affects you in many ways. This was just her way of grieving."

I scrubbed a hand down my face and groaned. "Yeah. And she finally told me that Hayes told her we wouldn't stand a chance with me signing on with the NHL and her leaving for college all those years ago. He basically told her she'd be holding me back. That dude is such an asshole."

She chuckled. "Are you really surprised? I mean, I feel terrible that he did that to her, and it explains a lot. She was so vulnerable back then, and Everly didn't want to bring anyone down. I get that. Your star was rising, Hawk, and she was drowning in grief. So she reached for a life vest and just suffered on her own. It doesn't surprise me if I'm being honest. It's who she is. And it's who Coach Hayes is. I've always told you that people show you who they are—you just need to believe them."

"I know who Everly is. I've always known. But she pushed me away, and I don't know, maybe I never really got over it. Because being around her again, it's—" I rolled my neck. "I don't know, Mom. It's fucking with my head. Forgive my French."

She laughed. "The French don't say fuck, son. And maybe it's messing with your head because you know it's worth fighting for. You respected her wishes back then, and you let her walk away. And that's exactly what she did. Maybe it's time you don't let her do that."

"How do you get through to someone that doesn't want to let you in?" I said as I forked some salad and took an oversized bite.

"I don't know. How do you get that puck in the goal when someone doesn't want to let you in?" She smirked, quite proud of her hockey analogy.

"You fight like hell. But at least you know what you're fighting for. I can't fight for something that she doesn't want. And I honestly don't know what she wants."

"Well, you've been here for a few weeks, and I'd say things have shifted. I mean, when you were getting ready to start working with her, you weren't sure how uncomfortable it would be. You hadn't spoken in years. And look how quickly you two have found that connection you once shared. Trust it. Don't run from it."

I shrugged. "I'm not afraid of fighting for what I want if I'm not alone in the fight."

"Well, you've got a lot to decide, son. So start with what you can control. How are you feeling about another season? Is it time to hang up the skates, or do you want to keep going?"

"Honestly, being back here has reminded me why I fell in love with the sport. Being on the ice every afternoon where it all started, skating with the kids—man, I love it. And all the guys are texting and calling, and I sure as fu—heck, don't want to let them down. I love my team. I'm their captain and that means something to me. But my disdain for Coach Hayes has only grown stronger. I've gotten a bunch of other offers, but if I'm not playing for the Lions, I just don't think I can lace up for another team."

She smiled, her eyes welled with emotion. "You've always been loyal, Hawk, and I can't tell you how much I admire that. You've had bigger money offers and you've never wavered from where you started."

"Thanks. I told you to call me out if I ever did. None of that even matters to me at this point. I've made more money than I know what to do with. I'm in great physical shape, and Everly has helped remind me about how much I love this game. So I'm leaning toward biting my tongue with Coach and going back. But I'm not ready to say that just yet because

Hayes will rush me back, and I want to take my time here. I'm enjoying being away from the chaos and the expectations."

"Honey Mountain will always be home." She shrugged. "Just take your time with everything. How about Darrian? I'm guessing that's over?"

"She's a damn good friend. We talked about me going to her event, and I would have gone for her, because I do care about her. But it's just a friendship for me, and I think it is for her too. She's probably just romanticizing things in her head, which brought her out here."

"I think she knows what a good man you are, and they aren't easy to find." She smiled. "But I've never seen a real connection with you two that was stronger than friendship."

"Yeah. It is what it is," I said, and she knew I was done talking about all this shit. We spent the next hour eating and laughing as she told me about how my father ate every pastry on the menu from Honey Bee's bakery yesterday and then went to bed at seven p.m. because he had a stomachache.

I hugged her goodbye. I swear, lunch with my mom was all I ever needed to put things into perspective. I made my way to my house to change for my run. Everly was sitting on my front porch, and she waved. I got out of my truck and made my way toward her.

"How long have you been sitting here?" I asked as I pushed the door open.

"Not long. I just didn't want to miss you."

"Give me a minute," I said. I needed to go change. My words came out harsher than I meant them to. Or maybe I did mean them to come out harsh. I didn't know anymore.

"Oh, okay," she said, and I barely heard her because I was

halfway down the hall when she said it.

It pissed me off that less than twenty-four hours ago, I'd had her splayed out on my kitchen counter crying out my name, and now she wanted to focus on working out. And if that's what she wanted, that's exactly what she'd get.

"You ready?" I asked, as I stood in front of her in running shorts and a tee, and she pushed to her feet.

"Yeah. Are we doing the usual five miles?"

"Yep." I walked to the door and we both made our way out to the driveway, as she stretched for a minute before I cracked my neck and raised a brow.

Buckle up, girl. You want me to get my head in the game... here we go.

Chapter 17
Everly

Dear God, I couldn't feel my legs. He'd never pushed this hard, nor did I realize that Hawk had another gear. So much for thinking I could take on the NHL's star player. When we hit mile four, I was fairly certain I vomited in my mouth. I glanced down at my watch to see we were running sub six-minute miles, which was not the norm. We normally ran about thirty seconds slower per mile and then sprinted it out on the last half mile.

Today was definitely different.

He obviously had a point to prove. I was just a workout buddy now, when I wasn't trying to psychoanalyze him, as he liked to say.

We turned the corner with a half mile left to go, and he took off. Mind you, the man had already killed it in his morning practice according to Wes, who'd shared that Hawk had been in a mood this morning. I shrugged it off even though I knew I was at the root of it.

I pumped my arms as hard as I could, but he was gone. Maybe there was symbolism there. He thought I was always running or pushing him and everyone away, and now he was doing it all on his own. I came down the final stretch. Stiffness had set in, and my legs were not cooperating. I came to a stop beneath the tree and gasped for air before completely embarrassing myself and vomiting right there in front of him. He didn't try to comfort me or touch me, but he handed me a water.

"Here you go. Drink this."

I wiped at my mouth and took a long swig. "Thank you."

"You got it," he said, but there was no warmth in his tone.

We stood there for a bit while I waited for my breathing to calm. "That was a great run."

"Yeah. I figure you can tell Coach that I'm doing great, right?"

"Hawk. Come on. That's not why I run with you, and you know that."

"Yes. You're here to work on my head, even though you don't have your own head screwed on right." He raised a brow.

"Does that make you feel better to call me out? Have at it, Hawk! I'm a mess. Is that what you want to hear?" I hissed.

"Not particularly. But I'm just calling it as I see it. You dropped a fucking bomb on me this morning, and you don't want me to have a reaction? I'm just supposed to talk about my love for the sport with you? It's bullshit, but I forgot… you're the queen of bullshit." He started walking toward the lake, and I huffed behind him.

"That was low. I just wanted to remember what we were here for. I have a job to do," I shouted.

"So fucking do it." He tugged his T-shirt over his head and tossed it on the ground. His tanned and chiseled abs were on full display, and I found it hard to look away. "I have a job to do too, Ever. I'll see you at Sunday dinner. You can have the night off. I'm tired of talking about hockey."

He kicked off his shoes and dove into the water.

I glanced down at my watch and realized it was almost time to meet with Lala. I wanted to jog, but considering my legs were completely shot, I walked as quickly as they would take me. I guess the superstar had been holding out on me these past two weeks.

I grabbed a water after I walked into my house, as there was no time to shower at this point, and opened my laptop as I sat at the kitchen table. Lala's face appeared on the screen.

"There she is. I see you're out there getting your vitamin D while I'm cooped up in this office," she said. We'd always joked about our differences, yet our connection was strong. Lala was tall at five feet, eleven inches, and fair-skinned with gorgeous long, red hair. My olive skin kept me tanned most of the year, and I was at least six inches shorter than her and with dark hair. The girl was stunning and brilliant, and she could make me laugh on my darkest days.

"Sorry. Just went for a run. Luckily you can't smell me through this screen because I'm sure I'm in desperate need of a shower. How are you? How's Grayson?" Grayson had attended NYU with us, and they were a fabulous couple.

Her head fell back with a chuckle. "He's great. But I refuse to get caught in your devious ploy at small talk. The fact that you finally reached out had me completely checked out with my morning clients because I want to know what's going on."

I took a long sip of water before setting the bottle beside my computer and letting out a long breath.

Let's do this.

"So, I told you I'm working with Hawk."

"Yes. Which I think is a great idea. The fact that you avoided the man for almost a decade and were willing to work with him now says a lot. You're ready to move forward." She pulled her pretty hair over one shoulder as she waited for my response.

"Or I just needed a job?" I shrugged, knowing that wasn't the truth. I'd been terrified when the offer came from the Lions, but I'd also been excited for the first time in a long time. Because I'd missed him terribly, and as nervous as I was... the thrill of seeing him was stronger.

"I call bullshit. You're brilliant, and you took a temporary job instead of holding out for a permanent one. So, tell me how it's been going. And not the surface answer, Ev. You've already told me that you're training together and spending time together and that you're just friends, blah, blah, blah." She laughed. "I know, not very professional. But seeing as you're my best friend, I'm not going to be standing on ceremony with you. Spill it, girl."

I shook my head because there wasn't anything I didn't love about Lala, and I was okay with talking about it. Hell, maybe that was progress in itself. I didn't want to hold this in. I hated that he was mad at me. I wanted to fix it, not run from it. I didn't want to go another decade without talking to him.

"So, we had a moment of weakness. Actually, two moments of weakness."

"Details, please," she said, raising a brow with a mischievous smirk on her face.

"We went to dinner at his parents' house a few weeks ago, and Darrian Sacatto was there. She surprised him."

"Wasn't she in *Blood Stripes*? Wow. She's my fashion icon," she said before her eyes widened, and she winced. "I mean, if you're into tall, blonde bombshells. I'd take a petite, tan goddess all day long."

I laughed and rolled my eyes. "She's just as gorgeous in person. Anyway, seeing her kind of fawn all over him did something to me. I think I actually got jealous. But they aren't together, they're just friends. So, I hid in the bathroom, deciding if I was going to sneak out the back door, and Hawk came in there. And somehow, my lips landed on his. It truly was an accident."

She fell forward in a fit of laughter. "Sure, it was. So, what happened next?"

I filled her in on all the details about the ridiculous car ride home. How she left the next day, and we got back to normal and just pretended the kiss never happened. I assured her that I made every effort to be professional, up until the night Brad and his friends showed up at the bar. I gave her all the details, everything that happened outside of the fact that I cried out his name twice that night. Because a girl has to have some pride, right?

She was listening so intently, as if this was the most fascinating story she'd ever heard.

"Say something. You're scaring me. You're a therapist, for

god's sake. You must hear more messed-up stuff than this?" I groaned.

"Oh, trust me. I've heard it all. Weird sex fetishes. Commitment-phobes. But this... it's so romantic and sweet. Like something you'd see in a movie."

My mouth gaped open. "Did you not hear the part about him being furious with me?"

"Well, let's think about this." She leaned back in her chair and crossed her arms over her chest. "The man gives you all the orgasms and takes nothing for himself while you sleep naked in his bed, and then you wake up and tell him that his coach is an even bigger asshole than he already knew, and you follow that with a reminder that you need to go back to being professional. Seriously, Ev? You're giving me whiplash."

I buried my face in my hands and groaned. "I'm such an asshole."

"You really are," she said before we both lost it, laughing.

"Listen to me. There's something here. You never stopped loving him, Ev. All these feelings are coming up for you again. It's been a long time, and you've dated so many boring, shallow assholes ever since."

"Wow. Tell me how you really feel." I played with the ends of my ponytail.

"You know I'm a straight shooter. I've told you many times that I thought you chose unappealing men on purpose. You can't get super attached to a guy who is emotionally stunted, right?" Her lips turned up in the corners, and her eyes softened. "You're ready to move forward or you wouldn't have gone home. You had the money to keep your apartment here in the city until you found a job. You went home because

I think you're tired of running. Hell, you've got to be. And the only way to find happiness is to face it."

"What does that even mean? I'm here. I'm facing it all." I swiped as a tear escaped and rolled down my cheek. "Hell, I cry all the time now. You'd be so proud."

"Oh, Ev. You're doing great. You've put yourself right in the middle of it. It's so you to face the death of your mother and the only guy you ever truly loved all at the same time."

"Well, you know I'm an overachiever," I croaked.

"Honey, listen to me. Keep doing what you're doing. It sounds like all the feelings are still there with Hawk. Don't run from that."

"He's not even speaking to me."

"Because you hurt him. You're sending mixed signals. But I'm telling you, if he's as amazing as you say he is, he'll understand. All the people who love you want you to be happy. You need to allow yourself to be happy. It's time."

I sighed as the tears poured down my cheeks and I didn't try to stop them. "Being here reminds me so much of my mom. I've spent so much time trying not to talk about it, but it actually feels good to feel her presence here. And I do."

"That's a good thing."

"And being with Hawk, it just feels—right. But where can that go? I mean, I'm most likely not going to get hired by the Lions. And he'll probably go back and play. And I don't think I could recover if I let this thing go too far and then we have to leave each other again."

"Stop overthinking. I think that's a coping mechanism for you. But stop trying to figure everything out. Just see where it goes. If this is the real deal, you guys will figure out a way to make it work. People do it all the time, Ev. I think you know that. I think you're afraid of it actually working out. Afraid of loving that deeply again."

I nodded because I knew she was right, but I didn't know how to let that fear go. I couldn't speak because the lump in my throat was too big.

"I know that loving someone is a risk. But it's so worth it, my sweet friend. You deserve to love and to be loved. By a good man. By someone who makes you happy and fulfills you. Just tell him how you feel, and I'm willing to bet he feels the same way."

I covered my face with my hands and let out a long breath before looking back up at her. "And what about the fact that I'm his sports psychologist? How does that look if I'm dating the guy I'm working for?"

"Well, technically, you're working for that dickhead Hayes." She shrugged. "None of that matters in the big picture. If it works out and you two want to give it a shot, you can keep this under wraps from the team until you've settled into the job. It's not like Coach Hayes doesn't know you have a history. Hell, that connection you two had probably scared the hell out of the guy, which is why he tried to kick you to the curb."

"Okay, this is a lot to process. Let me think on this."

"Do you know how proud I am of you? This is big, Ev. Just keep pushing outside of that comfort zone, okay?"

"I will. Thank you. I don't think I could have had this conversation with anyone else."

"Damn straight, girl. Your secrets have always been safe with me."

"Right back at you. I love you, Lala. Give that hubby of yours a big hug from me. I miss you."

"Miss you and love you too. Call me later and let me know what happened."

I blew her a kiss and ended the call.

And then I crawled into bed and let myself do something I hadn't done before. I lay there thinking about my mom. About Hawk. About all that I lost.

I cried and sobbed and wailed.

And it felt damn good.

Chapter 18

Hawk

"That was nice of Everly to invite me to Sunday dinner. I could use a good home-cooked meal," Wes said.

"Yeah, the Thomases always have an open-door policy. Jack's a damn good cook, and all the girls kick in and make side dishes. You'll definitely be well-fed." I laughed, but I'd had a pit in my stomach since I saw Everly last. I probably didn't handle things well, but I was pissed at what she'd said. I didn't know if she'd ever fully let me in, and I was surprised that I was right back in the same place with her that I'd been nine years ago.

Nothing had changed.

At least not for me.

And whether or not she felt the same, she sure as fuck wasn't willing to own it. She didn't fight for us nine years ago, and she wasn't fighting for us now.

"Sounds like a great family," Wes said as I walked inside, and Dylan and Charlotte met us at the door. I introduced my trainer to them and then we all walked into the kitchen where Everly stood making a salad. Her gaze locked with mine as Dylan continued introducing Wes to her father, a few firefighters, and the rest of the group.

"Hey," she said. "Did you get your workout in this morning?"

She was wearing a long white sundress, her hair pulled up in a ponytail that ran down her back, and she looked fucking gorgeous.

"Yep. We did a good weight workout this morning. How about you?" I asked, my hands fisting at my sides because it took everything I had not to reach out and touch her.

"No. I'm pretty sore from that ass-kicking yesterday," she said with a shrug. "Obviously, you've been holding out on me."

Her smile made my chest squeeze, and I silently cursed myself for being such a pussy when it came to Everly Thomas.

The one girl I'd never been able to deny.

"Nah. I just had to work some stuff out of my system."

"Yeah? Did you get it all worked out?" she asked, and her voice cracked a little bit as her gaze searched mine.

"I'm not sure I can." It was the honest truth. Getting Everly Thomas out of my system wasn't an option. Not being this close to her at least. I'd be all right once we went our separate ways, and she made it clear she wanted nothing to do with me.

Again.

"Hey there. Thought you might want a beer. Wes was

just telling me you survived a brutal workout," Jack said as he handed me the cold brew and clapped me on the shoulder before turning to his oldest daughter. "Burgers and dogs are ready."

"All right. All the side dishes are already out there, so I'll bring the salad." She poured some sort of dressing over the giant bowl of lettuce and chopped veggies and carried it out of the kitchen.

There was a long table out on the screened-in porch, and everyone was taking their seats as I followed Jack and Everly out there.

I sat beside Wes as he and Niko were deep in a conversation about MMA fighting. Everly took the seat across from me, and Jace leaned over and clinked his beer with mine from the other side of the table. Ashlan and Charlotte were fawning over Jace's little girls, Paisley and Hadley, and Gramps, Big Al, and his wife, Lottie, sat on the other side of me. It was a lively group, but I'd grown up with all these people, so there was always a comfort here.

Vivian passed the potato salad to me, and Dylan rubbed her hands together excitedly.

"Is that Mom's potato salad?" Dylan asked.

"Yep. I know it's a crowd favorite." Vivian smiled before quickly turning to look at Everly to make sure the mention of their mother hadn't upset her.

Jack looked between his two daughters, and it was almost as if everyone at the table understood what was happening because the conversation came to a halt. I glanced over at Wes who had so much food piled on his plate, looking utterly confused by what was happening.

"It's okay to talk about her." Everly let out a long breath, her gaze finding mine as her eyes welled with emotion. "I think I owe all of you an apology."

"You don't owe anyone anything, sweetheart," Jack said, watching his daughter with concern.

"No. I do. I really do. It took me a long time to realize why I left here as fast as I could. Why I didn't come home as often as I should have and always wanted you guys to come visit me at school." She looked between her sisters and her father.

"Ev, you don't need to say anything. We all understand," Vivian said, reaching over Niko to grab her sister's hand.

"I do though. The truth is, I've been running scared for a long time. After Mom died, I had so much guilt about Vivian being the one who was here, and me not being there with her. But seeing Mom deteriorate every day those last few weeks," her words broke on a sob, and she held her hand to her chest as the tears started to fall. "It scared me. It made me feel so sad and so out of control—I don't know how else to describe it. And after she passed, I never wanted to hurt like that again. I made a promise to myself that I wouldn't ever let myself feel that kind of pain again."

Dylan was on her feet now and hurrying over to hug her sister. Charlotte and Ashlan were both watching with tears running down their faces. And I just watched the girl I loved break all those walls down. I stared at her with amazement as she allowed herself to be honest and vulnerable.

"I know, sweetheart. It wasn't fair, and I think we all just did the best we could." Jack clasped his hands together, as everyone watched with emotion-filled eyes.

"But I was the only one who ran. And I'm sorry about that." Her gaze turned to me. "I'm still running in a way, aren't I? And I'm so tired of running."

That was it. I couldn't stand by and watch her suffer without saying something.

"Ever mine," I whispered. "You're okay."

She shook her head and looked directly at me. "But I'm not, Hawk. I'm really not. And you're the reason I know that. I loved you so much and that terrified me. That's the truth. I ran from home, and I ran from you. From all the people I loved most in the world."

"Well, Coach Hayes didn't help anything," I said as I stared into those Honey Mountain blues.

"I could have told you. I also could have told him to keep his advice to himself. But I was looking for a reason to run, right? It's what I do. But I don't want to do it anymore." She buried her face in her hands, and all of her sisters were around her now, doing what they could to comfort her. I just waited for a sign. Waited for her to tell me what she wanted.

What she needed.

"I love you, Ev," Vivian said.

"I love you too," she sobbed.

Her head lifted, and her gaze was back on mine. "I love you, Hawk. I'm sorry it took me so long to say it. I know this is highly unprofessional," she said as the table erupted in laughter. The pent-up emotion causing everyone to lose it.

"Come here, baby," I said, pushing my chair back, because there was no chance of me breaking through that sister barrier currently going on across from me.

Everly pushed to her feet and came running around the

table and fell into me. I wrapped my arms around her as she settled on my lap and hugged me tight. "I love you too, Ever mine."

"All right, does this mean we can eat?" Gramps asked. He was the oldest firefighter in the group, and I'd known him most of my life.

"Go ahead and eat, you old grump," Big Al said and there was more laughter.

"I'm enjoying the show if I'm being honest," Dylan said as she wiggled her brows.

"Of course you are." Charlotte laughed as all the girls returned to their seats.

"You want to go talk in the other room?" I whispered.

"Nope. No more running and no more hiding," she said. "I'm not afraid to say how I feel in front of anyone here."

"Could we not get too sappy, please? Every damn dinner, someone's proclaiming their love for someone," Jack said, and even I had to laugh.

"Personally, I look forward to these tender moments at the Thomas house. Hell, with Cap riding our asses at the firehouse, it's nice to have a Hallmark movie moment every now and then," Rusty said, and Big Al gaped at him.

"I told you, you're too soft, Rusty." Niko smirked.

"Says the dude who keeps talking to his wife's belly like it's going to talk back to him." Rusty reached for another roll.

"Babies can hear voices, and our baby will know his or her father's voice when they enter the world." Vivian leaned into Niko as he kissed the top of her head.

Everly's head tipped back, and she looked up at me. "Do

you forgive me?"

"Nothing to forgive, unless you wake up tomorrow and tell me we need to act professionally," I said, not making any attempt to hide my sarcasm.

"Well, I still wouldn't let Hayes know this is a thing. He's asked me a couple times about you two, and I've assured him nothing is going on," Wes said as he reached for his beer. "He's a spiteful dude, and I wouldn't put anything past him."

"What happens at the Thomas table *stays* at the Thomas table." Charlotte smiled and glanced around at everyone.

"I'll drink to that," Dylan said, holding her glass up as everyone did the same. Everly wrapped her hand around mine which was holding the beer.

"What happens at the Thomas table *stays* at the Thomas table," everyone shouted at the same time with a chuckle.

But I didn't miss the concern in Wes's eyes. Coach wouldn't like it, and I didn't want to ruin her chances of getting hired. He would not hesitate to destroy anyone who got in the way of what he wanted. I knew it, and Wes knew it. But we would deal with that later.

"I'm happy for you guys. I've been wondering how long it would take for this to happen." Wes smirked as he bit into a roll.

"You and me both. It was like watching a fire build slowly. With each gaze, the flames were fanned, but neither were giving in," Dylan sang out, and Jack coughed on the water he'd just sipped.

"Could we not compare my livelihood to my daughter's dating life, please?" He held up his hamburger and took a bite.

"I'm glad you're home, Ev," Ashlan said, as she watched her big sister and smiled. "It feels like we're all figuring things out."

Everly nodded and tucked her head against my chest. "It does."

"Well, I can tell you something, girls. Your mama would be so proud of each and every one of you," Lottie said, and Big Al wrapped an arm around his wife's shoulder.

"She definitely would. Now can we eat some of her potato salad and stop all this crying?" Jack said, looking from one daughter to the next.

"I can eat and cry. I'm special that way." Dylan stood and reached for the potato salad and scooped some on her plate.

"You sure are special," Rusty said, his eyes wide and smile playful.

"Give it a rest, Rusty," Dylan hissed as Jack smacked him on the back of his head.

"Can I get through a meal without you hitting on my daughters, please?"

"Of course, Cap. But a guy's got to take his shot."

"Maybe take it a little less often," Jace said, scooping some corn onto Hadley's plate.

"Agreed," Tallboy said with a laugh.

The banter continued, but I focused all my attention on the girl sitting on my lap. I handed her my burger, and she took a bite and smiled up at me once again.

"You'll need fuel for what I've got planned for you," I said, whispering in her ear, making sure no one else could hear.

Her cheeks flushed pink, and she grinned. "You best fuel up, too."

I didn't know what any of this meant or how long it would last, but I wasn't going to question it. She'd been strong for so long, and her armor was tightly locked around her—so the fact that she'd set it down for me...

I'd call that a win.

And this was one win I'd hold on tight to.

Chapter 19

Everly

I felt like I'd just run a marathon with how fatigued my body was from my emotional meltdown. But I sort of had that same rush of pride that I'd done something good.

I knew I had.

I felt it in my gut.

That didn't stop Hawk from hurrying us out of my father's house and giving me a piggyback ride the few blocks home. Wes had hit it off with everyone and stayed to sit around the fire pit and drink beers and roast marshmallows.

"How are you feeling?" he asked as I rested my chin on top of his head.

"A little zapped but good. I'm relieved to have this weight off my shoulders. I've felt it for a long time," I admitted. Now that I'd told the truth, I couldn't seem to stop spilling everything that I felt.

"Yeah?"

He was still being cautious, and I didn't blame him. "I felt it the first time you walked into the house a few weeks ago. But if I'm being honest, I felt it every day since the day we ended things. Every time I saw your photo in a magazine or on social media, it hurt. That's why no one could talk about you to me. Because I missed you every day."

He came to a stop in front of his house and somehow managed to unravel me off his back and into his arms, holding me like a baby, which made me laugh ridiculously loud. He just laughed right along with me and carried me inside, dropping me on the couch before settling beside me.

"Thank you for telling the truth. That's how I've felt. I've never stopped missing you. Never stopped loving you. And just hearing that you felt the same, it's something I knew in my gut, but I don't know... I guess I needed to hear it."

"I don't care if Coach Hayes knows or the whole world knows. I'm sorry for acting the way that I did after we spent the night together. I was scared, and I'll probably get scared again, but I'll do my best to talk to you."

"I'm the only one who needs to hear it, Ever. I don't think it's any of Coach's business or anyone else's, for that matter. He'll use it against you. Trust me. This was never about you telling Coach or the world how you felt about me. This is about you and me."

I nodded and climbed onto his lap. Now that I'd admitted how I felt, I couldn't get close enough. Needing him was terrifying, but loving him was worth it. I knew it in every bone in my body.

"So, I guess what happens at the Thomas table *stays* at the

Thomas table." I rubbed my nose against his.

"I don't want him messing with you. I'd say he's interfered enough with our relationship for a fucking lifetime. But he's a devious dude, Ever. I'm not going to let him mess up what you've worked so hard for. This is just for us for now. When we go to the event, I'll just tell Coach that I'm bringing you and Wes because we're working together. He probably thinks I'm still with Darrian, so he won't question it. I don't involve him in my personal life because it's none of his fucking business."

I tried to push away the pit in my stomach. "It took us a long time to get here, and I don't want anything to ruin it."

"I'll fucking protect it with my life."

"So, we're doing this?" I threw my hands out to the side and chuckled. "You and me. We're really doing this?"

"You said you loved me, right?" he asked with a sexy-assin smirk on his face.

"I love you. Always have. Always will."

"That's all I need, *Ever mine.*" His mouth crashed into mine. Claiming and needing and wanting.

"You're all I need," I said as he pushed to his feet, pulling me along with him. My legs wrapped around his waist, and he tangled his fingers in my hair, pulling my mouth down to his again.

We made our way to his bedroom, and he dropped me on the bed, my body bouncing on the mattress, making me laugh.

"Tell me what you need, baby," he said, as he climbed on the bed and hovered above me.

"You."

His green eyes burned with desire, and I reached up to stroke his cheek.

"I'm all yours. I always have been."

His mouth crashed into mine and my fingers tangled in his hair. He pulled back, reaching for my hands and sitting me forward as I raised my arms over my head while he found the hem of my dress. I pushed up so he could pull it past my butt.

"I need you naked, now," he said, his voice gruff.

I chuckled as he tugged it over my head and tossed it on the floor. He unsnapped my bra and his fingers moved beneath the straps, slowly sliding them down my arms as goose bumps spread across my skin in anticipation.

"Fuck, Ever. You're so beautiful." He tipped me back and his mouth came over my breast, and I moaned.

The sensation was too much.

Yet I wanted more.

He took turns moving from one breast to the next. Licking and sucking and driving me mad.

My fingers tugged at his hair. "Hawk, please."

He pulled back, lips red and swollen from kissing me and his eyes wild with desire. "You want more, baby?"

I nodded, unable to speak, and he laughed. "I've thought about these tits, this mouth, this body for nine fucking years. I'm not rushing this."

My breaths were coming hard and fast. Needing this man in a way I couldn't wrap my head around.

He kissed his way down my neck, and I tipped my head back, granting him better access. He continued his slow worship of my body as he moved down my stomach, kissing and ravishing every inch of me. I writhed and shook beneath his touch as he seared his path down my body, setting my entire being ablaze.

His fingers moved beneath the lace of my panties, and he pulled back to look at me as he glided them down my legs. My body trembled.

Anticipation and desire and want.

"It's too much," I whispered.

He reached for my hands and intertwined his fingers with mine. "It's always been too much with us. That's why nothing else has ever compared."

"I missed you."

"I missed everything about you." He leaned down and claimed my mouth before sliding down the bed and settling between my legs. "I need to taste you again, baby."

I nodded as he buried his head between my legs.

Making me feel everything.

Making me remember what it felt like to be this close to someone.

To trust someone completely with my body.

My heart.

He slipped a finger inside me, and I nearly came off the bed. His mouth found my most sensitive area as he continued to bring me right to the edge, before pulling back.

My body began to shake as the overwhelming need for release took over.

My vision blurred.

Stars exploded behind my eyes.

I tugged at his hair. He didn't stop this time. He took me right over the edge, and I cried out his name as I rode out every last bit of pleasure.

I gasped for air as I tried to calm my breathing. A lump formed deep in my throat, and I fought hard not to cry again.

But my body shook in response as I tried to control my emotions.

He pulled back, moving up to hover above me. He studied me. "Are you okay?"

The concern in his voice overwhelmed me. The empathy in his green gaze caused my heart to expand in my chest. The vulnerability I felt was both terrifying and exhilarating.

"You make me feel all the things, Hawk Madden."

He nipped at my bottom lip. "Buckle up, baby. Get ready to feel even more."

"You have too many clothes on."

He pushed off the bed and yanked the T-shirt over his head. His chest and abs were chiseled perfection. Tan and defined and glorious just like the man beneath.

He shoved his jeans off, and I propped myself up on my elbows to watch the show. His erection tented his boxer briefs, and I bit down on my bottom lip as I took him in.

Every inch of him large and hard and impossible to look away from.

He wiggled his brows before pushing the fabric down as his overzealous erection sprung to life.

"Oh my."

"He's excited to be inside you again. It's been too long, baby," he said as he dove onto the bed, propping himself above me. His erection throbbed against my lower belly.

"Your penis has emotions?" I half laughed, half moaned as he settled between my legs and ground up against me.

"He sure as shit does when it comes to you."

"What are you waiting for?" I whispered, my breaths growing more rapid.

He stretched his long arm over my head and reached for

his nightstand. He pushed back on his knees and tore the top of the condom wrapper off with his teeth and then tossed it on the floor. He slowly rolled the latex over his long, thick erection, and his gaze never left mine.

He settled between my legs again, and his tip teased my entrance. He covered my mouth with his before moving forward, slowly inching inside me.

I gasped at the intrusion, and he paused, giving me a minute to adjust to his size.

"Don't stop," I said, and he shifted his hips, hitting me exactly where I wanted him.

We found our rhythm, moving together. His gaze locked with mine.

The light from the moon filled the room and as I looked up at him, I let go of all the fear.

I embraced the moment with this man.

The man I gave my heart to so long ago.

Reality hit me hard when I realized that I'd never gotten it back.

We continued to move faster.

Lost in the moment.

Lost in one another.

His hand moved between us, touching me exactly where I wanted him.

Where I needed him.

Our bodies slapping together.

Breaths gasping.

Lips searching for more.

"Hawk," I shouted as lights burst behind my eyes and my body exploded.

Oh my god.

He moved again, thrashing his hips into mine before he went right over the edge with me.

"Fuck," he gasped.

Our breaths filled the room as we both rode out our pleasure.

"I fucking love you, Ever mine," he said as he fell to the side, pulling me along with him.

"I love you," I whispered.

Because I'd never stopped, and I never would.

But that little voice in the back of my head was there the moment I admitted my feelings to myself.

And that creeping feeling that the rug would be pulled out from under me reared its ugly head.

Hawk pushed the hair away from my face as he took me in.

And I pushed that fear away.

At least for now.

Chapter 20

Hawk

"Ramping things up, are we?" Wes asked when I wiped the sweat from my brow and leaned over to catch my breath. Coming home to Honey Mountain had been a good move for me, and not just because Ever and I had found our way back to one another. But physically and mentally, I'd really needed this. I was pushing myself harder than I had in years because my head was clear. I'd shut out all the noise and come back to my roots.

"Something like that." I glanced over at Ever who was sitting a few feet away watching me. Sitting there in her little running shorts and driving me out of my mind. She pushed me in the afternoon workouts and usually just came for moral support in the morning, all under the ruse of sports psychology. She claimed she was analyzing my workouts, but I believed she was just here to check my ass out.

"Good work, man. Hayes is going to be impressed, pending you decide to play for him." Wes smirked.

"Yeah. Joey's so far up my ass it's hard to see straight," I said of my agent. The dude wanted to get this deal done, but I wasn't quite there yet. And after years of having to make decisions based on money, I didn't need to do that anymore, and it felt damn good.

Ever's phone rang, and she glanced down at the screen, holding her finger up to me and walking away as she answered the call.

"You've got more to think about now than you did when you first arrived here," Wes said.

"Meaning?"

"I've been with you a long time, Hawk. It's really nice to see you happy. She definitely makes you happy."

I nodded. He was right. Ever and I were taking things one day at a time, but I'd be lying if I didn't admit it was a big factor in my decision. I knew Coach would hire her if I negotiated that into my deal, but she didn't want to get hired that way. I also didn't like the idea of him having any power over me or her. Finding out that he'd contributed to her walking away from me all those years ago only reminded me that he'd do whatever it took to keep me focused on the game. And playing for a man I despised and didn't trust had lost its lure. I didn't need him. I didn't have to tolerate his manipulating ass.

"She does."

"Remember, there is more to life than hockey. And if you tell anyone I said that to you, I'll be forced to kill you." A loud laugh boomed from his chest.

"I'm sure it's not easy for you being away from Marlene

and the kids this summer. You must be ready to get back."

Wes commuted home to the city twice a month.

"With FaceTime and Zoom and all that hoopla, it's been manageable. They're busy with camp during the week, and I get to be there for all the fun on the weekends. They'll be coming for a week after camp ends. A little mountain air will do those city kids some good."

"Yeah. I appreciate you going with me to the event this weekend. You can cut out early if you want."

"Nah. I'm happy to be there to see you receive that award. And I know you need me, so Hayes doesn't question you and Everly too much. I assume he's going?"

I'd asked Wes to attend the event as well, because it would keep Coach from getting too curious about my relationship with Ever. I didn't need him in my business or messing with hers. And I'd put nothing past that man when it came to getting me to sign.

"Yeah. I think he's going to try to close me. I've told him I'll give him my decision in a few weeks when we head back. Until then, I don't owe him a damn thing. He's got a great backup for me. The team is young and there is a lot of growing that's going to happen either way. With or without me."

"Having you on the team means another chance at the Stanley Cup. I don't see them having much of a chance without you. And having Everly and me both there will definitely keep him off your tail. I've worked with him a long time as well and I wouldn't put a lot past the man. He cares about winning, not much else matters."

"Guess what?" Everly shouted as she sprinted toward me,

and I held my arms out as she dove into them.

"What?" I laughed.

"That was Coach Rayburn from the Gliders, the team I worked for back in New York. Jason Peters, the sports psychologist I trained under just told them this would be his last year. They're offering me an assistant job, with the potential of taking over for him when he leaves."

I spun her around before setting her feet back on the ground and Wes clapped her on the shoulder. "Congrats, girl. You're the best I've ever worked with."

"Well, I'm the only one you've ever worked with, but I'll still take it," she said with a chuckle before turning back to look at me.

Hell, I wasn't thrilled about the idea, but it didn't mean I couldn't be happy for her. After spending nine years apart, the last thing I wanted to do was put miles between us. I was all-in. I just needed to make sure that she was.

"That's amazing. What are you thinking?"

"Well, there are a few factors to consider." Her brows pinched together as she thought about it, and she twirled the end of her long ponytail between her fingertips. "First off, the pay is pretty horrible, as they really don't need an assistant. But I think they are afraid I'll be scooped up if they wait until next year. I'd have to live in a dump that first year, and there is no guarantee they will offer me the full-time position when he retires. Plus, it would be far away from you, pending you go back to the Lions when we have to go back to reality."

I chugged my water and nodded. There was a lot to unpack here, and I was glad she was opening the door to discuss it.

"Well, that's my cue. I'm going to head to the grocery

store and grab a few things, and then I think I'll be stopping by your sister's bakery for some of those cupcakes," Wes said as he saluted us and walked toward his house.

Everly and I made our way to my truck and climbed inside.

"You're being awfully quiet," she said, as she buckled her seat belt and I backed out of the driveway.

"I was waiting until we were alone." I pulled in front of my house which wasn't far from Wes's place at all, but we'd grabbed bagels from the Honey Mountain Café this morning before practice, so we'd taken the truck.

She turned to face me. "All right. Lay it on me."

"First off, don't let money be a factor, Ever."

"Of course, it's a factor. It's my salary."

"I make a shit-ton of money. I have more than I know what to do with. So, if this is your dream job and it's important to you, do not let that get in the way. I'll cover your expenses," I said, holding my hands up before she could start arguing. Which she was biting at the bit to do. "Just that first year, until they start paying you right." Hell, I'd support her forever, but we'd have to take baby steps. The girl didn't like asking for help or needing anyone, so this was new.

"That's your big concern? Helping me cover my bills?" she teased.

"Listen. I'm never going to lie to you. You know that."

"I do."

"Obviously, it took us a long time to find our way back to one another. I'm not in any hurry to be away from you now. So, the idea of you going to New York is something that affects me, and I'll need to factor that into my decision."

"The GOAT of the ice is going to base his decision on

where his high school girlfriend is going to be an assistant sports psychologist?" She smiled and shook her head. "That doesn't seem right."

"Well, is what I do a factor in your decision? Where I decide to play?"

She reached for my hands. "Of course, it is. But Coach Hayes only asks about your decision lately. He hasn't brought up me coming on the team permanently in a few weeks, and I worked really hard to get here. I know I don't make the big bucks like you do, but my job matters to me. I need to feel like I'm accomplishing something."

I tugged her onto my lap and pushed the hair back from her pretty face. "You accomplished something last night, when you rode me into oblivion."

A pink hue crept up her cheeks and I fucking loved it. Loved that I could still make her blush when we'd been naked in bed for the past week every time we weren't working out or eating.

"You know what I mean. I think you're right. People probably shouldn't find out that we're together before I sign a contract, wherever it is. Everyone will say that I slept my way to the top."

I didn't give a shit what anyone thought, but I'd never do anything to hurt Everly. And being a woman in this industry wasn't easy. I respected the shit out of how hard she'd worked to get here, and the last thing I'd ever do was mess that up.

"It's our secret. Wes has agreed to go to the event this weekend, and we'll act completely professional around Coach Hayes. Hell, he keeps asking about Darrian, so he clearly thinks we're still together."

She scrunched her nose and frowned. "Do you still talk to her a lot?"

I laughed. "You jealous?"

"Totally."

I wrapped my hand around her ponytail and tugged her closer, studying her gorgeous blue eyes. "There's no one I want but you. Darrian and I are friends, so we text occasionally. I did ask her to keep our breakup quiet for a bit longer, as it just makes things easier for you and me. She knows that we're together, and she's happy for us."

"And what happens if I go to New York and you go to San Francisco?" Her lips were so close, and my tongue swiped out to stroke her bottom lip.

"Ever mine, it doesn't matter where you live. As long as you want me, I'm yours."

My mouth crashed into hers and she ground up against me, but when she leaned back, the horn sounded, causing us both to startle.

Everly glanced over her shoulder and then covered her face with her hands. "Oh my gosh. Mrs. Fork was watching us."

"Well, maybe she'll go inside and fork Mr. Fork." I waggled my brows.

Her head fell back in laughter. "That was a good one, Hawky player."

"Yeah, you like that." I pushed the door open and pulled her right along with me. Her legs came around my waist, her hands tangling in my hair as I walked up the driveway to my house.

"I like everything about you, Hawk Madden," she

whispered once we stepped inside.

"You're going to kill me, woman. Wes just kicked my ass, but you know I'm always down to fork you in the shower." I nipped at her bottom lip and carried her down the hallway.

"I wish we could stay right here forever," she said when I set her ass on the bathroom counter and moved to stand between her legs.

"We can do whatever the fuck we want."

"We both still have to live our lives. You've got a lot of people counting on you, and I, well, I want to make a name for myself."

"I prefer *Ever mine*." I wrapped her ponytail around my hand and tugged her closer.

"I don't mind that one either."

"We've got dinner at your dad's tonight, right?"

"Yeah. He's making ribs."

"Ah... my favorite." I stepped back, letting her hair fall over her shoulder, and I yanked my T-shirt over my head. I dropped my shorts, and her eyes widened as she took me in.

"It's really good to know that your favorites haven't changed." She reached for my hand. "I don't really need to shower since I haven't worked out yet, but seeing you naked has me feeling like a shower might be a great idea."

I reached for the hem of her tank top, and she raised her arms above her head as I pulled it off of her and tossed it on the floor. I helped her to her feet and slipped my fingers beneath her waistband, tugging her shorts and panties down her legs. I kissed her toned stomach before pushing to my feet.

"Any time I can shower with you is a good day."

I picked her up and tossed her over my shoulder and gave her ass a playful swat as she laughed.

And I knew that being away from this girl ever again was not going to work for me.

It just wasn't an option.

Chapter 21
Everly

"I'm excited for you to go to the city with him. You'll get to see where he lives and cheer him on as he accepts his award, even if you have to act professionally for his asshole coach. I do think it's wise to keep this a secret, at least until you have a job. Unfortunately, us women get judged for everything we do, most especially in a male-dominated industry." Lala rolled her eyes and shook her head.

"Yeah, Hawk even reserved me a room at the hotel, just in case his crazy coach were to check into it. That's how much he doesn't trust this guy. He's so worried that he'll try to do something to leverage him with me."

"He sounds very twisted."

"He really does. But it'll be great. I'm glad I get to be there with him. And I'll get to meet a few of his teammates."

"I think it's so cool that he's being honored for his charity work. A man should not be allowed to look that hot and be philanthropic." She raised a brow and I laughed.

"Yeah. He's amazing."

"Oh my." She dropped her glasses back down on her face and studied me. "I have never seen you all dreamy about a man. Mind you, you've always dated very uneventful men before now."

"That's a good point."

"In all seriousness, it's got to be tough for Hawk playing for a man he doesn't care for?" she asked.

"Yep. For sure. He said if Coach Hayes wasn't there, it would be a no-brainer about returning for one more year. But he doesn't appreciate the way he manipulates the players and he just doesn't know that he can play for the man another year. But he loves his team. I know he wants to go back."

"And what are you thinking as far as the Gliders? You know I'd be thrilled to have you back here."

"I know. They told me I could have a couple weeks to decide. They know I've been working with Hawk, which I think is probably the reason they're actually considering hiring me. Everyone's waiting to see if I fixed the golden boy of the ice during the off-season."

"Did you?" she asked. My best friend had a gift for asking the right questions in order to pry information out of you.

"Wait. Is this a session? We don't meet professionally until next week."

"Well, can't a friend ask her bestie questions without being accused of being a therapist?" She laughed.

"Fine. The truth is... Hawk didn't need fixing. He's in fabulous shape physically and mentally. He just doesn't respect his coach, doesn't know that he wants to be held accountable for a young team, and—"

"And?"

"He said he always felt like something was missing, and he doesn't feel that way anymore."

"Because he found it, didn't he?" She used her hand to fan her face.

"I don't know. I don't know what any of it means. But we can save that for next week's conversation."

"No, ma'am. I can be a friend and a therapist. What do you mean you don't know what it means?"

"I just don't like that so much is up in the air. I mean, we're here and we're playing house. I can't believe how easy it was to fall back into this with him. We just have such a comfort with one another, and I love it. But what happens when he has to decide? What if he goes back to San Francisco and I'm in New York?"

"I thought he said it didn't matter," she asked, watching me intently through her computer screen.

"I can't help but feel this sense of panic. And things are so great right now that I don't want to start asking the hard questions, you know? It'll ruin it."

"What are the hard questions?"

"How do you make something work if you're living across the country from your significant other? We'd both be traveling with our teams all the time. Hell, marriages of twenty-some years end due to this kind of stuff. So, how does it work?"

"He's a wealthy man, Ever. He can fly to you whenever he has time off. He can fly you to him. You make it work. What are you not saying?"

"Nothing. I just don't know how realistic it is. He's going to go back to his life in the spotlight. Women will be fawning all over him. I might be the most exciting thing in Honey Mountain for him—but out in the real world? I don't know that that's true."

"I thought you said he was honest to his core?" She raised a brow.

"He is. But still, that's a lot of temptation. And, I don't know. The thought of him leaving me makes me feel physically ill." I pushed to my feet and shook out my hands. I'd been agonizing over this lately, as so much was up in the air for both of us.

"Whoa, whoa, whoa. Slow your roll, girlfriend. You just jumped from the long-distance conversation to him cheating and leaving you. Do you not remember that he told you no one has ever compared to you? He's had nine years to get hitched, and he never did. I know he's had girlfriends, but nothing like what you two have. And I know for a fact that you've never felt it with anyone else either. Why can't you have faith in that?"

Why couldn't I? Why was my instinct to flee?

Fight or flight.

"I know you, Everly Thomas. You're having an internal battle with yourself over your whole fight or flight philosophy, aren't you?"

A loud laugh escaped from my throat, and I moved back to my chair to sit down. "It's the natural reaction when you're feeling like things are too good to be true at the moment, right?"

"First off, nothing has happened. He hasn't made his

decision," she said, holding her hands up to stop me from interrupting because we both knew he was most likely going back. "And you could get offered the job from the Lions, and none of this will be an issue."

"It's a lot of ifs." I chewed on my thumbnail. "I just hope I haven't been too quick to go all-in. To put my guard down. I mean, in reality, it's been a few weeks. He's back home, and we're both feeling nostalgic. But the closer we get to this deadline, the more panicked I feel. If he left me, Lala..." I shook my head and let out a few breaths. "I'm so scared that this is going to end."

"You haven't been too quick. And it's about damn time you put your guard down. It's got to be exhausting protecting yourself all the time." Her eyes grew wet with emotion. "Listen, Ev, I know that you've been hurt and that losing your mama when you did was really hard. And really unfair. But the truth is—it doesn't mean that everyone is going to hurt you. It just doesn't. You tend to expect it to happen and you're so busy preparing yourself for it, that you run before you can let yourself be happy. What if just this one time, you did something different?"

"Like what?"

"Like you didn't run. You embrace these feelings, and you have faith that it will all work out. It's time to stop running, Ev."

I swiped at the tear running down my cheek. "I have never cried more since being back here, and now you're making me cry too. I hate it."

"Maybe that's all part of healing?"

"What if I'm broken?" I finally whispered, because that

was the part that scared me the most. What if I never allowed myself to be truly happy because the fear of losing the person I loved was too much?

"You're not broken, Everly Thomas. You're just a little wounded, that's all."

She wasn't saying what we both knew.

Not all wounds ever fully heal.

But I was damn well going to try not to mess this up.

Because it felt good to be happy. Truly happy to my core.

And that was worth fighting for.

"Ever mine," Hawk shouted. He'd gone with Niko and Jace to help set up a few things for the baby reveal party at Vivi and Niko's. I'd been over there this morning with my sisters, and we'd set up all the tables and decorations. I couldn't wait to get over there to find out if I was having a niece or a nephew.

"All right, he's home. We'll talk later. Love you."

She gushed at Hawk when he came into the room, and we said our goodbyes. They'd met on FaceTime several times, and he was looking forward to meeting her in person soon.

He was so confident about our future, I longed to feel that sure that things would work out. To know that this wasn't just a fantasy or a fairy tale I was living in. Because everything about Hawk felt like it was too good to be true.

"You had a session?" he asked, scooping me up and sitting on the bed, pulling me onto his lap.

"No. We were just catching up."

"Yeah?" His gaze locked with mine and he studied me. The man knew me too well. "You sure? Is something up?"

"Nothing is up aside from what's going on beneath your zipper." I wiggled my butt against his erection that was currently poking my behind and laughed.

"You're going to kill me, woman," he said, pushing to his feet with me in his arms. "I just can't get enough of you. But we need to go."

"That's a good thing, right?" I asked as my legs wrapped around his waist.

"It's the best thing, baby." He kissed my cheek and carried me out to the living room. "Come on, little spider monkey, I'm starving."

I pushed away every doubt I had.

Everything was going to work out just fine.

"You know I could get used to being carried everywhere." I ran my fingers through his dark hair.

"Good. I don't plan on letting you go anytime soon." He pulled the door closed behind him and dropped me on the seat of his truck before leaning forward to kiss me hard.

I was still panting when he made his way around the car and climbed into the driver's seat.

When we pulled up to Vivi and Niko's house, several cars already lined the circular drive. Dylan and Charlotte had come early to help Vivi set up. Hawk's parents' car was out front, and I recognized another dozen cars lining the street. Firefighters, locals, and family were all here. They'd invited everyone out for an end-of-summer barbecue and a baby reveal.

"You ready for some good food and a baby reveal?" He interlocked his fingers with mine and led me up the driveway. We walked around back, and country music played through the speakers. There were tables dispersed around the yard with white linens covering them and fresh blooms filling the vases on each table.

There was a large blue and pink balloon arch in front of all the tables, and a small table sat there with a large cake on it.

Hawk and I took turns hugging everyone. I swear the whole town turned out for this party. Most of the firefighters were here, Dylan sauntered over and introduced us to two guys, Collin and Ben, who were a grade ahead of her in law school. I remembered her telling me that Collin was cute, and I think she brought Ben to set up with Charlotte. Ashlan came walking into the backyard, and Dylan leaned in between me and Hawk and whisper-shouted loud enough that anyone in a one-mile vicinity could hear her. Clearly someone had been dipping into the keg early on.

"It's Henry. The hot dude Ash just started seeing a few weeks ago."

Hawk laughed, and Ashlan rolled her eyes as she glanced up at Henry and shrugged before introducing all of us.

These were the things that I'd missed most when I'd been far from home. These moments of just gathering with all the people I loved most in the world. There was nothing here that I wanted to run from anymore. I wanted to stay put, right here. Right now.

"Hawk, I'm, uh, I'm a massive fan." Henry extended his hand as he fumbled over his words, and the two guys next to Dylan moved in front of her.

"Yeah, dude, we did not believe Dylan when she said you were dating her sister. You're the fucking GOAT, man," Collin shouted, and Dylan rolled her eyes.

"Take it down a notch, *Colon*." Dylan smiled and took a

sip from her red Solo cup.

"Uh, it's Collin, not Colon." He raised a brow at her.

"Not if you don't stop fangirling all over my future brother-in-law. You're acting like an ass."

Ben barked out a laugh and so did Hawk. I was still processing the fact that she'd referred to him as her future brother-in-law, and no one flinched.

Including me.

Hawk posed for pictures with all the guys, and I made my way through the yard, hugging Jada and Rook, Jilly, and Garrett, my father and all the guys, Big Al, Rusty, Samson, Tallboy, Gramps, Hog, and Little Dicky. Niko and Jace pulled me into a bear hug before I dropped down to hug his little angels, Paisley and Hadley, who were playing with Niko's niece, Mabel.

"There's our girl," Dune said, and I sat down at the table beside Hawk's parents.

"You excited for the big baby reveal?" Marilee asked me. "Awfully sweet of your sister and Niko to invite everyone out today."

"Yeah, this is nice. I am really excited."

"You got any guesses?"

"I go back and forth. I think it's a girl and then I think it's a boy." I shrugged.

"Well, we sure are glad we get to be here to share this moment with them," Marilee said. "And the fact that they wanted to serve Dune's beer was a double win."

He laughed. "Damn straight. Best beer in Honey Mountain."

"Okay, it's time," Niko shouted, and everyone turned their

attention to the center of the yard, where a table stood with a tall cake. "I know we were supposed to eat first, but the truth is, I can't wait any longer. So, we're doing this."

"That looks more like a wedding cake to me," Dune whispered. "Although in my day, you didn't have a party to tell what flavor baby you were having."

Marilee and I both giggled, and she slapped his chest. "These baby reveals are a big deal."

"I guess Jilly and Jada baked this creation after Niko and Vivi gave them the sealed envelope from the doctor a few days ago. They all decided not to have Dilly help because they didn't think she could keep the secret."

"That was a wise move," Hawk said with a chuckle as he lifted me up and set me on his lap.

Niko stood behind my sister and his large hand covered her small one. They pushed the knife into the top layer of cake and Vivi gasped, using her free hand to cover her eyes as she was clearly overcome with emotion. Niko set the knife down and wrapped her up in his arms, kissing the top of her head as tears streamed down her face.

"Uhhhh, the rest of us are waiting patiently," Dylan shouted, and everyone laughed.

Niko looked down to make sure Vivi was okay before scooping the slice onto the plate and holding it up.

"It's a girl. We're having our own little Honey Bee," he said.

Vivian swiped at her eyes before looking out at us. "We wanted to share the name with you once we knew the sex."

Everyone cheered.

"We're going to name our little girl Beth Everly West.

Named after the two strongest women I know." Vivian's voice cracked, and Niko looked down at her like she set the sun.

"A little Ever mine," Hawk whispered in my ear.

I kissed his cheek before I hurried toward my sister, completely overcome with emotion. Honored that she would name her child after our mother and me.

"You're lucky you didn't say the two best-looking women you know," Dylan said as she, Charlotte, and Ashlan joined in on our group hug, and we all laughed.

Our sisters started passing out cake, and Vivian turned to me, eyes wet with emotion. "I hope she's just like you, Sissy."

And just like that, my heart exploded in my chest.

Chapter 22

Hawk

"Are you ready?" Everly called out from the bathroom. She wouldn't let me see the dress she bought for the event, and I waited patiently on the bed for her to come out. Dylan was in there helping her get ready, and I sat there listening to them argue about whether Everly should wear her hair straight or wavy as I read a few emails that my agent, Joey, had sent over.

"I'm ready."

The door flew open, and Dylan came out first and laughed as she took me in. "Is that what you're wearing, Hawky player?"

"Yeah. This is my standard attire when I'm not in uniform. I've got a sports coat I'll put on when we get there."

"You look great," Everly said, as she stepped out and twirled around.

I nearly lost my breath at the sight of her. A gray gown

with layers of something fancy that flowed down to the floor. It tied behind her neck and her back was completely bare. She looked like a living, breathing princess. Her blue eyes looked more gray as the sun filtered in through the windows, and she did a little curtsy before I pulled her into my arms. "You're fucking beautiful."

"Thank you. I thought it was formal?" she asked, looking up at me with confusion.

"It is. This is just my version of formal."

"I like it," she said. "It's very... *you*."

I leaned down and claimed her mouth before Dylan cleared her throat. "Let's move it, people. I want to take a quick picture of you guys before you leave."

We took a few photos on the property before heading to the truck. We were meeting Wes at the helicopter which was already waiting for us. It was a quick up and down, and we'd stay over one night because I wanted to show her my house in the city. It's where I hoped she'd move into if all went well.

"Looky here," Wes sang out when we arrived. Of course, he wore a suit, and they both looked far more appropriate for a formal event than I did, but this was who I was and I was good with it. We made our way onto the helicopter and I helped buckle Everly in. "I see Hawk has his typical attire on."

"It suits him, don't you think?" She winked at me.

Don, the pilot, introduced himself to Ever and then gave me a thumbs-up before firing things up and getting us up in the air. Everly had a death grip on my hand before she finally relaxed and enjoyed her views out the window.

When we landed, there was a car waiting for us, and I

slipped on my sports coat in the car. We'd already agreed that Everly and Wes would get out first, we'd circle around, and then I'd meet them inside.

I squeezed her hand and she slipped out of the car, and then Don took me around the block. When I stepped out onto the red carpet this time, there were flashes going off and I waved.

"Where's Darrian?" several people shouted, and I just continued striding toward the entrance.

Coach Hayes was there when I stepped inside, deep in conversation with Everly and Wes, and my desire to move between them was strong, but I controlled my anger as I approached.

"No Darrian tonight?" Hayes asked as he straightened his already straight tie.

"She's filming. I told you that."

"Yes. That's right, you did. And Everly sure looks stunning."

I didn't like the way his eyes scanned her from head to toe. My hands fisted at my sides, but I refused to give him a reaction.

"She does. How about we go take our seats?" I said, clearing my throat and placing my hand on Everly's lower back as Coach led us inside.

I intentionally had Wes sit between Everly and me. Coach Hayes on my other side. My eyes locked with hers and she smiled. She knew I was doing this to protect her.

Protect us.

"So, both Wes and Everly tell me you're doing amazing things back home. Apparently, I should have sent you there a while ago," Coach said.

I didn't appreciate him insinuating that he'd sent me there. It had been my choice. But this was his MO. Take credit for anything that goes right and blame others for everything that goes wrong.

"Things are going well, yes."

"I heard Darrian took a trip out there to see you," he asked, and I glanced over to see Everly smile, and I knew she'd planted that seed.

"Yep. Honey Mountain's not really her speed, but it was nice of her to come check on me."

"So, any chance you're going to make your announcement tonight? That would be great press for everyone."

"Nope. Tonight is about giving back to the community. It's not a publicity stunt. I scheduled a meeting with you in two weeks, which I already discussed with you. We agreed that I'd make my decision a few days before I'd officially need to be there for practice. You'll get your answer then, and Joey will be present for that meeting."

He nodded and put his hands up. "I'm not trying to push you. Just saw an opportunity to make a splash in the press."

I didn't even know why he was here. This was more of a charity event than a sports banquet, but he was sending a message to every sports team out there that we were close. Even though we weren't.

The man would trade his firstborn for a top draft pick.

"There he is," Buckley shouted as he clapped me on the shoulder. He was our goalie, and I loved the dude.

"Thanks for being here, brother," I said, pushing to my feet and hugging him. I introduced him to Everly, and he turned back to look at me. "I'm glad I'm not the only asshole in jeans, even if I'm not the one being honored."

"I only wear suits for weddings and funerals, I've told you that." I laughed.

"Well, well, well. If it isn't the sports philanthropist of the year," Tony sang out, as he and Will both pulled me in for a hug.

We were big and tough and got vicious on the ice, but these dudes were like brothers to me, and we didn't hide that.

Wes introduced them to Everly, and it was challenging for me not to let them all know that she was mine. But in a few more weeks we wouldn't need to hide anything.

Will flirted his ass off with her, and I just laughed every time she glanced over at me with wide eyes.

"Is she staying here, at this hotel?" Coach Hayes asked, and I leaned back in my chair to look at him.

"Yep. And we fly back tomorrow. I want to check on my place and make sure everything's good there. Wes will stay with his family for a few days." I didn't need to check on my house, I had a lady that took good care of it. But I wanted to spend a night in the city with Everly. Show her my life here and convince her that she'd love it here too.

"Of course. Just checking. Looks like the three of you are getting along just fine."

"We are." I kept it short. He was looking for something because the man was twisted and was always working every angle.

Thankfully, the speaker took the stage. He talked about the charities that they worked with and thanked everyone for helping to contribute. Several people received awards and I watched as Everly clapped for each one. She laughed at the guys as they made their jokes and took their shots at flirting with her.

But every time she looked over at me, I knew she was mine.

Hell, she'd always been mine.

Food was served, the drinks flowed, and music boomed through the speakers. Coach Hayes was off schmoozing after insisting we take a few photos together. Tony and Will were talking Everly and Wes's ears off and Buckley leaned in, holding up a glass of champagne for me to toast.

"You look good, brother. I have a hunch Everly has something to do with that." He smirked, keeping his voice low. "I see the way you keep looking at her. And the fact that she isn't remotely moved by Will and Tony's attempts—well, that's something."

I glanced over my shoulder to see where Hayes was. "Keep it between us for now, all right?"

"Always. Not gonna lie. It's fun seeing Will and Tony strike out." He laughed and I couldn't help but join in. "I get it. Protect what you hold dear, my man."

"Absolutely." I trusted him with my life. He knew I was leaning toward coming back. We talked often and he was a big factor in my decision.

When the host took to the stage, Coach returned to his seat beside me. I got an overly generous introduction that didn't feel necessary. I didn't donate my time or my money helping inner-city kids because I wanted praise. I did it because I could. I was fortunate enough to come from a home where I'd never wanted for anything. I'd never been hungry a day in my life, and I'd been very blessed that my career had allowed me the resources to give back. It was important to me to help others get their start. We'd opened a hockey center for kids, which offered after-school care, as well.

I winked at Everly as everyone applauded, and I moved to my feet and headed for the stage. I didn't write a speech ahead of time because I wanted to just talk from the heart.

When I took to the podium and glanced out at the audience, there was one girl drawing all my attention, just like she always had. I forced myself not to just stare at her, but to move my gaze around the audience.

"So, I see I'm only one of two dudes in jeans." Laughter filled the space and Buckley stood and saluted me. "All joking aside, thank you all for having me here tonight. Being able to take part in projects like opening the ice rink for the kids and providing food and clothing for those in need—those are the things that inspire me. Yes, I enjoy making goals and winning games. But, giving back to others, isn't that what it's all supposed to be about? Listen, I've been fortunate in my life, and I don't take any of this for granted. I'm a lucky man. But nothing is as rewarding as knowing that you're impacting others, right? Especially kids. So, I want to thank you for supporting me on this journey, because it takes a village, man."

"Are you coming back to play for our city?" a man shouted and I chuckled.

"Listen, I'm trying to figure out how to maneuver this next part of my career. I haven't made my decision yet, but I promise you that I'll let you know soon. I can tell you this, my physical game is strong, thanks to my trainer Wes, and mentally, I've never felt better. For all of you athletes out there who get to a place where you need to be reminded what you're playing for, find yourself a sports psychologist like Everly Thomas. It's the real deal. She's been a game changer for me, because sometimes we just need to remember that we love what we do," I said, and my gaze locked with hers. "But anyway, back to the reason we're all here. Give back where you can. Give your time, give your money, and give your energy. It matters, man. Thanks again." I held up my hand and waved as people moved to their feet and cheered.

This was the part of my celebrity that I liked. Joining with good people and doing good things. I glanced over at Coach as I walked to the table, and I didn't miss the irritation. He was mad I didn't mention him.

He was the king of self-promotion, and he wanted a shout-out any time his players spoke. But he wasn't part of this journey that I was currently on. I was just trying to decide if I wanted to return to a place that he was part of. After all these weeks, I realized I wasn't tired of the sport or lacing up my skates... I was tired of playing for a man who didn't inspire me or those around me. He'd been given this gift to impact athletes in this sport, and he'd squandered it.

"I'm going to head out," he said, and we gave one another a fake-ass bro hug. "I'll be in touch. Looking forward to having you back in the city soon."

A reminder that my time was ticking.

He turned to Everly and extended a hand. "I'd like to talk to you soon about a possible future with the Lions."

Her entire face lit up. "That would be amazing. Thank you."

Coach left, and a weight lifted off my shoulders.

Wes and I shared a glance before he moved to his feet and said his goodbyes.

"Thanks for being here," I said, clapping him on the shoulder.

"Always."

Everly and I spent the next hour at the hotel bar with Buckley, Tony, and Will. I didn't doubt they all knew something was going on between us, but they were my brothers, and they wouldn't say a word until I talked to them about it.

After everyone left, she and I sat at the table, and I finished the last of my cocktail. "I need you out of that dress, *Ever mine*," I said, leaning close so only she could hear as my lips grazed her ear.

"Yeah?" Her voice was breathy.

"Yeah."

"You did good tonight. I'm proud of you," she said, shaking her head. "Such a good man."

My chest squeezed at her words. "Thank you. That means a lot."

"That speech was something."

"Well, hopefully giving you that shout-out will force Coach Hayes's hand. Because he might have some competition getting you to sign with him." I leaned back in my chair, my tongue swiping out to wet my lips as I watched her.

This growing need for her so strong it caught me by surprise.

"So, how do we get out of here without drawing attention?"

"We already got your hotel key," I said, typing a message into my phone for my driver to pull around. "Nothing stopping us from getting a nightcap elsewhere. But just to be extra cautious, you go out first and slip into my car with Don. I'll wait five minutes before walking out. Tell him to pull up around the corner."

"You're awfully sexy when you're conspiring."

"I want you naked in my bed sooner rather than later. I'll conspire all day long to make that happen." I set my phone down. "He's out front."

She nodded and waggled her brows. "Have a good night, Mr. Madden."

"I plan on it, Ms. Thomas."

She walked through the bar, and I didn't miss the way every man watched her leave.

She wasn't even aware of how gorgeous she was.

But all that mattered was she was mine.

Ever mine.

Chapter 23

Everly

Hawk kissed me senseless as we drove to his place in the city. He lived in a high-rise across the street from the water. We pulled up in front of the building and said our goodbyes to Don. A doorman greeted us as we stepped out of the car and walked inside.

"Good evening, Mr. Madden."

"Hey, Russ. Good to see you." His hand was clasped with mine and he led me through the extravagant foyer. The building was modern and sleek in architecture. The interior in grays and blacks with white floral arrangements and contemporary light fixtures hanging above.

Hawk guided me onto the elevator that only had a button to the penthouse, the parking garage, and the lobby.

"Is this your own elevator?" I gaped.

He chuckled. "Yeah. When I'm here, I'm a bit more into

my privacy. Honey Mountain has been a nice reprieve from that."

I nodded as the doors opened to a sprawling great room. Floor-to-ceiling glass windows covered the entire back wall which looked out at the water, lit up only by the light of the moon.

"You'll like waking up to it. It's a little different being this high up to the view of the bay, but Honey Mountain Lake is no slouch."

I stood in front of the windows, looking out before turning toward him. "I can't believe this is your place. It's beautiful."

He reached for my hand. "I'm glad you finally get to see where I live."

"This must be gorgeous during the day."

"It is. Come on, let me show you around," he said. He walked me through the palatial space, and I took a minute to look around his modern, sleek kitchen. The cabinets were gray, the counters a sleek white marble that ran up the backsplash, and there was an oversized island with seating for eight. He showed me his home gym, the two gorgeous guest rooms, and then led me through his bedroom.

"There is no way you decorated this place," I said with a laugh as I hurried over to sit on his bed.

"It was the model unit and I bought it furnished." He sat beside me.

"Is it weird that we've both got these other lives that we don't know anything about?"

"Listen, you're my past and you're my future. If we have to catch up on the present, I don't have a problem with that. I want to know everything about you."

"Well, you're in luck. I gave up my apartment in New York, so the current rental and Sunday nights at my dad's are kind of my digs for now." I laughed. "But I'd love to take you to New York sometime and show you where I lived. Show you my school and all my favorite haunts."

"How about this? Once we figure out where we're going, and we don't need to keep this secret from my crazy ass coach… we spend some time here, and I can show you all my favorite places. But since it would be hard to hide in this city right now, since this is where I've played for the past eight years, I say we leave tomorrow and head to New York."

"What?" I asked.

"I can go undetected in New York City much easier than I can here. Show me where you've been, Ever. Show me where that dream of yours took you."

"You're serious?"

"Yeah. I mean, I'm ready to say this to you because I want you to know where I'm at. I'm good to go back to the Lions and play another year, if you're on board with that. And if that's the case, we may as well enjoy this time before the season starts."

I searched his gaze. "If I'm on board?"

"Ever, I want this." He motioned between us. "It's what's been fucking missing from my life. So yeah, what you think matters to me. Let me talk to Coach about bringing you on. I won't say we're together. We can let that come out later. But let me help make this happen."

"And you aren't going back for me? You want to play another year?" I asked, my eyes wet with emotion, which made it hard to see.

"I want to play another year, and I want to be with you. So, let's do this."

"Okay. Yes," I said, as I threw my arms around his neck. "Are we really doing this? We're going all-in?"

"I've been all-in with you most of my life. I'm just glad we found our way back."

He tipped me back and kissed me hard.

"You look so fucking gorgeous sprawled out on my bed in this beautiful fucking dress. Prettiest girl in the world."

My breath hitched at his words. No one had ever made me feel things the way Hawk did. Maybe that's why I'd been so lonely since we'd ended things all those years ago.

"I love you, Hawk Madden." I pushed up to sit and undid the button of my dress that rested behind my neck before letting the halter portion of the gown fall forward. He pushed back to stand as he watched me.

"I love you, baby." His thumbs grazed over my nipples, and my head fell back. "If I'd known you weren't wearing a bra this whole time, I would have dipped in here earlier."

His voice was all tease, but I didn't miss the desire in his voice.

I reached for the hem of his shirt, and I pushed to stand in front of him as I pressed up on my tiptoes and shoved it over his head. His hands were on me, moving behind my waist to unzip the bottom of the dress. A puddle of tulle surrounded my feet, and I kicked off my heels as he shoved his jeans down his legs.

I slipped my white lace panties slowly down my thighs, making a show of it, as his tongue dipped out to wet his lips.

"Ever mine," he whispered.

I moved back and dropped onto the bed before he shoved his boxer briefs down, and his mouth covered mine. He somehow positioned us both on the center of the bed and extended his arm over my head, reaching for the nightstand.

"Wait." I wrapped my fingers around his wrist. "Have you been tested? I have, and I've also never been with anyone without a condom."

"Neither have I. And yes, I test regularly."

"I want to feel you. Feel everything," I said, as his gorgeous green gaze locked with mine. He knew it meant that I was all-in. I'd never consider something like this if I wasn't, and neither would he.

"Me too, baby." His mouth covered mine, our tongues tangling in a wicked dance of need and desire.

His lips traveled down my jaw and my neck, tasting and kissing every inch of me. He covered my breast with his mouth, and I gasped as I arched in response, only wanting more. He took his time moving to the other breast, and my breathing was out of control. My fingers tangled in his hair as I got lost in the moment. Lost in this man.

I'd never wanted anyone or anything more. I'd never felt so desired.

He kissed his way down my stomach, taking his time before burying his head between my legs. He worshiped me like I was his prized possession. His tongue working its magic exactly where I needed him.

I writhed and groaned, begging for my release. "Please."

But Hawk took his time. Making sure I felt everything. A layer of sweat covered my body, and my hands moved to fist the sheets beside me as the building sensation was too much.

And I exploded. Every inch of my body was set on fire. Bursts of light behind my eyes. Tingling and free.

I gasped for air as I tried to catch my breath, all while riding out my pleasure against his mouth. He climbed over me and pushed the damp hair out of my face.

"That's just round one, baby. Now I need to be inside you."

I chuckled as I studied his handsome face. His jaw was peppered in dark scruff, and my fingers traced along his lips. "Not just yet, hockey star."

I shoved against him, and he followed my lead, rolling on to his back as I kneeled beside him.

"You going to take control, baby?" He ran his fingers down my shoulder and then my arm. My body was still coming down from the epic orgasm he'd just given me.

I took my time kissing him, my tongue slipping in for just a taste before I kissed my way down his body. Worshipping his chest and abdomen, my fingers moving ahead of my mouth as they traced every muscle and line on his body. His breaths were coming hard and fast now, and his hands found my hair as I gripped his erection in my hand, stroking him slowly as I looked up at him.

"So fucking beautiful, Ever," he whispered, as my mouth covered his shaft and I slowly took him in.

I wanted to please him the way that he'd pleased me. So I took my time. My hand at the base as my mouth moved forward.

We found our rhythm, and I loved the way he groaned and bucked against me. Loved that he reacted to me this way.

I moved slowly. Intentionally.

"Baby," he whispered, sending a quiet plea in the air.

I moved faster, knowing he was close.

Wanting to take him over the edge the way he'd taken me.

He tugged at my hair and cried out my name, making every attempt to pull me away before he lost control.

But I stayed right there.

I didn't pull away.

I wanted to feel everything.

He continued to jerk his hips a few more times before he settled, and I pulled back to look at him, wiping my mouth with the back of my hand and smiling.

"Wow," he said, his voice gruff.

"Glad I'm not the only one that gets to feel that way." I leaned over him and kissed his mouth as he maneuvered my hips over his body so I was straddling him, and I could feel his erection grow hard again.

"What are you doing to me, Ever?"

"The same thing you're doing to me." He found my hands and our fingers intertwined with one another's, and he lifted me up enough to position me just right.

"You ready for round two?" he asked.

"I'm ready for everything, Hawk."

Because I was.

• • •

New York City was one of my favorite places in the world. I'd always loved it. My mom had taken me to the rink at Rockefeller Center when I was a kid, just me and her on a girls' trip, and I swore I'd live there someday.

Being here with Hawk was special because I was sharing

my favorite place with my favorite person. He'd booked us a room at a swanky hotel in the city, and we'd spent the day sightseeing. We'd been to Rockefeller Center, Bryant Park, the New York Public Library, and Grand Central Station. We'd shopped, we'd eaten, and we'd laughed. I showed him the dumpy apartment building I used to live in, and he gasped and wrapped his arms around me as if he could shield me from anything.

Tonight, we were meeting up with Lala and Grayson, and I couldn't wait to introduce my best friend and her husband to my boyfriend. Yes, it was official. Even if me, Hawk, and the people in Honey Mountain were the only ones who knew it. And of course, Lala and Grayson were also aware.

Only the people that we trusted most.

It hit me when I realized that the entire town I'd grown up in fell under that umbrella. I'd been running from a place that I loved dearly. Running from the people that I loved the most. Honey Mountain was home.

Yes, it was the place where my mother had taken her last breath, but it was also the same place I'd fallen in love with Hawk as a teenager, and again today. It was the place where my sisters lived, my father, and our extended family. It was the place where my sweet little niece would be born in a couple of months, and the place that held my favorite memories.

I'd been running from both my heart and my home. And though I still worried the rug would be pulled out from under me—I was content and happy.

"I love it here. That was definitely the best pizza I've ever had." Hawk turned off the TV as he sprawled out on the couch in the living area of our suite. "You look gorgeous."

We'd flown back home after leaving San Francisco, and we literally packed our bags and left for New York that same day. It had been a whirlwind. I'd never been an impulsive person. I was a thinker when it came to... everything. Yet I'd say the past forty-eight hours were the happiest of my life.

Unplanned.

Unpredictable.

Untamed.

"Thank you. And yes, the pizza is hard to compete with."

"I'm glad you brought me here. I like seeing where your life was those years that we were apart, even if your apartment was terrifying." He shuddered, and I threw a pillow at him.

"It was not that bad."

"I saw cockroaches running toward the street. Even they wanted the hell out of there," he teased.

"Well, we don't all have million-dollar contracts. I was surviving on student loans," I groaned, and he sat up and tugged me onto his lap.

"You should have called me. We didn't need to be together for me to help you. You know that, right?"

"I didn't need help." I kissed his lips gently and looked into his emerald-green gaze. "It was an adventure."

He nodded. "I get it. I just hate the idea of you struggling."

"This is the same journey that brought us back together, right?" I rubbed my nose against his.

"I guess. But no more struggling. Not on my watch."

"Just you being here makes everything better."

"Good. Then I've been doing my job. Let's go meet your friends." He pushed to his feet and pulled me up along with him.

I liked sharing this part of my life with him.

I liked sharing everything with him.

And for the first time in a very long time, that didn't freak me out.

Chapter 24

Hawk

We pulled up to the three-story brownstone in Brooklyn and Everly practically ran to the door. She couldn't wait to see Lala, and I was looking forward to meeting these friends of hers that she said were more like family.

The door flew open and both girls moved in a blur as they shrieked and hugged and laughed. I stood behind Everly and looked up to see a dude shaking his head with a goofy smile on his face.

"Hey, I'm Grayson." He moved around them and extended his hand.

"I'm Hawk. Nice to meet you."

"Do not play it cool, my dear hubby. I'm Lala, and this guy is a superfan of yours. He grew up in San Francisco and stayed loyal to his sports teams back there." She wrapped her arms around me and hugged me tight. When she leaned back, she just studied my face for a long minute and smiled. "I've heard about you for years, Hawk Madden. It's nice to finally meet the only boy who ever had my girl's heart."

"Okay, good doctor. Let's invite them inside before you go too deep," Grayson said, and Lala and Everly laughed.

Ever took my hand and led me inside. "Isn't this place gorgeous?"

"Yes, beautiful."

We moved through the entryway into the living space, and Grayson poured us each a glass of chardonnay. We sat on the couch—Everly beside me, and Grayson and Lala across from us in two armchairs. The home finishings were modern, and the vibrant art hanging on the walls gave a hip, cool vibe.

"I ordered dinner. I don't know if Ev told you, but I'm not much of a cook." She grinned. "So, it'll be here soon. I just thought we could visit first."

"I'm dying to know if you're going back to the Lions, but my lady made me promise not to ask. I have a hunch she knows the answer and is holding it hostage from me." Grayson took a sip of wine, and Lala gaped at her husband.

"Way to play it cool." She shook her head.

"Listen, Ever considers you both family, which makes you family in my book. I'm planning to go back for one more year. Just not quite ready to announce it because my coach will be so far up my ass for me to get back there, and I'm trying to convince my girl to go with me."

Grayson jumped to his feet and fist-pumped the sky. "Yes. Dude, your secret is safe with me. I give you my word."

"Well, I'm guessing Coach Hayes is going to feel the pressure to hire Everly now. She's going viral on Twitter.

Apparently, that speech you gave the other night has every sports team in the country talking about the value of sports psychologists, and Everly Thomas is at the top of the list."

I'd received a few messages today from my agent that the speech had made a blast, but I didn't realize just how large that reach had gone. Everly looked between me and her friends and shook her head. "Really?"

"Get ready to have choices," Lala said, and Everly peeked up at me with wide eyes.

She stressed far too much over this shit. It didn't matter where she went. Hell, I wanted every team in the country to make her an offer. She deserved that. I knew she worried about us being apart, but I didn't. Because I'd come to realize that nine years and thousands of miles hadn't changed a thing between us.

We still loved one another fiercely.

Would I prefer to have her close? Absolutely.

Was it a deal-breaker? Not even close.

"Well, my first choice would be to be near Hawk. We've spent a lot of years apart and I just don't want to do it anymore." Everly sipped her wine.

I was determined to make it happen, because I knew the distance was an issue for her. I knew I could negotiate it easily into my contract. Hell, I was fairly certain Coach Hayes would give me his firstborn if I asked him to. And this ask wasn't a stretch. Our team would benefit from her expertise. She'd helped me more than she even knew. The guys would love her, and it would make life a hell of a lot better if we were together.

"I'm guessing he has the power to make that happen," Lala said.

"That's not really the way to try to get a job. I mean, I know he's the GOAT and all…" She winked at me. "But I'm pretty damn good at my job. I'd like to get offered a contract because someone believes that I can help."

"But you know you can," Grayson said. "Does it really matter how you get in the door? I mean, if it does—then I've really shit the bed. I'm only at my firm because my uncle Toby is a partner. But I'm moving up the ranks because I'm damn good at helping people part ways amicably." He smirked.

"Says the happily married divorce attorney," Lala said.

"A therapist and a divorce attorney. It sounds like a perfect match." I raised my glass and they followed suit.

"A hockey star and a sports psychologist are a damn good team as well," Grayson said as our glasses clinked together.

"A damn good team." Everly nodded as she winked at me.

Now I just had to figure out how to make sure we played for the same damn team in real life.

We moved to the dining room once the food arrived, and laughter filled the room as we talked and they told me all about Everly and Lala's early days in college. I loved hearing about this part of her life that I hadn't been a part of.

We cleaned up the takeout, and Everly received a call from an unknown caller, so she excused herself and stepped into the next room. Grayson left to go grab another bottle of wine from their bar, and Lala leaned against the kitchen island and smiled.

"I've waited a long time to meet you, Hawk. You really were always present… even when you weren't. I hoped for a long time that you'd find your way back to one another."

I nodded and cleared my throat. "I did too. Nothing's ever

been right since she left."

It was the truth. Sure, I'd had some fine relationships and met some great women, but it never felt quite right. Something had always been missing, and I knew it in my gut. That no one would ever fit just right.

"Be patient. She's coming along, but she's definitely scared. And all of the unknown tends to make her want to run. Get away before she gets hurt, you know? It's her favorite coping mechanism."

"Yep. I'm working on it. I think the Lions will hire her. We'll both be there for the year, and then we can go wherever she wants after that." It was the truth. I'd follow this girl anywhere she wanted me to.

"Sounds like it's all going to work out perfectly. Even if they don't hire her, you'd only be committing to one year, and then you could go wherever she is."

"Exactly."

"If it's any consolation, she never did get over you. I can't tell you how many times I heard her cry herself to sleep during our first two years in college. The few times I was able to get her to open up, it was always about you."

My chest squeezed at the thought of her hurting like that. Hell, I'd been completely lost when she'd left me. Felt like my heart had been cut from my chest.

"Well, I'm here now and no matter what we face, I won't let her go this time."

"You're *good people,* Hawk Madden. You're the first guy I've actually given a thumbs-up to, by the way." Lala laughed.

"Trust me, I met Brad. If he's any version of who she'd been dating over the years, I'm not surprised."

She covered her mouth with both hands and shook her head. "You know, I think she just might be the reason I chose the path of psychology. My bestie was both complicated and easy to read—all at the same time. But I diagnosed her early with *ass-pass disorder.*" She laughed again and reached for her wine. "All the assholes pass her dating screening process because they're safe. How attached can you really get to an asshole? There's literally no risk. It never goes deep. If they leave, you just go find another asshole."

"Cheers to ass-pass disorder," I said, holding my glass up and clinking it with hers.

"Oh no. Who has ass-pass disorder now?" Everly waltzed into the kitchen and looked between us.

"Girl, you may have been the first one I diagnosed with ass-pass, but it turns out there are a whole slew of women suffering from this particular disorder. Girls with daddy issues, relationship-phobes, abandonment issues... there is just something about seeking out an asshat that can't hurt you."

"Um...I'd like to reintroduce the *bitch-switch disorder* that you diagnosed my brother with," Grayson said as he walked in carrying a bottle of red and reached for the wine opener.

"Is Garrett still with that she-devil?" Everly asked as she wrapped an arm around my waist.

"Nah. She broke his heart and when he picked up all the pieces, he just found himself another domineering lady who likes to boss his ass around and treat him like shit."

"And this is called the bitch-switch?" I laughed as Grayson handed me a fresh glass of wine.

"Yes. They act super sweet when he first meets them, and then they spin him around in their web and hold him hostage as they slowly verbally abuse the poor guy. If I'm being honest, I believe it stems from *mama-trauma disorder*, which is another Lala-only diagnosis," she said with a nod. "I mean, your mom is a little bit terrifying."

Grayson gaped at her and then laughed. "Baby, my mother loves you."

"Um... we've been together for six years and she still calls me Britney." Lala raised a brow, and we all laughed. I could tell it was all in good fun with her and Grayson, but then she turned her attention to her best friend. "So, who was on the phone?"

"It was Lyle Gallager, the head coach for the Los Angeles Rucks. They want me to fly out next week, and he said they were going to make me an offer." Everly shrugged, and she forced a smile when she looked at me. "Apparently, everyone thinks I've healed the GOAT of the ice. That's a direct quote."

She healed me in more ways than she knows.

"I guess it's time for the Lions to shit or get off the pot," I said, pulling her close and kissing the top of her head.

"I'll try to hold them off as long as I can. I can fly out there and meet with them, and hopefully by then, you'll know what's happening with the Lions."

"It's all going to work out. I promise." And I wasn't a man who made promises I didn't intend to keep.

"I know it will," she whispered before reaching for the glass of wine Grayson handed her.

"Cheers to being cured of ass-pass disease and all of us cheering on the Lions this year, with both of you on the same damn team." Grayson held up his glass.

"I will drink to that all day long," Lala sang out.

Everly and I both tipped our glasses, and she beamed up at me.

We were going to be just fine.

Chapter 25

Everly

When the call came shortly after Hawk and I landed back in Honey Mountain and just walked through the front door, I nearly dropped my phone at the sound of Charlotte's voice.

Hawk hurried over and took the phone from my hand as she repeated what she'd just told me.

Vivian was in the hospital. Niko had found her on the floor in a ball when he'd arrived home from the grocery store an hour ago.

"We're on our way," Hawk said, grabbing my purse beside the door and reaching for my hand. He ended the call and led me out to his truck and buckled me in without a fight. I was completely numb. Panic coursed through my veins, and I sat in silence as I processed what Charlotte had said.

"She's going to be fine." Hawk held my hand in his and pulled into the parking spot in front of the hospital. We hurried inside to find Dylan, Charlotte, and my father all there.

"Hey," I said, as I took the chair beside Dad and leaned my head against his arm.

"Hi, sweetheart. We're just waiting to hear from Niko. The doctor took him back to see Vivi," he said.

"More like he had a meltdown and pushed through the doors, demanding they bring him to see his wife." Dylan continued pacing in front of us.

"Have you seen her yet, or were they both in the back when you arrived?" Hawk asked as he took the seat beside me and reached for my hand.

"Niko was here when we got here, but then he got upset that they'd taken her back and he was tired of waiting." Charlotte shrugged.

"So, we don't know anything?" I asked.

"Not yet," Dylan hissed. "And I'm about to shove through those doors myself."

"Slow your roll, Dilly," Charlotte said. "We don't need to cause a scene. Niko is back there, and he'll find out what's going on."

"It's too early to have the baby," I whispered, leaning into Hawk.

The doors flew open, and Niko stalked toward us, pushing his hair away from his face. Dr. Prichard was behind him, trying to keep up.

"She's going to be okay, the baby apparently has an attitude and got pissed at her placenta or some shit like that. Shocker. Of course, my kid can't cooperate." Niko scrubbed the back of his neck.

"That's not quite what happened," Dr. Prichard said with

an empathetic smile. "Vivian has a placental separation, but it's not severe. That explains the vaginal bleeding and the cramping she experienced. We were able to see it on the ultrasound, and we will continue to do fetal monitoring for the next forty-eight hours. The baby's vitals are good, and if all continues, she can go home in two days, as long as she takes it easy and rests."

"How in the hell do we make her rest?" Niko scrubbed a hand down his face and blew out a frustrated breath.

"She doesn't have a choice. We don't want the placenta to completely detach. I've spoken to her, and she knows how lucky she is, so I don't think she'll give you a hard time about taking it easy. It's what the baby needs." He clapped Niko on the shoulder. "You can all come back, but let's keep it short and let her get some rest."

"I'm not fucking leaving," Niko grumped as we followed him down the hall.

"I figured as much. Just let her rest, all right?" Dr. Prichard said as he shook his head.

"I'll make sure she does." Niko pushed her door open first, and we all stepped inside.

Vivian was lying back but propped up, and she swiped at her falling tears when she saw us. "Sorry for scaring you guys. I hope you didn't call Ash. She's swamped with that internship this week, and I don't want her to feel pressure to come back here."

"I'm texting her now," Dylan said as she typed into her phone. "I'll let her know you're okay."

"What happened?" I asked, as I moved to sit in the chair beside my sister. The strongest woman I knew.

"I just had really bad cramps. My back was throbbing. I thought it was just a pregnancy thing, but then I looked down and saw blood, and the pain grew more severe."

"I don't like seeing you that way, Honey Bee," Niko said as he moved to the other side of the bed and took her hand. "Finding you on the floor scared the shit out of me."

"I'm sorry, baby. That last cramp hit me really hard, and I couldn't stand. I'm sorry I scared you," she whispered.

"Don't ever apologize to me. It's my job to take care of you." He leaned down and kissed her cheek.

It hit me right there. Just how precious life was. We were living examples of it. We'd lost our mother at a young age, and we knew all too well how fragile life could be. How cruel and unfair, and the thought of my baby sister losing her little one before it even entered the world.

Fear gripped me tight, threatening to take me under.

"Baby, you have to take it easy. Dr. Prichard said you need to be on bed rest, or at the very least take it *real* easy," Niko pressed as he studied her face to gauge her reaction.

"I can cover the bakery." Dylan continued pacing because the girl could never sit still in a situation like this.

"I can be there too. School doesn't start for a few weeks, so consider me at your beck and call. And Jilly just texted me that she can work as many hours as you need her to," Charlotte said. "You just take it easy."

I knew things were about to get busy for me, and the thought made my heart ache. I didn't want to live across the country from my family anymore. I wanted to stay close. See my niece grow up. Be here when things like this happened.

Hawk's hands came over my shoulders and he leaned

down. "You all right?"

I nodded as the lump in my throat threatened to steal my breath. "Yeah. I'm just glad I'm here."

"Hey, I'm all right. This is just part of life, Ev. Things happen when you're pregnant. I'm going to be just fine." Vivian squeezed my hand.

"I don't like it either," Niko hissed. "I'm going to watch you like a hawk." Niko glanced over at my boyfriend as the words left his mouth and chuckled. "No offense, dude."

"None taken."

My father just stood in the corner watching us, not saying a word. He looked exhausted. The fear had taken a toll on him even if he wouldn't say it.

Why were we all so afraid to admit that we were scared? Niko was brave enough to say it.

"I was really scared. For you and the baby," I admitted, and my words broke on a sob.

"Oh boy. We're doing this," Dylan said, as she fanned her face to keep from crying. "Everything is fine."

"Everything is not fine," I shouted, startling everyone. "Our sister was in a ball on the floor and she's almost six months pregnant. Everything is not fine!"

My father's eyes doubled in size, and Charlotte hurried over and reached for my hands as Hawk wrapped his arms around me from behind.

"Don't cry, Sissy," Charlotte whispered.

"It's okay to cry." I pulled back to look at her. "If I've learned anything over the past decade, it's that bottling up everything doesn't help. That's probably why I've been a weepy mess for weeks since I returned home. It's okay to say that I was scared. Hell, Niko forced himself through those doors because he was terrified. It's okay to be afraid. We don't always have to be brave."

"Says the one who never cried before now," Dylan said with a laugh as tears streamed down her face. "I try to be brave in front of you because you can't handle when we get upset."

"She's telling the truth," Charlotte said, swiping at her cheeks. "She cries behind closed doors all the time."

"Snitches get stitches, little girl," Dylan hissed, and the room erupted in laughter.

"She's your twin, you fool," Vivian said over her laughter, as she shook her head and let the tears fall. "I'm glad we're all letting it out now. I was tired of trying to be strong for you guys."

"Does this mean we're going to have waterworks for everything from zits to breakups?" my father grumped as the nurse, Sierra, who happened to go to school with me, pushed into the room. Her eyes widened as she took us all in.

"I'm sorry to break this up, but we really need to let her get some rest. I understand that you're staying, Niko, but everyone else needs to say goodbye."

"It's fine. Charlotte said there's a hot dad from her class last year that's doing open mic night at Beer Mountain. Let's go get a drink." Dylan kissed Vivian on the cheek and wrapped her arms around Niko. "Goodbye, gentle giant."

He laughed and moved to his feet to hug each of us, giving Hawk a fist bump. We all kissed Vivian goodbye and walked out of the hospital.

"That's my cue. I have zero interest in finding out what

a hot dad is. Love you girls. I'm heading to the firehouse to check on things, and then I'll be home." My dad kissed us each on the top of the head and clapped Hawk on the shoulder before heading to his car.

"I'm tired," I said, exhausted from traveling, followed by all the crying and the emotions of the day. "I think we're going to go home."

"I'm tired too," Charlotte said, and Dylan rolled her eyes.

"Help me out, Hawky player. They're going to go home and mope. Let's go have some fun. Vivi's okay, the baby is okay, and we'll come back in the morning. Plus, I want to see what Charlotte considers a hot dad. He moved to town the second half of the school year last year, and I'm fairly certain he was hitting on her those last few weeks of school."

"He was not." Charlotte gaped. "I ran into him this morning when I was getting coffee and he just asked me to come to be nice."

"Please." Dylan put her hands together like she was praying and looked between us. "All this stress makes me anxious. I don't want to go home and just think. Plus, open mic night at Beer Mountain. Come on. Think of all the drunk turds that will be on stage acting ridiculous."

"Fine. One glass of wine and I'm going home." Charlotte shrugged.

I peeked up at Hawk, and he wrapped an arm around me. "You up for it?"

"Sure. I've wondered what open mic night meant, and I could use some comedy to take my mind off things."

We hopped in our car and drove to Beer Mountain.

"I'm glad you let it all out back there," Hawk said as he

pulled into a parking spot behind the bar.

"It's exhausting."

"What is?"

"Feeling all the things." I laughed before hopping out of the truck.

"It's all part of life. Let's go check out the hot dad."

I chuckled as my fingers interlocked with his and we made our way inside. A few people stopped to gape at Hawk and asked for a selfie and an autograph, and he took it in stride, per usual. Dylan and Charlotte were sitting at a table, and there was a man standing beside Charlotte who looked at her like she was his next meal. He was good-looking, quite a bit older than her, and clearly a little intoxicated.

We took our seats after Charlotte introduced us to Mr. Milkin, Austin's dad, who she'd taught last year. He waved goodbye and made his way backstage.

Darla Swanson was on stage firing off some jokes that got a few laughs, and Dylan leaned in and whispered so only we could hear her.

"Lame dad jokes are not going to cut it for me tonight. Not after this one had an emotional meltdown, Niko lost his shit, and Vivi got rushed to the hospital. Let's hope Charlotte's hot dad can bring it."

Hawk, Charlotte, and I all fell over laughing, and Darla beamed on stage because she thought we were reacting to her joke about waddling penguins. She continued doing some sort of penguin walk on stage, mimicking her husband at the office, and even if it was ridiculously silly, I had to admit, it felt good to laugh.

None of us felt much like drinking and we barely sipped

our wine, opting to drink our water as we watched the show.

"And now, I'd like to bring on a new resident who moved to Honey Mountain this past year, Jacque Milkin. Jacque is a poet, or did you already know it?" Arnold DeAngelo cracked, as the resident MC.

Dylan groaned as we all chuckled because she was less than impressed with the show thus far.

"Jacque? I thought his name was Jake?" I asked.

"He said he uses a stage name." Charlotte shrugged.

"A stage name for Beer Mountain? Ugh. Hot dad better be good," Dylan whisper-hissed.

"Good evening," Mr. Milkin said in a deep voice.

"That's more like it," Dylan said, and Charlotte slapped her shoulder and shushed her.

"He's Austin's dad. Be respectful."

I don't even know Austin, Dylan mouthed to me and Hawk.

Hawk wrapped an arm around my shoulder, and I scooted closer to him. I didn't miss the way several women stared at us, taking in the handsome hockey star.

Back the hell off, ladies. He's mine.

I'd never been the possessive type, but when it came to Hawk Madden, I was possessive as hell.

"I wrote a little something for a beautiful woman who happens to be out in the audience tonight," he purred into the microphone.

"Oh, hell yeah," Dylan said, elbowing Charlotte in the side.

Charlotte's cheeks flushed pink as she sipped her water and tried to ignore the fact that people were looking at her because the poet was staring directly at her.

"This is called, *In the Wake of the Luscious Bosom*."

Dylan spewed water across the table, and Hawk barked out a laugh.

Mr. Milkin cleared his throat, his gaze focused on my baby sister. "In the mornings, when I'd see her—I longed for a touch. A taste, a squeeze, a feel and such."

He walked to the other side of the stage but returned his watchful gaze to Charlotte. "Supple bosoms—called to me. Her brassiere holds them, set them free. Two handfuls that light my fire, scorching erection that will never tire."

"What the actual fuck is happening?" Dylan whispered as she wiped the table with her napkin.

"Dear Lord, make it stop." Charlotte looked at me and Hawk, trying hard not to move her lips and forcing a smile as she continued watching him.

"Nipples that can ring my bell, my son was in her care. I must be going to..." he paused and raised a brow in my sister's direction. "Hell... ooo, operator. I beg you to set me free. My erection in my grip like she belongs to me."

"Oh. My. God." Charlotte did not whisper this time, and Mr. Milkin winked as if that were a positive response.

"Cheers to you, Miss Thomas," he said, and a few people clapped and looked awkwardly at my sister as he left the stage.

"Holy hell, that was so worth *coming* out for. No pun intended." Dylan pushed to her feet after Charlotte stood and grabbed her purse.

"Let's get out of here. That was quite possibly the most unprofessional experience of my life, and that's saying a lot, seeing as Brandon Carver's dad asked me out in front of the kids." Charlotte shivered, and Hawk and I stood.

"Do you want me to go talk to him? The guy is a total creep," Hawk said.

"No. Let's go. Austin's not in my class this year, so it'll be fine. The guy barely spoke to me last year. I'm guessing he just had liquid courage tonight." She shook her head, and we walked out the door.

"Well, I feel kind of dirty sitting through a five-minute poem about your boobs and your nipples and his erection." Dylan acted like she was dry heaving in dramatic fashion as we walked them to their car.

"These ladies have never had so much attention." Charlotte laughed.

"He's a pig. His kid was in your class. Who the hell does that?" Hawk's veins were straining against his neck.

"I love when you go all Papa Bear on us." Charlotte pushed up and kissed his cheek before hugging me tight. "Don't worry. I'll talk to Principal Peters when we go back to school next week, just to make him aware of the situation."

"Love you, Hawky player. Love you, Sissy." Dylan hugged us both, and we moved toward the truck.

Hawk held my hand as we drove home.

And even with all that had happened tonight, I realized one thing.

I was okay. I didn't run.

I was exactly where I wanted to be.

Chapter 26

Hawk

"It's going to be fine, baby. Have faith. I will get this handled. You just go hear them out in Los Angeles. Don't sign anything until we talk." I pulled up to the airport and got out of the car to grab her and Charlotte's luggage.

Dylan was staying with Jilly to cover things at the bakery while Vivian remained on bed rest. I didn't want Everly to be alone in LA, and I had a meeting set with Coach Hayes, Joey, and upper management in San Francisco later today. The sun was just coming up as I'd scheduled her on the earliest flight out, so she could be there in time to meet with Coach Gallager this afternoon.

"I won't. It'll be fine. I have complete faith in us. But mostly in you," she said with a laugh.

"I have complete faith in you, Ever mine. Go let them kiss your ass and make an offer, and I will try to get the Lions to top that. But remember, we're okay no matter what." I kissed her hard and heard Charlotte sigh beside us.

"Ugh. Airport goodbyes are so romantic. I really need a boyfriend. The closest thing I've got is a creepy dad who writes poetry about my boobs." She shrugged, and I covered my mouth to keep from laughing.

"I think you mean your luscious bosoms?" Everly teased.

"Go sign that contract, superstar. This is a win-win. We can be together and still be close to home. I love you."

"Love you more." I kissed her once more before jumping back in the truck and taking off for the city. I was anxious to get this done and get a deal for Everly as well. I'd discuss how much she'd helped me and sing her praises, urging Coach Hayes to bring her on, and we'd both be part of the Lions' organization. Hell, he had the money. It was no hardship and I figured if I played nice, he'd do the same.

I blared music as I coasted down the highway when my phone rang. It was my agent, Joey, and I could hear the edge in his voice right away.

"Hawk, you on the road?" He was meeting me at the Lions' office to help negotiate my deal.

"Yeah? What's wrong?"

"A story broke today and it's going viral. Jim Brown, the coach for The Breakers, claimed in some interview that they've all but got the ink on the dotted line and you're going to play for them. I'm guessing Hayes is losing his shit about now."

"I haven't even talked to Jim Brown, but I like the dude. Why the fuck would he do that?"

"Politics, brother. Apparently, Hayes hooked up with

Brown's sister a few months ago and then ghosted her. There's bad blood, and I think he just wants to fuck with him a little. Everyone knows that you're Hayes's golden boy."

"Fuck. Well, hopefully, this helps me get what I want." I already missed the mountains and the trees as the city came into view in the distance. The honking of horns and traffic.

Welcome to city life.

"Hayes is obviously buying this shit because they are in some sort of public Twitter war now. Hayes is claiming he'll seal the deal today when you arrive, and he made some really crude comments about Brown's sister that have him now receiving a shit-ton of backlash."

"I've been in the car for less than three fucking hours. How did he manage to go sideways so quickly?"

"Not a clue, brother. I think something's going on with him—he appears to be unstable. I'm parked outside of the offices. I'll meet you there in twenty minutes. Let's just hear him out and then negotiate the shit out of this deal."

"The priority is getting them to agree to bring Everly on. The money isn't a deal-breaker for me. I'll bend there. But we've got to do it slyly or he'll suspect something with her, and I don't trust the asshole as far as I can throw him."

"The money's kind of a big deal, considering I get a piece of the pie." He laughed. "But I hear you. I plan to get you everything you want."

"All right. I'll see you soon."

I continued my drive, and the phone rang. I answered via Bluetooth. "Hey, baby. Did you land there safely?"

"I can't believe you put us in first class. So bougie." I could hear the smile in her voice. "But damn, once you go first class,

I'm guessing flying coach is going to pale in comparison."

"You deserve the best," I teased as I saw the press lined up outside of the building.

Fuck.

Of course, Hayes made this a show. The dude loved making everything public. I pulled into the underground parking and turned off my car. "All right, I'm here. Are you heading to your meeting?"

"Yeah. Charlie and I dropped our bags at the hotel, and I had time to change. Thank you so much for setting us up in such a beautiful place. She's still in the room stretched out on the bed eating candy." She chuckled. "I'm heading to my interview now. I'll call you after?"

"Yep. I love you, Ever."

"Love you more. I'll talk to you in a little bit. At least today we should finally know what the future holds, right?" I could hear the stress in her voice.

"Absolutely, baby. Don't worry about a thing. It's all semantics. It doesn't change a thing for us. We're solid. No one can change that. Not this time." Anger rose again as I thought about the fact that I was meeting with an asshole who'd already done something cruel to the person I loved most in the world. And he didn't give a shit then nor did he give a shit now.

I'd be wise to remember that.

"Yes. I'm here. I'll call you soon," she whispered, and I ended the call.

I took the elevator up and when the doors opened and I stepped off, Joey was waiting for me.

"Hey, Hawk." Tawny batted her lashes and smiled. She'd

worked for Coach Hayes for the past year. The man changed personal assistants every single year, and there were rumors that he'd been sleeping with one after the next. "He's ready for you."

When she pushed the door open, I was surprised that Duke Wayburn, the owner of the team, wasn't here because he and I were close. I was guessing Hayes didn't invite him.

"Where's Duke?" I asked, dropping into the chair across from him.

"Close the door, Tawny," Hayes hissed. "I'm fine if it's just you and me. You're going to get what you want, so you don't need Joey or Wayburn here."

All right. This was going to be heated. He was clearly already hostile, and I was not going to bite.

"He's my agent. He stays."

"Did he go with you to meet with Jim Brown?" His hands were fisted on the table and I wanted to laugh. The man was coming unraveled over nothing.

Right in front of my eyes.

"I've never met with Jim Brown. I've been upfront from the start. I would either retire this year or play for the Lions. Have I received calls and offers from other teams? Yes. But I've never met with anyone."

"Listen to me. I'm done being dicked around by you, Hawk. You come in here all calm, like you don't have a motherfucking care in the world. I'm calling the shots now. Do you hear me?" he shouted and slapped a contract down in front of me. "You're going to sign this shit now, or I'm going to bring the wrath of God on you."

This was a bit much, even for him. I came here to sign the

fucking deal, but I sure as shit didn't need to do it because I was being threatened. That shit did not fly with me.

"Don't you fucking threaten me." I shoved the papers back at him.

"Do you think I'm fucking stupid? Do you?" He leaned over the table and shouted, and spit flew from his mouth like he was a rabid animal.

"You need to sit your ass down. You've managed to fuck this negotiation up royally. He came here to sign, and you knew that. You let some prick get in your head, and now you're acting like a fucking fool," Joey said, one brow raised as he studied Coach Hayes with concern.

"I know you've been dipping your dick into that sports psychologist of yours. The one that I fucking hired. You think I don't have people watching you? You think I don't know about your little jaunt to New York?" He pulled his phone out and held it up for me to see as he scrolled through several photos of me and Everly together.

"What the fuck is this?" I pushed to my feet and yanked his phone out of his hand before slamming it down on the table with anger. "You've lost it. You're having me followed? So what if I'm dating her? I don't give a shit who knows. And you're the fucker who messed it up the first time around. I just didn't want to give you the chance to do it again, you piece of shit."

"I will fucking ruin her. You sign this contract right now, and all of this goes away. I can hire your fucking sidepiece if that's what you want. But if you don't sign this contract today, I will call every coach in the fucking NHL, NFL, and NBA and ruin her name. Let them all know that she's a little whore who sleeps with her clients."

That was it. I was over the table and on top of him before I could stop myself. Joey was shouting and pulling me off of him, but it all happened in a blur.

I finally stepped back, letting out a long breath to get my breathing under control.

"I wouldn't play for you if you were the last fucking guy on the planet. Do you hear me?" I screamed as he moved to his feet, panting like a little bitch. I walked around the table and grabbed the contract, tearing it into little pieces and throwing it at him. "Fuck you. We're done."

He leaned over the table, and I squared my shoulders, ready for round two, but he snatched my phone instead and threw it as hard as he could against the wall, shattering it to bits.

"Does that make you feel good, you pathetic piece of shit? I'll get a new one. Good luck finding a new captain." I flipped him the bird and sauntered out of his office with Joey behind me.

Tawny stood there gaping at us, unsure about what to do, as she'd obviously heard the fight that just went down. Hell, I was as shocked as her. I hadn't expected him to come undone the way he did, but in a way, I was glad. I already struggled with playing for a man like him, but he'd showed his true colors and there was just no fucking way I could lace up after what he'd said about Ever. I was done.

"Holy shit," Joey said after we stepped on the elevator and the doors shut.

"He's fucking lost it."

"He sure has. I think we should take this over his head.

The man is out of control." We stepped off the elevator and walked through the lobby. "Let's go get a coffee next door and talk about what the fuck just happened."

When we stepped outside, the press was there. I'd completely forgotten the madness that came with this side of my job. I'd been away long enough that I didn't have the patience for it at the moment. I shielded my eyes from the sun as several cameramen moved closer, invading our space.

"Hawk," a familiar voice shouted, and I looked over their shoulders to see Darrian getting out of a car and hurrying toward me.

What the hell was she doing here?

Cameras were clicking and flashing as she rushed in my direction with a look of panic on her face.

"Hey, what are you doing here?" I asked as she moved close and leaned up to speak into my ear.

She squeezed my hand. "I need to speak with you now. I tried calling, but you didn't pick up. It's important, Hawk."

I glanced at Joey and he watched us with wide eyes. He'd met Darrian several times and they were friendly enough. She smiled at him and turned her attention back to me.

"We're going next door to get a coffee. Come on." I led her away from the cameraman, but several guys stepped in front of us and shoved their lenses in her direction.

"Back off, asshole," she hissed.

I wrapped an arm around her to shield her from the madness as we pushed our way past the aggressive dudes who continued to run beside us, snapping pictures.

Once we were inside, the manager noticed the ruckus and stepped outside. I wasn't sure what he said, but they moved away from the door. I apologized once he stepped back inside, and he waved me off.

"Not your fault. I told them if they entered the premises with their cameras, the police would be called. This is private property. I don't need anyone harassing my customers."

I nodded in thanks, and Joey asked what we wanted and said he'd place our order. I led Darrian to the back corner, and one of the fuckers with a camera was trying to get photos through the glass. I leaned over the table and held my hand up against the side of my face to shield myself as much as possible from him.

"What are you doing here?"

"I came to meet with Duke Wayburn about something that happened with Coach Hayes." She chewed on her thumbnail. The woman never looked anything but confident, but she was clearly shaken.

"What happened with Hayes?"

"Hawk, he called me last night and then he was standing outside my building this morning."

"Coach Hayes called you? Why the fuck would he reach out to you?"

"Yes. I tried to call you last night, but you didn't return my call." I'd seen the missed call, but I figured she was just saying hi, and I hadn't opened her text this morning just yet.

"You didn't leave a message."

"This wasn't something I could say over a message. Plus, I didn't realize how serious this was until he showed up this morning and got in my face."

"About what?" I leaned back in my chair, completely baffled at how off the rails this man had gotten.

"Hawk, he offered me money to take photos of you while you were in town. He wanted me to get photos of you in my bed or…" She shook her head and looked away. "He offered me drugs to stage and then photograph you with them. I don't know what the hell is wrong with him. I told him to fuck off when he texted me last night, and then he showed up this morning and offered me even more money."

"Are you fucking kidding me?" I asked as Joey came over with our drinks and set them on the table.

We spent the next thirty minutes filling him in on all that Darrian had told me and discussing a game plan. She'd recorded the conversation this morning outside her building because he'd scared her, and she wanted proof of the harassment.

I ran a hand through my hair. I wanted to call Everly, but I didn't have my fucking phone with her number in it. And right now, I needed to deal with this shit before this man blew up everything she'd worked for.

I'd be fine either way. Hell, I could retire now and call it done.

But Everly was just starting out. And he was not going to fuck this up for her.

"We've got to go to Wayburn. It's time to go over Hayes's head. The man is unstable, and that's not good for the Lions whether you play for them or not," Joey said.

"I had my agent call and he got me in to see him now." Darrian pushed to her feet.

"Let's go."

Time to put an end to this shit.

And the buck stopped here.

Chapter 27

Everly

Coach Gallager had taken me over to the stadium and showed me the workout facilities. He was very nice and had made it clear that they would like to bring me on board. We discussed my philosophies, and obviously, he'd asked quite a bit about Hawk, but I'd expected that.

We were heading back to his office, and I glanced down at my phone. Still no word from Hawk, which was strange. I figured his meeting with the Lions would be done by now. They wanted him and he was willing to go back. He figured he'd be in and out.

I slipped my phone back into my purse and followed Coach Gallager back into his office.

He motioned for me to take the seat across from his desk, and I set my purse in the chair beside me as I settled in the brown leather armchair.

"So, I'm going to get to the point. We've got some guys who could benefit from your expertise. I'm an old-school guy, never much thought we'd ever get to this point." He chuckled, and it was genuine, so I didn't take offense. "My wife says it's time for me to get on board. I don't know, I guess I came from the school of hard knocks, so I always thought asking for help was weak. I've been a believer in the suck-it-up and grow-some-balls mentality." He winced at me apologetically.

"I get it. We're evolving about all things concerning mental health. I'm not proud to admit it took us far too long to get here."

"Thanks for not passing judgment. And the truth is, we've got trainers and physical therapists and massage therapists. We've even got a lady who leads weekly meditation now for the guys to help ground them or something." He shrugged with a smile. "I think you could be a valuable asset to this team. I didn't believe in the whole psychology thing, but I've heard you worked wonders on Madden, and the guy is the best of the best, so I'm impressed. We've got plenty of headcases for you to work with here."

I smiled and nodded. "Thank you. It truly means a lot that you would consider me. Can I think about it?"

"Yeah. But I've already met with two other people, and I wasn't impressed with either of them. Didn't even take them to tour the stadium. You've impressed me, Ms. Thomas. I think you could handle my players just fine." He slipped a piece of paper across the desk, and I zoomed in on the fact that the salary was triple what the Gliders had offered me to come on as an assistant. I tried to control my features and not show him how impressed I was by his offer.

"I'm honored that you think I would be a good fit. I do have other offers that I'm considering, so if you'll just give me a day to think it over, it would be much appreciated." My heart was racing, and I clasped my hands together.

"How about this? Give me an answer tonight, and I'll double that salary. Sign with me before you leave Los Angeles, and I'll make it worth your while."

I could barely contain my smile. It felt damn good to have someone want me to be part of their organization this badly, and the fact that he'd just offered to double my salary with an obscene amount of money. It was a lot to consider.

"All right. I'll get back to you tonight before I head home in the morning."

"Sounds good. I hope we'll be welcoming you to the team."

I pushed to my feet as he came around his desk, and I shook his hand.

"Thank you, Coach Gallager. It's truly been an honor."

He escorted me out of his office, and I made my way down the elevator, hands shaking as I hurried out to the street. I walked over to the fountain in the courtyard and let out a loud scream, and a few people glanced over at me and laughed.

I didn't care.

I'd just nailed my first interview. And if they wanted me that badly, there was no reason to think that the Lions wouldn't. Hell, I'd worked with their star player all summer and he was returning stronger than ever.

I checked my phone again and there was still no text

from Hawk. I tried calling his phone and it went straight to voicemail.

"Baby. How did your meeting go? I just got out of mine. It went so well. I can't wait to fill you in. I need to give him an answer by tonight. Call me as soon as you can. I love you." I left him a voice message.

Maybe they'd gone to lunch or extended the meeting to work out all the details. I googled his name as I walked to the hotel that was just two blocks away, to see if there'd been an announcement in the press or anything on Twitter about his return to the Lions. The first photo that popped up was of Hawk and Darrian. It had to be an old photo, right?

I zoomed in and saw today's date. He was wearing what he'd worn this morning.

Why would he be with Darrian?

I reached the hotel and leaned against the outside of the building as I continued to scan my phone. There were endless photos of Hawk and Darrian taken today. He was hugging her and had an arm around her, holding her close. They were leaning over a table at what looked like a restaurant. He had his hand up to block his face.

What the hell was this? Was he leaning in to kiss her?

My heart raced, and my palms were sweating as I read the headline. Article after article.

Hawk Madden and Darrian Sacatto, stronger than ever! The Lions' superstar meets with his coach and his biggest supporter, movie star Darrian Sacatto, was right by his side.

What was this? I dialed his phone again, my chest pounding so hard I could hear the drumming sound in my ears.

Voicemail again.

"Hey, it's me. I've called several times. I don't know what's going on. I saw the photos of you and Darrian. I didn't know she was attending the meeting with you. I don't know why you would be with her, Hawk." I swiped at the tears as they started to trickle down my cheeks before ending the call.

Had I been played?

Would he do that?

It didn't make any sense. I hurried inside the building and made my way to the elevator. It moved slowly up to the top floor, where Charlotte was waiting for me.

I knocked on the door and she whipped it open, a smile spread clear across her face before it fell as she took me in. "Oh no. What happened?"

"It went really well, Charlie." I moved across the room and dropped on the bed and covered my face as the tears started to fall again.

"That's a good thing, Ev."

"Yeah." I swiped at my cheeks and nodded. "It is. He offered to double my salary if I sign tonight."

"Wait. I thought we were just buying time and hoping that you get offered a contract from the Lions after Hawk signs? What's happening? I'm confused."

I held up my phone. "I haven't heard from Hawk, but apparently he and Darrian are splashed all over the press and social media because she is right there by his side."

"What? That doesn't make any sense."

"Oh my god, Charlie. Could he be playing me? I don't understand what's happening."

"Hawk? No freaking way. That man is crazy about you.

There has to be an explanation." She picked up her phone and dialed him, shaking her head in disbelief.

"He'll just send you to voicemail, which is what keeps happening to me." I fell back on the bed when his voicemail picked up, and she ended the call.

"Something doesn't add up."

"Maybe I'm cursed? Everyone I love leaves me, and I'm going to suffer forever from ass-pass," I said, and my words were muffled by sobs and laughter because the whole thing was ridiculous. My emotions and adrenaline were running the gauntlet, and I couldn't make sense of anything.

"Oh, yes. Lala did diagnose you years ago with that. But I think you've outgrown it with Hawk."

"I thought so too. Why wouldn't he answer his phone? Why would he be with her?" Although things weren't adding up, I knew deep down he wouldn't lie to me. He said they were friends, but that wouldn't stop her interest in him. *Calm down.*

My phone rang and I sprang forward, only to be disappointed when I saw Dylan's face light up on my screen. "Hey," I grumped.

"Wow. Glad I FaceTimed you and all," she hissed as she sat on the counter at the bakery. "Things just slowed down here, and I wanted to see how your interview went and if you've heard from Hawk?"

I groaned and spent the next ten minutes filling her in on all that had happened and fielding four hundred rapid-fire questions from her that I was unable to answer.

"This makes no sense." Her gaze moved to the ceiling as if she were deep in thought. "Absolutely none."

"Um, we know that. This isn't helpful." Charlotte's head rested beside mine on the bed as I held the phone above us so Dylan could see both of our faces.

"If I were there, I would suffocate you both with a pillow until you woke the hell up and started fighting. I can't do the sad-sack Thomas girls' shtick right now," she said, rubbing her temple with her free hand. Dylan had invented the ridiculous suffocation game when we were young, and we'd all chase each other through the house and see who could get away the quickest. Vivian had surprised everyone with her physical strength when we were young, but we were all fairly strong, and Dylan liked to say we were tiny but fierce. I chuckled at the thought and looked back at the screen.

"What, pray tell, do you recommend I do when he isn't picking up his phone?" I snapped and sat forward because I was frustrated, and she was pissing me off in the way only Dylan could.

"*Pray tell*, so fancy, Dr. Thomas. You're a freaking psychologist, do the math."

"That makes no sense," I shouted into the phone and Charlotte sat up and nodded in agreement.

"Math isn't really her specialty," Charlotte said with a shrug.

Dylan groaned dramatically. "Must I be everything to everyone in this family? I'm over here making motherfreaking red velvet cupcakes, I'm teaching Dad how to online shop, I'm helping Niko learn how to play nursemaid for his challenging patient, and now I'm playing psychiatrist to you. No. I'd rather suffocate you," she said, closing her eyes and letting out a couple of slow, dramatic breaths. "But I'm better than that.

Pull your shit together, Ev. Charlie, stop being an enabler. This doesn't make sense, so we aren't going to react to it. You know him. He wouldn't do this. Stop expecting everyone to let you down, and maybe they won't."

I sat in silence waiting for her rant to end, processing everything she'd said. It actually made sense. "Okay."

"Okay? What does that mean? Come on, girl. Think."

"I am. That's why I said *okay*. Stop shouting at me."

"What did we used to do when one of us wanted to give up on something when we were young?"

"I'm not suffocating her right now when she's vulnerable." Charlotte raised a brow in challenge.

"I appreciate that," I said.

"Fine. I'm going to the vault for the Rocky Balboa speech. Desperate times call for desperate measures. Get on your feet, bitches!" she shouted, and I cracked up, because even when I felt like my world was crumbling, my sisters could still make me laugh. Dylan moved to stand on the countertop at the bakery, and Charlotte and I both shook our heads because Vivian would not be okay with her dirty shoes touching her pristine counters.

"Get down from there," I hissed as Charlotte and I both pushed to our feet to appease her.

"Give me your phone, Jilly," she yelled, and Jilly must have handed her the phone because Dylan disappeared and Jilly smiled at the screen.

"Oh, hey, girls. How did the interview go?"

"Not the time, Jilly." Dylan's voice was loud over the booming *Rocky* theme song she had playing in the background now. Her face appeared on the screen again, and she used one arm to punch at the ceiling like a raging lunatic. "You're a tomato, Rock!"

"Oh my gosh. Not the tomato speech."

"Get up, Everly Thomas. Fight for what you want. Life is going to knock you down, girl. Stop running and start fighting. You're a freaking tomato!" She was screaming now, and the phone fumbled, and Jilly yelped and turned off the music as she looked into the phone.

"Uh, she fell off the counter. Let me make sure she's okay," Jilly said.

"I'm fine. Give me the phone back."

Charlotte and I were laughing so hard that tears were blurring my vision. "Okay, Rock. We've got it. Go on back to the cupcakes."

"Are you going to sign that contract tonight?" she pressed. "Don't do anything you can't take back, you stubborn ass."

I nodded. "Thanks, Dilly. I love you."

I ended the call and dropped back down to sit on the bed. "She's insane."

"She sure is. Definitely the kookier twin. Am I right?"

I laughed. "I don't think anyone would argue with that. But she's right about one thing."

"What's that?"

"That I need to fight for what I want."

"Well, I'm sure glad you didn't say that you wanted to play suffocation, because I'm not up for it," she said with a laugh before she reached down for my hand and clasped her fingers in mine.

"Nope. No suffocating one another and no running. Not anymore. Come on. Let's go."

"Where are we going?" Charlotte asked as she grabbed her purse.

"To see Coach Gallager. I made my decision."

Fight or flight.

I was going to fight.

Chapter 28
Hawk

"So, we've got a deal?" Duke Wayburn asked as he pushed to his feet and watched me sign my contract.

"We've got a deal. Thanks for making this happen." I extended my arm and shook his hand.

"Absolutely. We're grateful for all you've done for the team, Hawk. This is your home. I'm just glad you agreed to everything."

I nodded, and Joey's eyes were wide as he glanced at me behind Wayburn's back. I moved toward Coach Bulby, and he clapped my shoulder.

"It'll be an honor to continue working with you, Hawk." He'd been the assistant coach for the past five years, and I respected the hell out of the man.

Joey and I left the office and when we stepped on the elevator, I laughed, and he leaned over to grab his knees as he gasped a few times.

"What the fuck was that?"

We'd spent the entire afternoon. Five long hours discussing all that had happened this summer. Coach Hayes had tested positive on a drug test, and his current secretary, Tawny, had filed a sexual misconduct complaint against him this morning. Darrian had shared their interaction and the recording of him threatening her, all in hopes of catching me doing something inappropriate to blackmail me to play another year.

You couldn't make this shit up.

And the dumbass was too blind to see that I'd planned to come back. But he'd played his cards and lost. Apparently, Coach Bulby had already been offered the job, and they were planning to fire Hayes after our meeting today. They thought Hayes and I were close, and they didn't want to complicate my contract with the changes in the coaching staff.

"I don't have a fucking clue, but I can't imagine things could have gone any better."

"And you've got Everly's contract for her to sign?"

"Yeah. The best part is that they wanted to hire her before I said a word."

"Yep. And that asshole just wasn't going to tell you that the owner had already said he wanted to hire her. I can't believe Bulby is the new coach. That dude is so much better than Hayes."

"Yeah." I scrubbed the back of my neck. "But that dickhead shattered my phone, so I don't know how to reach Everly. All my contacts were in the phone. Give me yours. Let me try to call the hotel." I'd booked them at my favorite place when I was in Los Angeles, and I needed to let her know what was going on.

"Shit," Joey said as he looked down at the phone. "I'm getting a ton of texts. Apparently, your photos with Darrian went viral today, and everyone is assuming you signed with the Lions with your famous girlfriend by your side."

"Fuck me. Everly won't believe that shit," I hissed as I glanced at his phone to see photos of me with my arm around Darrian and us in the coffee shop. It was amazing how things could appear out of context. I knew nothing had happened, and Everly knew me. She wouldn't believe this bullshit.

Unless she's looking for a reason to run.

Wouldn't be the first time, but I wouldn't allow her to do it this time.

I just hoped she wouldn't do anything rash and sign with another team when everything we'd wanted was right in my hand.

I dialed the hotel, and they buzzed her room three times before I gave up.

"Fuck," I shouted, as we stepped out onto the street and several photographers stormed me.

Man, I had to give it to these guys, they didn't give up. They'd camped out here all day.

"Hawk! Did you sign? Are you coming home?"

I walked over to him and nodded. "I did. I'll be playing for the Lions. But I'd like to clear something up. Darrian Sacatto and I are no longer together and we haven't been for quite some time. We're good friends. Nothing more."

Cameras were snapping and photographers gathered around, salivating at how open I was being.

"Congrats, man," one of the dudes said. "So, are you

dating anyone?"

"I don't normally discuss my personal life. But today... I'm just putting it all out there. Yes. And she knows who she is. I'm coming to get you, baby. Go ahead and print that."

Joey chuckled as we walked toward his car.

"Hey, I have no fucking phone. Can you call the hangar and see if someone can get me out today? Like, right now."

He shook his head as he started dialing. It wouldn't be the first time he'd booked me a flight via the private airlines I usually flew. "Isn't your car in the lot? I suppose I need to get that taken to my house?"

"Unless you want to drive it to Honey Mountain?" I teased.

He chatted as I climbed in his car, and he headed toward the hangar. "They can get you out of here in ten minutes. I'll have your car brought to Wes's house. Isn't he heading back to Honey Mountain tomorrow?"

"This is why you make the big bucks."

Laughter filled the inside of the car. "Damn straight, buddy. I'll hitch my horse to your cart any day."

"Thanks, dude. Truly, I'm lucky to have you."

"So, you've got the job. Now you just need to go get the girl."

"Oh, I'll get the girl, come hell or high water. She's not getting away this time."

I meant it.

Everly Thomas was mine back then, and she was mine today.

• • •

This was by far one of the longest days of my life. I flew to Los Angeles, and thankfully, Joey pulled out a spare phone because apparently, all agents had more than one phone? Anyway, it allowed me to arrange for a car service to be waiting for me when I landed and took my ass to the hotel. Now I just needed to talk to Everly.

I'd been at the front desk taking selfies with the dude behind the counter for five minutes because he insisted that it was hotel confidentiality laws that kept him from telling me her room number, even though I'd booked the room with my credit card. However, once he recognized me, he completely flipped his stance and gave me all the information I needed, pending I take a half dozen photos with him first.

"Dude. I really need to go now. Thanks for your help."

"Congrats on the signing today," he sang out as I made my way through the lobby, only to see Dylan and Ashlan standing at the elevators and Vivian in a wheelchair.

"What the hell is this?" I asked as I strolled up.

"Well, look what the cat dragged in. What the hell is happening, Hawky player?" Dylan asked.

"Um, I could ask you the same thing."

Ashlan sighed. "Dylan called a Thomas family emergency and booked all three of us on flights to LA. I'd just arrived home for the weekend and never even made it in the house before she hauled my ass to the car, and we took off for the airport."

"And you?" I raised a brow at Vivian.

"Yeah. This isn't embarrassing at all. Niko refused to let me go even though Dr. Prichard said flying was fine as long as I wasn't on my feet much, but my crazy-ass husband insisted on a wheelchair."

"Oh, please," Dylan groaned. "You've been riding high, girl. I'm the one who had to push your pregnant ass all the way through the airport."

"That's beside the point," Vivian hissed. "What in the world happened to you, Hawk? She's called you dozens of times. We all have."

"And then you're seen all over the place *canoodling* with the movie star," Dylan growled as the doors opened, and she pushed Vivian onto the elevator and raised a brow at me.

"It's a long story. But there was no canoodling. My phone was smashed. And I tried calling the fucking hotel dozens of times, and she didn't pick up."

"Because she went back to meet with the coach here. He offered to double her salary if she signed today," Ashlan said with a frown.

"You're fucking serious?" I questioned.

"We don't know anything." Vivian reached for my hand. "Charlotte just told us that he needed an answer today, and that's the last we heard from them. They were on their way to talk to Coach Gallager. They don't even know we're here."

"Fuck me," I said under my breath.

Had she really given up on us that easily?

"I'd start with an apology over an f-bomb." Dylan studied me. "But nice job on the top floor when you booked the hotel room. I do love me a penthouse."

She pushed Vivian, and I ran a hand through my hair, preparing for the fact that this was now a conversation I'd be having with all of her sisters. I didn't mind it nearly as much as finding out that she'd signed with another team instead of having faith in me.

In us.

She'd seen the pictures and jumped ship. And that shit pissed me off. She was still one foot out the goddamn door.

"Hey, just talk to her." Vivian smiled up at me when Ashlan knocked on the door.

"What the hell," Charlotte shouted as she pulled the door open, and we all laughed because her words slurred, and her cheeks were pink.

"You're three sheets to drunkville?" Dylan asked, leaving Vivian outside the door and walking into the room. "Pour me a cold one. Ugh. The drama of this day has been a lot."

"Don't worry, I've got you," Ashlan said as she pushed her sister's wheelchair through the door.

"What are you guys doing here?" Charlotte was still laughing, and I stood in the doorway searching for Everly, who just opened the bathroom door and walked out. Her mouth gaped open and then she turned to me.

Honey Mountain blues.

"Hey. You sure have been hard to reach today." She moseyed over, her words not slurring nearly as much as her little sister's. But her cheeks were flushed, and I knew she'd probably had a couple glasses of wine. She was unusually unfazed, considering we'd all just crashed her hotel room.

"Come out here and talk to me." I reached for her hand and tugged her out into the hall, and she let the door close behind her, even though Dylan was begging her to keep it open.

"I tried to call you dozens of times," she whispered.

"Hayes lost his shit, Ever." I filled her in on everything

that had gone down—from him admitting that he'd had us followed, to him smashing my phone, to Darrian showing up to tell Duke Wayburn what had happened. She listened. She nodded. And she took it all in.

"Is that why you had your arm around her?" She tapped her lips with her pointer finger and raised a brow.

"No. I had my arm around her for all of thirty seconds to get her through the crowd of photographers, and obviously, they photographed it. I don't want her, you know that. She and I are friends. She knows it, and I know it. You're it for me, Everly Thomas. Always have been. And if you can throw in the towel so easily and give up on me and sign with another team because you're pissed, maybe I'm not it for you."

"Stop pouting, Hawk Madden." She smirked as she moved closer, her hands gripping the sides of my shirt. "You've always been it for me."

I reached in my pocket and pulled out the contract from the Lions. "I said I'd deliver this to you. I never even had to negotiate on your behalf. They were going to offer you the job, with or without me. That is, before they knew you'd accepted another fucking offer."

"Ahhh... you heard about the offer they made me, huh?" Her lips turned up in the corners. "Cha-ching. It really was an impressive offer."

Was she fucking with me?

"They offered to double your salary, even though money isn't a fucking issue for you because we're together. Period. Even if you jumped ship because you didn't have faith in me." I tucked her hair behind her ear and stroked her cheek.

How can I be mad at her and happy to see her all at the

same time?

"Is that so?"

"That is so." I leaned my forehead to rest against hers.

"Well, who's jumping ship now? For your information, I did not sign with the Rucks. I went back there because I promised to give him my answer today. He'd been really decent to me, Hawk. I felt like I owed him more than a phone call."

"Okay. What did you tell him?"

"I told him that I had to turn him down. I said that I'd fallen in love with a stubborn ass who wasn't answering his phone, but it didn't really matter if he did or not, because I was going to be standing beside him whether we were working together or not. We've spent too much time apart, and I wasn't willing to let you go this time."

My mouth covered hers, and I kissed her like my life depended on it. Because in this moment, I needed Everly Thomas more than I needed to take my next breath. And that was the God's honest truth. When I pulled back, her breaths were coming hard and fast as she smiled up at me.

"Fight or flight, baby," I whispered. "What made you stop yourself from running this time?"

"Well, if you must know. Dylan went all crazy-town on me. She blasted *Rocky* music and gave me the tomato speech."

I laughed. "So, shall I send a thank-you card to Sylvester Stallone?"

"Maybe. But the truth is, after I thought about it—it didn't add up. I know you. I know your heart. And I trust you."

"I can't ask for more than that." I kissed her again.

The door flew open, and I gripped her shoulders to keep

Everly from falling backward into the room.

"Um, sorry to interrupt this make-out sesh... but apparently, the pregnant woman is starving. You guys want something from room service?" Dylan asked as a pillow came flying at her head.

"Leave them alone. I'll order lots of everything," Ashlan said over her laughter.

"Fine. Looks like we're having a big slumber party." Dylan waggled her brows.

I leaned close to Everly. "I'll be getting us another room of our own."

"Counting on it, superstar."

She reached for my hand and led me inside.

And I was exactly where I wanted to be.

In a room full of crazy Thomas sisters and sitting beside the first, last, and only girl I'd ever loved.

Chapter 29

Everly

"You don't need to get back on the ice so soon, you know that, right?" I asked Tony, who'd taken a blade to the face two weeks ago and ended up with eighty-three stitches running from his nose to his jaw.

"I could get used to this, Doc." He chuckled. They all called me that, though I requested to be called Everly daily. But I'd fallen into a routine over the past few weeks since I'd come on board, and I was quickly finding my rhythm. "My mother was more of a tough love kind of lady, so having someone like you around—I don't mind it."

"Stop flirting with my girl or I'll put your ass back in the hospital," Hawk said with a laugh as he peeked his head into my office.

"Hey, she's actually motivated me to start thinking about settling down. It's nice to have someone care when your face gets split in half." Tony pushed to his feet, and loud laughter boomed around the office space. "Thanks for your help, Doc. But I'm ready to get back on the ice and kick some ass."

"Good, because we have a game in three days, and I wouldn't mind taking those Badgers down a few notches. They're rated higher than us at the moment, and we can't have that now, can we?" Hawk clapped him on the shoulder and studied the wound on his face. He acted like a big, bad hockey player in front of his guys, but they all knew the truth. He'd been the one pacing at the hospital, waiting to make sure Tony was okay. These guys were his family and he loved them, and that only made me love him more. Tony waved goodbye, and Hawk shut the door behind him.

"What can I do for you, Mr. Madden?" I teased as I leaned back in my chair and kicked my feet up on my desk.

"Damn, Ever. It's driving me a little crazy today. I can't focus knowing you're in the building, wearing that tight little pencil skirt that hugs your perfect ass just right."

"Highly unprofessional, Hawky player. Do you have an issue I can help you with before Buckley's appointment in five minutes?" I dropped my legs back down beneath my desk and raised a brow.

"Oh, yeah. I've got a real problem and you're the only one who can fix it." Hawk moved to his feet and came around the desk, rolling my chair back as the wheels skidded along the slick faux wood flooring. He placed an arm on each side of me, caging me in. "I can still taste you on my lips from this morning, and it's hard to lift weights with a raging boner."

My head tipped back in laughter as his lips teased mine.

"Well, we'll have to do something about that when we head home at the end of the day."

He kissed me hard before pulling back. "Definitely. Tell me how your day is going. Everyone treating you right?"

"Yep. Just the team captain who keeps harassing me."

He scooped me up and dropped down in the chair, settling me on his lap.

"Well, it goes without saying that you should do whatever the team captain wants you to do. He's the go-to guy. It would serve you right to follow his lead."

"Where are you going to lead me, Hawk Madden?"

"Right here, baby. Right by my side for as long as you'll have me," he whispered in my ear, and I laughed.

"I think forever might not be long enough for me," I teased, but it was the truth.

"I couldn't agree more."

There was a knock on the door, and I jumped to my feet, shooing him to the other side of the desk, and he barked out a laugh.

"You're adorable when you're flustered, baby. I'll see you later. Let's pick up takeout and eat at home."

Yes, I'd moved in with him the day after I signed my contract. We were done being apart, and we'd fought hard to find our way back to one another. Hawk had let everyone on the team know that we were together, so there were no secrets. They'd all chuckled, because his close friends had already figured it out.

"That sounds like a plan."

"And we need to FaceTime with the contractor. He's starting renovations on our place in Honey Mountain next week and wants to show us a few design options before they start."

Hawk had purchased the rental house I'd been staying in because we both loved it. It was right up the street from his parents' house and my dad's house, along with being within walking distance of Vivi's and Charlotte's homes. Dylan was thrilled because that meant she could continue living in the guesthouse, and she'd agreed to oversee the renovations. Ash had returned to school and would have a lot of options for places to stay when she graduated.

"I can't wait."

Hawk pulled the door open, and Buckley stood on the other side with his arms crossed over his chest. "Well, well, well. What a motherfucking surprise, you little pussy-whipped dicksack."

"I had an appointment." Hawk smirked. "And what the fuck are you doing here? You hate to talk about your feelings."

"For your information, Coach Bulby encouraged each of us to make an appointment with Doc so we could tell her a little about how we came about this profession. And to be honest with you, I like having someone who isn't a dicklicker and doesn't shame me for liking sunsets and long walks on the beach."

"Yeah, yeah, yeah. Nice try, asshat. Don't pamper him too much, baby, er, Doc. He's like a stray dog. If you give him too much attention, he'll never leave."

"I believe you're cutting into my emotional escape time right now." Buckley dropped into the chair across from my desk, and his laughter bellowed around the room.

"Goodbye, Mr. Madden." I smirked, and he pulled the

door closed behind him.

"Man, it's good to have him back another year. I was sweating that shit for months. This team just isn't the same without him. But if you tell him I said that, I will deny it until my dying day."

"Your secrets are safe here." I reached for my water and took a sip. "You know he's grooming you to lead this team in the future, right?"

"Yeah. He'll be an impossible fucking act to follow. Shit, am I not supposed to say *fuck* in here?" Buckley leaned forward, resting his elbows on his thighs. The man was close in size to Hawk, and he looked too big for the chair he was currently residing in.

"You can say *shit* and *fuck*. It's fine. My dad's a firefighter. I've heard it all." I smirked. "So, tell me what you love about this game."

"I fell in love with the ice as a young kid." He studied me, trying to decide how much to share.

"Who was the first person to take you skating?"

"My uncle. My mom was a single mom, and my uncle really stepped up to the plate and took me under his wing. The dude was a badass high school hockey player, but he taught me everything he knew."

And just like that, Buckley "the Destroyer" Callahan told me all about how he ended up sitting in the chair across from me. It was what I loved about this job. Feeling a part of something that was bigger than myself.

We spent the next forty minutes talking about his childhood and when he got drafted, and how making all that money had been the icing on the cake because he could take care of his mother.

Most of these guys were much sweeter than they let on. But the captain of both the ice and my heart, he was the one I couldn't get enough of.

My phone dinged with a reminder that I had a Zoom appointment with Lala, and I was done meeting with the guys for the day, so the timing was perfect.

I moved to make sure my door was closed and hurried back to my desk before accepting her call.

"Hey there," I said, tilting my head and smiling at my best friend.

"Hi. So, how has this week been? You've started seeing clients, right?"

"I have. Coach Bulby wants me to do a meet and greet with each one of them, and it's been surprisingly pleasant." I chuckled.

"I'm sure Hawk has booked you up for several meetings."

"You know him. He's in and out all day, and it's kind of amazing that we're here. Together."

"It's nice to see you happy, Ev. I'm really proud of you for not spiraling when you couldn't reach him, and not being afraid to follow your heart."

"Well, I spiraled for a minute."

"And then you figured it out. You stopped yourself from running."

"Yeah. It feels good."

"Now that you've had a taste of happiness, I think you'll be fighting for that from here on out," she said, and the corners of her lips turned up.

"You look different. What's happening here?" I asked as I

studied her face. "You're actually glowing."

"I'm pregnant!" she squealed.

"What? Oh my gosh, Lala. I'm so happy for you. What did Grayson say?"

"He was thrilled. I wrapped up one of those bibs that says *hot dad* on it and gave it to him. He started babyproofing the entire house when he found out about the baby last night."

"You guys are going to be the best parents. Oh my gosh. You and Vivi are both having babies. I can't believe it."

"Yeah? What do you think about that? You always thought you'd never get married or have kids, but look at you now, girl. You're living your best life."

"Damn straight. It took me a while to get here, but now that I'm here... I definitely think about it."

She whistled. "I'm guessing that hunky man of yours would be more than happy to put some babies in you."

My head fell back in laughter. "I guess I'm going to have to tell him he has a green light. Not today... but someday."

"Someday is good, Ev. I love you."

There was a knock on my door. "Okay, I love you too. I'm so happy for you. I'll call you tomorrow."

We said our goodbyes, and I called out, "Come on in."

"You ready to head home?" Hawk asked as he stepped into my office.

"Absolutely. I'm ready for all the things, Mr. Madden."

"Ohhhh. I like the sound of that. What kind of things are we talking?"

I closed my laptop and took a look back at my office. I didn't know how I'd ended up here. I never thought I would. I was absolutely living my dream. Working for one of the best

NHL teams in the league. Living in a city that I loved that was still close enough that I could go home and see my family all the time. And doing it all with the man I loved by my side.

"I've got something on my mind," I said, taking his hand as he led me down the hall and we stepped onto the elevator. Most everyone had already gone home for the day, and it was quiet.

"Tell me what's on your mind, Ever mine." He wrapped his arms around me, my back to his chest as he kissed my neck.

"Lala is pregnant. She's having a baby."

"Yeah? That's amazing. I'm happy for them."

"Me too," I said as we stepped off the elevator and made our way to the truck parked underground. He opened my door and lifted me up and set me on the seat.

"You going to let me put some babies in there someday?" he teased as he reached over and buckled my seat belt before resting his forehead against mine.

"Yes. How do you feel about that?"

"Like the luckiest guy in the world. Let's go home and start practicing."

"Sounds like a plan."

Because the future was all ours.

And it had never looked brighter.

Chapter 30

Hawk

"This is everything we've worked for," I said as the guys brought it in close for a huddle.

The Stanley Cup.

It was the Olympics for hockey players. And we'd made it.

Our team was young but strong and led by a coach who believed in us.

It had been an amazing season. We'd had ups and downs, but with the new coaching staff and the addition of our amazing sports psychologist who had done more for this team than she could even comprehend... we'd made it.

And it had been the best season of my life. Maybe it was knowing that this would probably be my last. Maybe it was having a coach that I actually respected. But I knew the truth—it was having the girl I loved by my side. Everly Thomas had been what was missing from my life for all those years. Everything was just better now.

"Thanks for leading us here, man," Buckley said, and I heard the emotion there.

"It's not like that, brother. We did this. Every single one of us. Now let's go kick some ass."

"You ready?" Wes asked as he clapped me on the shoulder, and his face was so pale he looked like he might pass out.

"Relax, man. We've got this. Now we get to enjoy all that hard work. And you helped to get us here, so you should do the same."

We lined up as our names were called over the speaker system, and each guy skated out onto the ice to roaring fans shouting their names. I was last in line, per Coach Bulby's insistence, and I just reveled in the moment. I clapped as each guy took to the ice, and Wes handed me the box that I'd asked him to keep safe.

"Proud of you, Hawk."

I chuckled and shook my head. The man gave me far too much credit, but I appreciated it. "Proud to call you my friend, brother."

"Let's get on our feet for the captain of the Lions' team... Hawwwwwwk Madden!"

I held up my hand, and he high-fived me before I walked my ass out of the tunnel and skated onto the ice. The sound of roaring screams filled the stadium as lights flashed all around me.

Hell, I'd loved this shit a lot, and this season had felt more like my first season on the ice. I waved and turned to look up as the lights turned on and the crowd settled down.

There, in the front, were my parents sitting beside Jack

Thomas and all his girls, aside from Everly. Niko sat beside his wife as she cradled their little girl who had gigantic headphones on to protect her little ears. I glanced in our box at the bench where Coach and Everly sat, and Wes skated over to join them.

The refs came over and gathered around me, and the guys on my team lined up behind me.

"You doing this, Hawk?" one of the refs I'd known for years asked.

"Abso-fucking-lutely. Go big or go home, am I right?"

"It's been an honor to be on the ice with you all these years," he said as he reached out for my hand.

I glanced over to see Everly looking between Coach and the guys and wondering why we weren't coming to the box.

"Go get her." I waggled my brows when I pulled my helmet off.

Coach, Wes, and Everly all stood to see what the problem was. Coach and Wes already knew what was going down. It was just my girl who was in the dark. I looked up to see Jack Thomas watching me, and he had a hand over his mouth as if he was overcome with emotion. Of course, I'd made a special trip home to ask his permission before I did this.

Dylan was waving her hands in the air trying to figure out what the holdup was, and Charlotte, Ashlan, and Vivian all stared at me as if they were just figuring it out.

Everly looked completely panicked as she held on to the ref's arm and made her way out on the ice.

"Ladies and gentlemen, let's all welcome the lovely lady to the ice," someone shouted over the loudspeaker.

The crowd applauded, but they had no idea what was going

on until I dropped down on one knee to deafening screams. Everly let go of the referee's arm and covered her mouth and shook her head.

"I love you, Everly Thomas. I loved you in kindergarten when you shared your fruit snacks with me. I loved you when you skated out on that ice like a freaking goddess in middle school. And I loved you the first time I kissed you, and every day since. Will you make me the happiest man in the world and marry me and let me put lots of babies in you?"

"Aww... man. That baby part wasn't what we practiced," Buckley groaned from behind me, and the guys laughed. My mic wasn't on, so the crowd couldn't hear what I was saying, but they still remained quiet as they waited.

"You sure don't do things quietly, do you, Hawk Madden?" Everly moved closer and put her hands on my shoulders. "You didn't even need to ask. Yes. It's always been yes."

I reached for her hand and slipped the ring onto her finger as music started booming, and the crowd went nuts. I picked her up, her legs wrapping around my waist, and I skated a lap with my future wife in my arms.

It didn't matter if we won or lost at this point, because I'd already won more than any one man deserved.

Nah, fuck that. I was a sappy ass when it came to Everly Thomas, but I still wanted to win.

I stopped at the box and set her on her feet and kissed her hard. "Thanks for saying yes."

She chuckled and pushed the hair away from her face. Her cheeks were flushed, and her eyes were wet with emotion. "Thanks for waiting for me."

"I told you once, forever isn't long enough with you."

"Uh, I hate to break this up, but this is the Stanley Cup," Tony said with a laugh as he clapped me on the shoulder.

"He's right. Now go win us a game," my future bride said.

I smacked her ass as she stepped toward the box. Each of the guys hugged her as she made her way to her seat.

I looked up to see my parents and Everly's family going wild with emotion, and I gave them a thumbs-up.

"You're a tomato, Rock!" Dylan shouted, and the crowd cheered even though they didn't know what the hell she was saying, but her sisters fell over in laughter and so did I.

"All right. Game time, boys," I said when I turned my attention to the guys. "Let's do this."

From the minute the puck hit the ice, it was game on.

There were punches thrown, body checks, and some dirty plays by both sides. We fought hard and so did they.

It was a little like life. You fought hard. You played hard. And you enjoyed every fucking minute because you were exactly where you wanted to be.

This game was a part of me. I'd be forever grateful for where it had taken me.

And at the moment, it was taking me solo down the ice heading for the goal because Tony and Will had protected my ass so I could break free.

I took my shot, just like I always had.

Sometimes you scored, and sometimes you missed. But if you kept taking your shot, you were bound to get it in there.

And today was that day.

I scored the winning goal for the Stanley Cup, sending the Lions home with the W. It was a good day.

I got the goal. I got the girl.

There were days that I thought it was okay to be a greedy bastard. And today was that day for me.

The buzzer sounded, and the lights flashed bright colors in our faces. The guys on the bench charged the ice, and the crowd roared.

I looked up in the midst of the chaos and found my joy.

Honey Mountain blues locked with mine.

My past.

My present.

And my future.

My life.

My home.

And my love.

My forever.

Epilogue
Everly

Ashlan's graduation party was massive. The last Thomas girl to graduate college.

"I'm just so thankful that I don't have to attend any more graduations for you girls," Gramps teased.

The man had been in our lives since we were little girls, and he'd never missed a celebration.

"Yeah, now you're just going to weddings and baby showers, old man." Rusty smacked him on the chest. "Frankly, I love the Thomas girls' parties. Good food. Good drink. Good sights." He waggled his brows, and Niko punched his shoulder.

"Why do you have to make everything dirty?" Niko hissed, patting his chest as baby Beth slept in the pouch that was strapped over his shoulders. Niko and Vivian were amazing parents, and my niece had her mother's rosebud lips and her father's eyes.

"Just saying, there's some good eye candy at these parties."

"Sometimes just keeping your thoughts to yourself is better," Jace said as he handed Paisley a cookie and she took off running.

"Any luck finding a new nanny?" I asked Jace, as his nanny had up and quit with no notice last week. We'd all been chipping in to help cover him while he was at the firehouse.

"I was actually coming over here to talk to you about that," Ashlan said as she walked up beside me with Hadley's little hand in hers.

"Yeah? You know someone?"

"I think I do." Ashlan kissed Hadley's cheek before she waddled off to play with her sister and the other kids. "You said the guesthouse is part of the deal, right?"

"Yep. They'd need to stay in the main house with the girls when I'm at the firehouse and then they'd have the other nights to themselves. But all living expenses are included."

I could feel the stress pouring from Jace, and my baby sister's face lit up. "I'd like to apply for the job."

His eyes widened.

Hopeful.

"Really? You just graduated from college. You sure there isn't something else you'd rather be doing?" Jace cleared his throat as he studied my sister.

"Actually, I've decided that I'm going to write. I have a story in my head that's just dying to come out. And you know that I love your girls, so it would be a perfect plan for me. I could write on my days off and be with the girls when you're at the firehouse."

"Paisley will be in school in the fall and Hadley will be able to start preschool in January, but this summer they'll need someone full-time." He sipped his beer, and his shoulders relaxed as this had been weighing on him heavily.

"I don't mind that at all. So, I've got the job?" Ashlan did a little dance, and we all laughed.

"You're overqualified for the job, Ash, so yeah, it's yours for as long as you want it. But if it gets to be too much or you find something else that you're better suited for, you know you can just tell me." Jace smiled.

"No. I have a good feeling about this. When do I start?"

"I'm back at the firehouse on Monday, so if that works for you, you can move into the guesthouse any time. How about you come by tomorrow? We can discuss the salary and go over the girls' schedules."

"Perfect. Thank you, Mr. King. It's a pleasure doing business with you," Ashlan teased as she extended her hand, and he took hers. I swear I saw something pass. Maybe I was reading into it. But the way Ashlan's cheeks flushed and Jace's tongue swiped out to wet his lips, hell, it was a sight, that's for sure.

"Holy hotness. What was that?" Dylan whispered in my ear, causing me to jump, and Ashlan ran off to tell Dad that she was going to nanny for Jace and the girls.

I tugged on Dylan's hand and walked her away from the group. "That was nothing. Don't make it weird. He's a family friend."

"*Hot daddy* is more like it."

I groaned as Vivian and Charlotte walked over to see what we were whispering about.

"What's going on?" Vivian asked.

"Nothing. Ash is going to nanny for Jace. Apparently, she has a book she wants to start writing, and she can live in his guesthouse and watch the girls while pursuing that dream of hers."

"I think that's awesome. Why does Dilly look like she's keeping a secret?" Charlotte raised a brow.

"And how exactly do I look when I'm keeping a secret?"

"A little devious and a little constipated," Charlotte said over her laughter.

"What are we laughing about?" Ashlan asked as she bounded back over.

"Dilly has the shits," I said as Dylan gasped. "So, what did Dad say about you working for Jace?"

"He thinks it's great. It means I don't have to move back home, which makes me feel a little more grown-up, you know? I like the idea of having my own place, and I can fix his guesthouse up cute. And I love Paisley and Hadley, and it will give me the time to write. It's a win-win situation."

Dylan raised a brow. "And Jace King? What's the story there?"

Ashlan rolled her eyes. "Of course, you took it to dirty town. Jace is a family friend. There is no story there."

I wanted to agree with Ashlan, but I didn't miss the way they looked at one another. Maybe it was my imagination. I'd noticed her acting weird months back at the bakery, and I'd thought it was Tallboy making her blush. Maybe it was Jace back then too. Or maybe I was completely dreaming all of this up. They were two extremely attractive people who shared a nice friendship.

I was definitely misreading it.

"Are you saying you don't think that man is hotter than sin?" Dylan pressed, as she watched Ashlan intently.

"He's like ten years older than me with two kids." Ashlan's cheeks flushed pink.

"I didn't ask how old he was or how many kids he had." Dylan tipped her chin up confidently.

"Oh, come on. Don't we all think he's hot?" Ashlan said as she laughed.

I wrapped an arm around her shoulder. "We all think he's hot. You're fine."

"It's just a job. I can help him out, and he can help me out."

"I'll bet you can," Dylan said over a fit of laughter.

"What's so funny over here?" my father asked as he walked up. "Never a good thing when the Thomas girls are huddled together whispering and laughing."

"We're just talking about Ashlan's new job and how she's going to write this book she's been talking about." Charlotte leaned into our father and rested her head on his shoulder.

"Yeah. So, what's this book about?" he asked.

"It's a romance, Dad. Probably not your genre." Ashlan smirked.

"I'll bet a steamy romance," Dylan whispered, but everyone heard her, and our father held up his hands.

"That's my cue. I think this is a great idea, Ash. You'll be helping out a family friend as well, so that's a good thing."

Dylan rolled her eyes when he walked away. "Well, that was a buzzkill. Let's go back to the steamy romance."

"No one said anything about it being steamy, you perv."

Ashlan chuckled before a few of her high school friends came through the door, and she ran off to see them.

"I need help in the kitchen, girls," our father shouted, and Dylan and Charlotte said they'd handle it.

Niko walked over with little Beth, and Vivian held out her arms, hugging her little girl to her chest. I stroked her dark hair and kissed the top of her head.

"She's so perfect. I love the way she smells too," I cooed as I kissed her cheek.

"Well, you should smell her when she's shitting black lava through her diaper," Niko said.

Vivian's head tipped back in a chuckle. "A little black lava never hurt anyone. I'm going to go sit down and nurse her." My sister smiled at me before she and Niko made their way to the living room.

"How are you doing, Mrs. Madden?" Hawk walked over and wrapped his arms around me. We'd gone to Paradise Island in the Bahamas and gotten married shortly after the Stanley Cup win. We didn't want to wait.

"I'm good. I can't believe my baby sister graduated from college. I'm so happy that I'm here for everything now. I love that we have two homes and can go back and forth. Thank you for giving me the fairy tale."

Hawk buried his face in my neck before pulling back to look at me. "Me too, baby."

Hawk had extended his contract another year, which had shocked and pleased his coach and teammates, as well as all of his fans. Turned out, he'd found a renewed love for the sport after spending a summer in Honey Mountain where it all started.

"Yeah. I'm surprised how much I love being here."

"Me too, baby. But anywhere I'm with you is home."

"You're right about that. I found my home right here." I placed my hand on his chest and he covered it with his.

"Dinner's ready," my father called out.

We walked toward the kitchen, as we'd be eating out on the back porch per usual. I glanced over to see Jace and Ashlan deep in conversation. He had his hands in his pockets, and she was looking up at him like he set the sun.

Hawk chuckled and tugged at my hand after he followed my gaze to Jace and Ashlan.

"You worry too much, baby. Let's eat."

"So, you see it too?" I whispered, and he wouldn't look at me.

"I don't know what you're talking about. I plead the fifth, Mrs. Madden."

"I'll bet you do."

Everyone gathered around the two big tables, and Dylan moved around with a bottle of wine asking who needed a refill or a topper. She paused when she got to me.

"Red or white, Ev?"

"I'm just having water tonight. My stomach's been a little off all day."

Dylan nodded and moved on, but my husband's head snapped up.

"You okay, baby?" he whispered in my ear.

"Yeah. But we may need to stop at the drugstore on the way home." I smiled.

I wasn't positive I was pregnant, but my boobs hurt, and I'd felt a little nauseous for the past few days. We'd been busy getting moved into the house here and preparing for Ashlan's graduation, so I hadn't stopped to really think about it until now.

"Should we go now?" His eyes were wild with excitement.

"No. It's Ash's day. We've got plenty of time."

"Forever will never be long enough, baby."

And he was right.

Exclusive

Bonus

Content

Everly

The day had been a whirlwind of emotions. Hawk was on his way home after being in the city with the team for the last two nights. I'd stayed back in Honey Mountain because I'd been under the weather and suffering from what I thought was a stomach bug.

But this morning when I woke up, I felt extremely nauseous again, my breasts were unusually tender—and that's when it hit me. We'd had a negative pregnancy test after we'd stopped to get one after Ashlan's graduation party a few weeks ago, so we'd just figured we'd go back to trying.

We didn't want to put any pressure on ourselves about getting pregnant, so we'd kind of put it out of our minds. Of course, my husband liked to tell me endlessly that he was enjoying all the trying that was involved when it came to making a baby.

So, I'd found one of the pregnancy tests in the bathroom vanity this morning, as we'd bought a few the first time we tested, and what do you know...there was a bright-pink plus sign on the stick.

"Baby, I'm home!" Hawk's voice called from the front door.

It took everything in me not to tell him the minute I'd found out earlier today. But I knew he was coming home tonight, so it was my opportunity to surprise him.

Hawk was going to be the most amazing father, so I wanted to tell him in a special way, seeing as we weren't together when I took the test.

"Hey," I said, walking toward him as he wrapped his arms around me. "I'm glad you're home. I never sleep well without you."

"Me either." He pulled back and studied me. "You look great. You're feeling better?"

"I am. It passed."

He hugged me against his chest again and kissed the top of my head. "I'm glad. I was worried about you. I don't like when you aren't feeling well."

"You don't need to worry. It was nothing big." I chuckled. "Come on. I made you dinner."

He followed me into the kitchen, and he paused when he saw the large box sitting on top of the kitchen island wrapped in gold paper with white ribbon tied around it.

"What's this?"

"Just something I got for you," I said, setting the plate of bruschetta down in front of him because this man was always hungry.

"Damn. You spoil me, baby. You haven't been feeling well. You didn't need to cook for me or get me a present. I wanted you to rest today." He tugged me closer where he sat on the barstool and pulled me to stand between his thick thighs.

"I like surprising you." I bent down and kissed him, my heart racing with anticipation. I couldn't wait for him to open it.

When I pulled back, he placed a hand on each side of my face, concern lacing his green eyes. "You sure you're feeling okay? Your face is flushed."

"You worry too much. How about you open your gift and then we'll have dinner."

He took one more large bite of bruschetta and pushed to his feet, reaching for the box. "You're too good to me, baby."

He tore the paper open, and I tried to remain calm and hide my excitement, or he'd be suspicious.

I'd met my sisters for an early lunch at the bakery today, and of course they'd all cried when I shared the news. And then we'd brainstormed the cutest way to surprise my husband, and we'd hurried to the sporting goods store just a little way out of town to get everything I'd need. And I'd come home and got to work putting it all together.

Once the gift wrap was set aside, he pulled the lid off the box and stared down at the hockey stick that read: *Congrats! You're going to be a daddy!*

He reached inside, finding the two little skates, one painted pink and one painted blue, and held them in his hands.

He still hadn't spoken, and I turned to look at him. I was caught off guard when I noticed the tear rolling down his cheek.

He made no attempt to swipe it away. He just stared at the little skates.

"Ever Mine," he whispered. "How did I get so lucky to get to spend my life with you?" he asked, setting the skates back in the box before turning to face me. "You're really pregnant?"

"I really am," I said, and the tears were flowing freely down my cheeks now. "I think we were probably pregnant a few weeks ago when we first tested, but it just didn't show because it was too soon."

He reached for the hockey stick, pulling it from the box. "This is pretty cool. We're hanging this in the gym so I can see it every day. And we'll hang the little skates right beside it."

"You're going to be the best father, baby," I said.

"I'm going to try damn hard. But this baby will be so lucky to have you for a mama that I'll just follow your lead, Mrs. Madden." He set the stick down and pulled me against him. "We're having a baby, Ever."

I chuckled. "We are. I can't believe it."

He pulled back. "You did it."

"We did it, Hawk. It takes two." I shook my head with a laugh.

"Is this why you haven't been feeling good?"

"I'm guessing so. I think it's probably morning sickness. That's why it passes later in the day. And now that I know what it is, I'll be able to work around it."

He moved his large hand to my stomach, looking down at me as the sides of his eyes crinkled when he smiled. "Our little baby is growing in here, Ever. We're starting our family, you and me and baby Madden."

"Yep. We're starting a new adventure together. The three

of us. Who would have thought back when we were just two teenagers in love that we would be here all these years later?"

His gaze locked with mine. "I thought it. I wanted it. I believed it. I always knew you were the only girl for me. Thank you for making me the happiest man in the world."

I sniffed as the tears continued to fall. "Thank you for loving me, Hawk Madden."

"Always have. Always will. Until I take my last breath," he whispered. "*Ever Mine.*"

He wrapped his arms around me, just the way he always did.

This man was the love of my life, my happily ever after, my husband, and the father of our child. I didn't know how I got so lucky, but I wasn't questioning it.

Life was about living every day.

The hard days.

The easy days.

And with this man by my side, I was doing exactly that.

Living.

Loving.

And enjoying every minute.

Like I planned to do for the rest of my life.

Keep reading for
a sneak peek of
Make You Mine

Chapter 1
Ashlan

I sat across from Jace at his kitchen table as he pulled out a notebook and cleared his throat.

"I can't thank you enough for doing this. And I mean it when I say that when you find what you want to do with your life, I'll understand that it's not this. I know this is temporary. Just give me a couple weeks' notice when you want to bail, all right?"

"Of course. But I'm planning to stay for a while if you'll have me," I said over an embarrassing giggle. I mean, this man was something straight out of a sexy firefighter calendar. He was tall with broad shoulders, glistening tan skin, and every inch of him was chiseled and hard. Well, I couldn't technically speak for every inch of him. "Is it hot in here?"

Oh my gawd. Did I just say that out loud?

He chuckled this sexy, gruff sound that sent chills down

my spine. "Let me check the thermostat. It is hot as hell outside today."

He moved to the wall beside the kitchen, and I quickly fanned my face frantically with my hand while his back was to me. He'd become a good family friend since he'd started working at the firehouse with my dad, and he'd been coming to our Sunday night dinners for the past few years. But lately, every time I was around him, I was a swoony fool. I didn't know what the hell was going on with me.

He was hot. Definitely hot.

And I was human.

"I've been setting up the guesthouse all day, so I'm probably overheated." I tried to make light of it, but the truth was—it could be snowing outside, and I'd be warm if I were sitting close to this man.

I wasn't proud of the thoughts I'd had lately, but I knew it would pass. I'd ended things with Henry, the guy I'd dated for a few months toward the end of school. It just wasn't going anywhere—he wanted to get serious, and I wasn't feeling it. So, I graduated from college and made my way back home to Honey Mountain.

I was going to write the book I had playing in my head for the past few years, and I'd taken a job to nanny for the two cutest girls on the planet, Paisley and Hadley King, while I pursued my dream.

Secretly crushing on my new boss was not a sin.

Was it?

Jace sat back down. His muscles strained against his white tee and my mouth went dry. He had blue eyes that were the lightest blue I'd ever seen. His brown hair always looked like he'd been tugging at it and managed to look sexy as hell with very little effort.

"Hawk and Niko helped me get a fresh coat of paint on the walls a few weeks ago. Looks like you and your sisters got everything moved and settled in there, yeah?"

Hawk and Niko were my sisters' husbands, and they were also good friends with Jace, so that didn't surprise me one bit that they'd helped out.

I nodded as I stared at his plump lips before clearing my throat. "Yeah. Thanks for letting me stay there. It's such a cute place."

"Well, you're saving my ass. Since Karla left, the girls haven't had any consistency. We've had more nannies come and go than I can count. A firefighter's hours aren't always the easiest for people to accommodate. This will be really good for the girls. They were thrilled when I said you'd taken the job."

Karla was his ex-wife who'd skipped town with some random guy and left her girls and Jace behind. I admired the way he stepped up for his daughters. My dad was an amazing father and it hurt like hell that we'd lost our mama to cancer, but I couldn't imagine how much it would hurt if she'd chosen to leave. But Jace took it all in stride.

"You know I love your girls. And honestly, I'm happy to have my own place and not have to move back in with my dad. It just makes me feel like I'm somewhat of a grown-up, you know?" I'd seen them interact at Dad's Sunday dinners, and although Hadley seemed a little shy and limited in her vocabulary, Paisley was more of an old soul. I'm sure their mom leaving had an impact on them both.

The corners of his lips turned up and my stomach fluttered. Jace was a serious guy, and after all he'd been through, I didn't see him smile all that often.

But when he did... I liked it.

Probably too much.

"Well, it's not much of a home with it being so small. But I'm glad you're happy with it. You know you can come over here any time if you want to cook in a larger kitchen." He slid over a set of keys. "These are to the main house. You'll stay here with the girls when I'm on duty at the firehouse, which is usually three nights a week. You know the drill, growing up with your dad. And then you'll have four nights to yourself. I may occasionally ask if you'd be willing to babysit a night here or there so I can go meet the guys for a beer or do a little work on one of the houses I'm renovating. But only if it works for you, and I'd pay you separately for that."

Did he date? My mind was spinning with questions that were too inappropriate to ask.

"Of course. You can ask me any time. And you're paying me plenty with the salary and the living accommodations." I knew Jace made money off of his house flipping side business that he did, which my brother-in-law, Niko, was now involved in as well. They were both talented when it came to renovating spaces, and apparently Jace King was doing quite well between flipping homes and being a firefighter, because this house was gorgeous.

"Well, I appreciate it. But I want to pay you for your time. My mom will watch the girls on the weekends for a few hours so I can work on whatever house we've got going at the time, but I don't like taking advantage of that. Hell, the girls are pretty good about chilling when I need them to in short doses. So, when you have to catch a shower or use the restroom, you just tell them to stay put until you come out. I usually put a show on in their playroom and they'll give you a quick fifteen minutes of peace. Just tell Paisley to keep Hadley with her."

I laughed. His girls were adorable. Well-behaved and sweet. "Okay. That sounds easy enough."

He handed me a piece of paper with a schedule on it. I have to say, I was impressed. It had everything laid out for me. What time they woke up, what time they napped, what they liked to eat. A lot of this stuff I'd already known because I'd spent a lot of time with them over the years, but I guess this cheat sheet would come in handy when it came down to all the details. He had the pediatrician's information at the bottom, along with his parents' phone number in case of emergency.

"So, a few things you should know that you probably aren't aware of from the time you've spent with them." His tone turned serious and when I met his light blue gaze, my chest squeezed at the concern I saw there.

"Okay," I said softly.

"Paisley is anxious about starting kindergarten for whatever reason. She's been in preschool and pre-K for the past two years, but she keeps talking about how scared she is for school to start in the fall. I don't know what's up with that, but let me know if she opens up to you about it."

"Got it. I think I was super nervous to start kindergarten too. It's all normal. You're doing a great job with your girls, Jace."

His smile was forced, and I saw it all in his gaze. The doubt. The worry. Maybe even some guilt about the fact that he was doing it on his own, trying to compensate for being a single parent.

"Thanks. I'm not sure how much damage her leaving will do to them, but I'm doing my best to give them a good life. As much as a grumpy firefighter can, at least." He shrugged and there was tease in his voice, but there was honesty too. "Anyway, Paisley will help out as much as you need her to. You know that. She's a go-with-the-flow type of kid. But she's got her quirks."

"Which are?" I hadn't noticed anything in all the time I'd spent with her. She was super polite and sweet and a ball of energy. Always helpful with little Hadley.

"She, uh, strips her clothes off when she goes to the bathroom." He barked out a laugh now. "Apparently, she takes them all off and folds them in a neat little pile by the door because she doesn't want her clothes to smell like poop."

My head fell back in laughter. I hadn't realized that's what she did, but it did make sense. "I did notice she takes quite a while in the bathroom, so now I understand why."

"Yeah. Her pre-K teacher was unimpressed about the little habit because a line was forming outside the bathroom every time she took her turn."

"Well, no one should be rushed when it comes to doing their business," I said with a laugh.

"Touché. Couldn't agree more. What I wouldn't give to have a few minutes alone in the shitter now and then. I have to practically bribe them to give me ten minutes in the shower."

Jace King in the shower must be a sight. Visions of him washing his golden, naked body under a hot spray of water... there I go again.

I'd blame it on the fact that I'd been reading a lot of romance books lately as I geared up to start writing my own book.

And I'd possibly had a few sexy dreams about this man in the shower over the past few months. But I couldn't control what my subconscious did while I slept, right?

"Yeah. I'm sure. And where would you like me to sleep when I stay here at the main house?"

"So, when Mrs. Tusley was with the girls for those last few weeks of school, she stayed in the guest room. The problem is, both girls have occasional nightmares, and they like to climb into my bed. The guest room bed is small, and Mrs. Tusley was not a believer in letting the girls come into bed with her, and I don't know..." He scrubbed the back of his neck. "Maybe I'm fucking them up by letting them come in when they're scared."

"No. My sisters and I always went into our parents' room when we were young and had a nightmare. That's when you need to be comforted. I don't mind if they come to bed with me at all. Heck, for the longest time I used to take turns sleeping with all my sisters after my mom died. I welcome the company."

He raised a brow and I realized what I'd said.

"I mean, the girls' company. I hardly have any company in my bed ever. I mean, not that I've never..." Please, make it stop. "The girls are welcome to come in if they get scared."

I reached for the glass of water that he'd given me and took a long sip, trying to regain my composure.

"I knew what you meant. And you're welcome to sleep in my room if you want. I'll make sure the sheets are clean for you. That way, if they come in, you'll still be able to get some sleep because the bed is plenty big."

"Okay. That sounds like a plan."

"I'm actually glad you brought it up. I, uh, I was hoping you'd understand if I asked that you not have any boyfriends stay over at the house when I'm on duty. Obviously, what you do in your free time in the guesthouse is your business, but I want the girls to feel safe when you're staying here with them. I've never allowed anyone to stay in my bed since Karla left, and I plan to keep it that way."

My face heated at his words, and I shook my head. "I would never do that."

"Fuck, I'm not trying to make you uncomfortable. Just needed to say it. You're young. I'm sure you have a million dudes chasing after you. But I just don't want to confuse the girls while you're with them. Obviously, you're welcome to have your sisters or a friend over any time. Just no strange guys." He chuckled.

My mind was still reeling that he'd just admitted he didn't bring women home. What did that mean? Did he just not have sex?

"I completely agree. That won't be an issue. I'm single." I held up my hands and fluttered them around like a crazy person. "I plan on writing when I'm not working."

"Yeah? I think that's great, Ash. What are you writing?"

I'm leaning toward writing about a sexy firefighter and his nanny.

Just kidding.

Not really.

"Um, it's a romance." I swallowed hard just as little Hadley came waddling over and walked right past her dad and over to me, holding her pudgy little arms up in the air for me to pick her up.

"Hey, sweetie pie. I'm excited that we're going to be spending lots of time together." I settled her on my lap, and she nuzzled her head beneath my neck. She smelled like sunshine and baby powder. Her light brown wild waves danced all around her face, and her hair didn't look like it had been brushed yet today. I knew Jace was doing the best that he could and the fact that he even attempted to do their hair was impressive to me.

"She still isn't speaking much, so maybe you can get her talking a little bit," Jace said, his voice low as he watched her with concern.

"Of course. I think we'll be just fine."

"Well, it's summer break, so they're going to be with you all day. You may be changing your tune here soon. A young girl like you probably wants to be hanging out at the lake with her friends, not hanging out with two little kids."

Young girl?

He'd pointed out my age twice now. I wasn't that young. I was twenty-two years old, turning twenty-three in a couple weeks. My mama always said I was an old soul. I never cared much for partying down by the lake or going out and getting crazy. Maybe it was because I'd lost my mother at a young age that I'd just become a homebody. I liked the comfort of being with my family. Always had.

"Don't worry about me, I'll be fine. I prefer staying home over going to Beer Mountain any day." I shrugged. It was the truth. And I was looking forward to getting lost in my words.

"So, I'll stay in your room when I'm here, and we'll see how it goes."

"All right. I've been having some plumbing issues in my master bathroom lately, but I have a guy coming over later today to get it fixed."

"Great. I'll just spend the rest of the day getting my place set up. I have a few pictures to hang, and Vivian made me some cute curtains."

He studied me. "Look at you. Making it all homey. I hope that's a sign you won't be quitting in a week."

"Not a chance."

Hadley squirmed to get down, and I pushed to my feet as the little angel wrapped her arms around my leg and kissed my knee which made me chuckle.

Paisley came walking into the kitchen wearing a princess dress with a tiara on top of her head. Her long brown hair ran down her back and she had her daddy's blue eyes. Both girls resembled Jace more than Karla, but Hadley had her daddy's coloring with big dark brown eyes and long lashes.

"Daddy, can Ashlan come over for pizza tonight?" Paisley asked as she stepped beside me and leaned her cheek against my side.

Be still my heart.

I'd always known I wanted to be a mother someday, and I couldn't wait for that to happen. I just hadn't found anyone I liked enough to date longer than six months.

"Not tonight, sweetheart. This is her night off."

Hadley moved toward her father and he plopped her on his lap and kissed the top of her head.

"Do you have another job?" Paisley asked me.

"I'm going to start writing a book," I said, and her eyes watered, her bottom lip quivering like I'd just broken her heart. "But I sure don't need to start that tonight. And pizza is my favorite."

Jace smirked, and his hand grazed over the beard that covered his jaw. "Don't let them be working you all the time, Ash. My girls may look sweet, but I swear they're little sharks."

"Well, seeing as tomorrow is our first day together, I think it would be fun to hang out a little tonight and they can show me some of their nighttime routine."

Jace smiled, and his face relaxed as he nodded. "If you're sure you don't mind."

"I'm sure," I said.

And just like that, my new life was getting started.

Acknowledgments

Greg, Chase & Hannah, thank you for always believing in me and supporting me! I love you forever!!

Willow, there are no words to thank you for all that you do for me. Thank you for always making time to read my words and working your magic to make them better. I love being on this journey with you! Love you!

Catherine, I am so thankful for your friendship, your guidance and your support!! Even when I'm spiraling, you are right there to talk me through it! Cannot wait to hug you SO SOON! Love you!

Nina, I'd be lost without you! So thankful for YOU! I told you I wished for you in my 2022 dreams…and you have totally lived up to the hype!! Love you!!

Christine Miller, I cannot thank you enough for all that you do for me. I am so thankful for YOU!

Kim Cermak, thank you for keeping everything organized when I'm certain that I don't make that easy for you!! I am so grateful for all that you do for me!

Sarah Norris, thank you for the gorgeous graphics and all that you do to make my releases extra special! It means the world to me!

Megan Corbett, thank you so much for helping to get my books out there on TikTok and being so supportive and patient!

Kelley Beckham, thank you so much for all that you do to help me get my books out there! I am truly so thankful!

Valentine Grinstead, I am so happy to be on this journey with you!! Looking forward to working together for many years!

Abi, Annette, Doo, Pathi, Natalie, Caroline, Jennifer and Lara, thank you for being the BEST beta readers EVER! Your feedback means the world to me. I am so thankful for you!!

Hang, thank you for bringing Hawk and Ever to life on this gorgeous cover!

I love working with you so much and I'm so grateful for YOU!

Sue Grimshaw (Edits by Sue), I love being on this journey with you. I am so grateful for your support and encouragement. Thank you so much for all that you do for me!

Ellie (My Brothers Editor), I am so thankful for you!! Thank you for being unbelievably patient and flexible, even when I sent you the wrong version and you had to edit it twice! Hahaha I am endlessly thankful for you!

Christine Estevez, thank you for all that you do to support me! It truly means the world to me! Love you!

Mom, thank you for your love and support and for reading all of my words! Ride or die!! Love you!

Dad, you really are the reason that I keep chasing my dreams!! Thank you for teaching me to never give up. Love you!

Sandy, thank you for reading and supporting me throughout this journey! Love you!

Pathi, I am so thankful for you! You are the reason I even started this journey. Thank you for believing in me!! I love and appreciate you more than I can say!! Thank you for your friendship!! Love you!

Natalie (Head in the Clouds, Nose in a Book), thank you for supporting me through it all! I appreciate all that you do for me from beta reading to the newsletter to just absolutely being the most supportive friend!! I am so thankful for you!! Love you!

Sammi, I am so thankful for your support and your friendship!! Love you!

A huge thank you to the JKL WILLOWS!! Your support means the world to me and I am so thankful for YOU!! Xo

To all the bloggers and bookstagrammers who have posted, shared, and supported me—I can't begin to tell you how much it means to me. I love seeing the graphics that you make and the gorgeous posts that you share. I am forever grateful for your support!

To all the readers who take the time to pick up my books and take a chance on my words...THANK YOU for helping to make my dreams come true!!

Don't miss any of the sweet and sexy small-town romances of Honey Mountain!

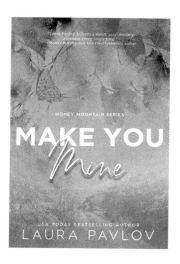

*Don't miss the exciting new books
Entangled has to offer.*

Follow us!

 @EntangledPublishing

 @Entangled_Publishing

 @EntangledPub